Nancy Kress is the author of twenty books of science fiction and fantasy, most recently *Probability Sun*. She has won three Nebulas and a Hugo. Nancy is also the monthly "Fiction" columnist for *Writer's Digest* magazine.

NEBULA AWARDS
SHOWCASE

2003

EDITED BY
NANCY KRESS

A ROC BOOK

ROC
Published by New American Library, a division of
Penguin Putnam Inc., 375 Hudson Street,
New York, New York 10014, U.S.A.
Penguin Books Ltd, 80 Strand,
London WC2R 0RL, England
Penguin Books Australia Ltd, 250 Camberwell Road,
Camberwell, Victoria 3124, Australia
Penguin Books Canada Ltd, 10 Alcorn Avenue,
Toronto, Ontario, Canada M4V 3B2
Penguin Books (N.Z.) Ltd, Cnr Airborne and Rosedale Roads,
Albany, Auckland 1310, New Zealand

Penguin Books Ltd, Registered Offices:
Harmondsworth, Middlesex, England

First published by Roc, an imprint of New American Library,
a division of Penguin Putnam Inc.

First Printing, April 2003
10 9 8 7 6 5 4 3 2 1

Copyright © Science Fiction Writers of America, 2003
Additional copyright notices can be found on page 231.

For Charles Sheffield, loved and remembered always

CONTENTS

Y ou always remember your first Nebula Awards banquet. Mine was Friday, May 3, 1985, at the Warwick Hotel in New York City. Young and starry-eyed, I was thrilled to be introduced to Donald Kingsbury and Harlan Ellison. At the banquet I sat next to A. J. Budrys and talked about advertising. William Gibson won Best Novel for *Neuromancer*. I lost Best Novella to John Varley for "PRESS ENTER." He was gracious, I was gracious, and everyone went around saying, "It's an honor just to be nominated."

The Nebula banquet held April 27, 2002, at the Westin Crown Center hotel in Kansas City both was and was not different. I knew nearly everyone, and they all looked older. The awards format was by now completely familiar (". . . and the nominees are . . ."). As in 1985, some of the works I wanted to win did so, some didn't. And everyone still went around saying, "It's an honor just to be nominated."

Oddly enough for a genre supposedly looking toward the future, SF generates a lot of nostalgia. People reminisce endlessly about the great editors, writers, and stories of yesteryear, with "yesteryear" sometimes defined as half a decade ago. Comparisons are made, trends dissected, time lines created. In one sense, all of speculative fiction is one huge time machine, in which past, present, and future are not distinctly separate entities but rather coexisting ones, like rooms in the same house.

That seems especially true of this year's Nebula ballot, in three ways. First, the nominees range from new writers like Kelly Link and William Shunn, who have yet to publish their first novels, to veteran Jack Williamson. At ninety-four, Jack is a time machine all by himself, able to entertainingly tell you about SF in 1929 or in 1999.

Second, nearly all of the fiction nominated for the 2001 Nebula was not published in 2001. The reason is the esoteric nominating rules. The effect is to create an impression of temporal fluidity, as if January 2000 sat side-by-side with December 2001, separated by no more than the second it takes to turn a single page.

Third, the stories themselves bend time. Severna Park's winner, "The Cure for Everything," is rooted firmly in present-day biotech explorations—with terrifying implications for the future. Lucius Shepard's "Radiant Green Star" and James Morrow's "Auspicious Eggs" take place in the future but comment witheringly on messes we've made in the past. Andy Duncan's "The Pottawatomie Giant" sets its events in the past—two pasts, take your choice—in the hope of shaping a more benevolent present. Jim Kelly cavalierly disregards any temporal barriers whatsoever as he careens around time in "Undone." Connie Willis's novel *Passages* goes one step further, discarding time altogether in the world the brain creates for itself during—and maybe after—that major event, death.

Among science fiction writers, a common question is, "When did you first enter the field?" Usually the answer is a simple number ("1968" or "two years ago"), but I think this question, like so much else in SF, is about more than the usual interpretation of time. The question also carries implications about the writing itself.

Look at that phrase "enter the field." All sorts of SF devices use fields, including, of course, time machines. A field can be defined as "a space in which there are electromagnetic oscillations due to a radiator." In one sense, we all enter the field every time we read a good SF story. It radiates, and our minds oscillate in response. In fact, more than our minds oscillate: eyes may widen, breath shorten, muscles tighten. (If symptoms become extreme, consult your physician.) The stronger the story, the greater the field strength.

Not everyone, however, oscillates to the same kind of speculative fiction story. Some like hard SF, some dark fantasy, some satire, some social extrapolation. This has been known to cause astonishment ("You voted for *that*?") or even hard feelings ("That story does not belong on a Nebula ballot at all"). But, in the long run, I think this diversity is a strength. Hard SF, social-extrapolation SF, space adventure, high fantasy, dark fantasy, urban fantasy, magic realism, satire, whimsy, alternate history, cyberpunk, apocalyptic SF . . . we are a rich field, or fields, ranging across category as well as across time, all radiating like mad. The Nebula stories in this volume, and the many nominees I did not have space to include, demonstrate that. You may not resonate with all of them. But I'm sure you will find among them at least some whose fields you enter with pleasure.

Go and oscillate.

—Nancy Kress

The Nebula Awards are chosen by the members of the Science Fiction and Fantasy Writers of America. On April 26, 2002, they were given in five categories: short story: under 7,500 words; novelette: 7,500 to 17,499 words; novella: 17,500 to 39,999 words; novel: more than 40,000 words; and script for a dramatic presentation. SFWA members read and nominate the best SF stories and novels throughout the year, and the editor of the "Nebula Awards Report" collects these nominations and publishes them in a newsletter. At the end of the year, there is a preliminary ballot and then a final one to determine the winners. The awards are then presented at a formal banquet.

The Nebula Awards originated in 1965, from an idea by Lloyd Biggle Jr., then secretary-treasurer of SFWA. The award itself was originally designed by Judith Ann Blish from a sketch by Kate Wilhelm. The official description reads, "a block of Lucite four to five inches square by eight to nine inches high into which a spiral nebula of metallic glitter and a geological specimen are embedded." Each award is different, and all are treasured.

BEST NOVEL

(winner) *The Quantum Rose*, Catherine Asaro (Tor)
Eternity's End, Jeffrey A. Carver (Tor)
Mars Crossing, Geoffrey A. Landis (Tor)
A Storm of Swords, George R. R. Martin (Bantam Spectra)
The Collapsium, Wil McCarthy (Del Rey)

The Tower at Stony Wood, Patricia A. McKillip (Ace)
Passage, Connie Willis (Bantam)

BEST NOVELLA

"A Roll of the Dice," Catherine Asaro (*Analog*)
"May Be Some Time," Brenda Clough (*Analog*)
"The Diamond Pit," Jack Dann (*Fantasy & Science Fiction*)
"Radiant Green Star," Lucius Shepard (*Asimov's*)
(winner) "The Ultimate Earth," Jack Williamson (*Analog*)

BEST NOVELETTE

"To Kiss the Star," Amy Sterling Casil (*Fantasy & Science Fiction*)
"The Pottawatomie Giant," Andy Duncan (SCIFI.COM)
"Undone," James Patrick Kelly (*Asimov's*)
(winner) "Louise's Ghost," Kelly Link (*Stranger Things Happen*,
    Small Beer Press)
"Auspicious Eggs," James Morrow (*Fantasy & Science Fiction*)
"Dance of the Yellow-Breasted Luddites," William Shunn
    (*Vanishing Acts*, edited by Ellen Datlow, Tor)

BEST SHORT STORY

"Kaddish for the Last Survivor," Michael A. Burstein (*Analog*)
(winner) "The Cure for Everything," Severna Park
    (SCIFI.COM)
"The Elephants on Neptune," Mike Resnick (*Asimov's*)
"Mom and Dad at the Home Front," Sherwood Smith
    (*Realms of Fantasy*)
"Wound the Wind," George Zebrowski (*Analog*)

BEST SCRIPT

O Brother, Where Art Thou?, Ethan Coen and Joel Coen
    (Touchstone/Universal)
X-Men, Tom DeSanto and Bryan Singer (story) David Hayter
    (screenplay), (20th Century Fox)
(winner) *Crouching Tiger, Hidden Dragon*, James Schamus, Kuo
    Jung Tsai, and Hui-Ling Wang (Sony Pictures Classics)
The Body, Joss Whedon (*Buffy the Vampire Slayer* episode)

"**S**everna Park" is the pseudonym of an artist in two media: ceramics and words. She lives in Maryland with her partner of almost twenty years and makes her living teaching ceramics, but her literary output is obviously far more than a sideline. Severna's first novel, *Speaking Dreams* (1992), was a finalist for SF's Lambda Award. Her second novel, *Hand of Prophecy* (1998) was a Tiptree Award finalist. *The Annunciate* (2001) made finalist for both awards. And in 2001, Severna's short story "The Golem" was on the final Nebula ballot.

And now, after all these finalists, Severna has won for a story about an unexpected peril of genetic engineering. "The Cure for Everything" is notable for not only its thought-provoking story but also for its rain forest atmosphere. Severna says that she has never actually been to the Amazon jungle, but she does have "a well-thumbed collection of *National Geographic*s and a burning desire to dance the lambada in Rio." Clearly, those sufficed.

THE CURE FOR EVERYTHING

Severna Park

Maria was smoking damp cigarettes with Horace, taking a break in the humid evening, when the truck full of wild jungle Indians arrived from Ipiranga. She heard the truck before she saw it, laboring through the Xingu Forest Preserve.

"Are we expecting someone?" she said to Horace.

Horace shook his head, scratched his thin beard, and squinted into the forest. Diesel fumes drifted with the scent of churned earth and cigarette smoke. The truck revved higher and lumbered through the Xingu Indian Assimilation Center's main gates.

Except for the details of their face paint, the Indians behind the flatbed's fenced sides looked the same as all the other new arrivals; tired and scared in their own stoic way, packed together on narrow benches, everyone holding something—a baby, a drum, a cooking pot. Horace waved the driver to the right, down the hill toward Intake. Maria stared at the Indians and they stared back like she was a three-armed sideshow freak.

"Now you've scared the crap out of them," said Horace, who was the director of the *Projeto Brasileiro Nacional de Assimilação do Índio*. "They'll think this place is haunted."

"They should have called ahead," said Maria. "I'd be out of sight, like a good little ghost."

Horace ground his cigarette into the thin rain forest soil. "Go on down to the A/V trailer," he said. "I'll give you a call in a couple of minutes." He made an attempt to smooth his rough hair, and started after the truck.

Maria took a last drag on the cigarette and started in the opposite direction, toward the Audio/Visual trailer, where she could monitor what was going on in Intake without being seen. Horace was fluent in the major Amazonian dialects of Tupi-Guaraní, Arawak, and Ge, but Maria had a gut-level understanding that he didn't. She was the distant voice in his ear, mumbling advice into a microphone as he interviewed tribe after refugee tribe. She was the one picking out the nuances in language, guiding him as he spoke, like a conscience.

Or like a ghost. She glanced over her shoulder, but the truck and the Indians were out of sight. No matter where they were from, the Indians had some idea of how white people and black people looked, but you'd think they'd never seen an albino in their lives. Her strange eyes, her pale, translucent skin over African features. To most of them, she was an unknown and sometimes terrifying magical entity. To her . . . well . . . most of them were no more or less polite than anyone she'd ever met stateside.

She stopped to scuff her cigarette into the dirt, leaned over to pick up the butt, and listened. Another engine. Not the heavy grind of a truck this time.

She started back toward the gate. In the treetops beyond Xingu's chain-link fence and scattered asphalt roofs, monkeys screamed and rushed through the branches like a visible wind. Headlights flickered between tree trunks and dense undergrowth and a Jeep lurched out of the forest. Bright red letters were stenciled over its hood: *Hiller Project*.

Maria waved the driver to a stop. He and his passenger were both wearing bright red jackets, with *Hiller Project* embroidered over the front pocket. The driver had a broad, almost Mexican face. The passenger was a black guy, deeply blue-black, like he was fresh off the boat from Nigeria. He gave Maria a funny look, but she knew what it was. He'd never seen an albino either.

"We're following the truck from Ipiranga," the black man said in Portuguese. His name was stenciled over his heart. *N'Lykli.*

She pointed down the dirt road where the overhead floodlights cut the descending dusk. "Intake's over there," she said in the same language. "You should have called ahead. You're lucky we've got space for them."

"Thanks," said N'Lykli, and the driver put the Jeep in gear.

"Hey," said Maria as they started to pull away. "What's a Hiller Project?"

Another cultural rescue group, she figured, but the black guy gave her a different funny look. She didn't recognize it and he didn't answer. The Jeep pulled away, jouncing down the rutted access road.

Maria groped in her pocket for another cigarette, took one out of the pack, then stuck it back in. Instead of heading for the A/V trailer, she followed them down the hill to Intake.

■

She found N'Lykli and the driver inside with Horace, arguing in Portuguese while four of Xingu's tribal staffers stood around listening, impassive in their various face paint, Xingu T-shirts, and khaki shorts.

"These people have to be isolated," the driver was saying. "They have to be isolated or we'll lose half of them to measles and the other half to the flu."

He seemed overly focused on this issue, even though Horace was nodding. Horace turned to one of the staffers and started to give instructions in the man's native Arawak. "Drive them down to Area C. Take the long way so you don't go past the Waura camp."

"No," said N'Lykli. "We'll drive them. You just show us where they can stay for the night."

Horace raised an eyebrow. "For the *night?*"

"We'll be gone in the morning," said N'Lykli. "We have permanent quarters set up for them south of here, in Xavantina."

Horace drew himself up. "Once they're on Xingu property, they're our responsibility. You can't just drop in and then take them somewhere else. This isn't a fucking motel."

The driver pulled a sheaf of papers out of his jacket and spread them on the table. Everything was stamped with official-looking seals and *Hiller Project* in red letters over the top of every page. "I have authorization."

"So do I," said Horace. "And mine's part of a big fat grant from *Plano de Desenvolvimento Econômico e Social* in Brasília."

The driver glanced at his Hiller companion.

"Let me make a phone call," said N'Lykli. "We'll get this straightened out."

Horace snorted and waved him toward Maria. "She'll show you where it is."

"This way," said Maria.

It wasn't that Horace would kick the Indians out if they didn't have authorization. He'd kick out the Hiller whatever-the-fuck-that-was Project first, and hold on to the Indians until he knew where they were from and what they were doing on the back of a truck. Indians were shipped out of settlements all over Brazil as an act of mercy before the last of the tribe was gunned down by cattle ranchers, rubber tappers, or gold miners. Xingu's big fat grant was a sugar pill that the *Plano de Desenvolvimento* gave out with one hand while stripping away thousands of years of culture with the other. Horace knew it. Everyone knew it.

N'Lykli followed her across the compound, between swirls of floodlit mosquitoes, through the evening din of cicadas. The phone was on the other side of the reserve, and Maria slowed down to make him walk beside her.

"So what's a Hiller Project?" she said.

"Oh," he said, "we're part of a preservation coalition."

"Which one?" asked Maria. "Rainforest Agencies?"

"Something like that."

"You should be a little more specific." Maria jerked a thumb in Horace's direction. "Horace thinks Rainforest Agencies is a front for the World Bank, and they're not interested in preserving *anything*. If he finds out that's who you work for, you'll never get your little Indian friends out of here."

N'Lykli hesitated. "Okay. You've heard of International Pharmaceuticals?"

"They send biologists out with the shamans to collect medicinal plants."

"Right," he said. "IP underwrites part of our mission."

"You mean rain forest as medical resource?" Maria stopped. "So why're you taking Indians from Ipiranga to Xavantina? They won't know anything about the medicinal plants down there. Ipiranga's in an entirely different ecological zone."

He made a motion with his shoulders, a shrug, she thought, but it was more of a shudder. "There's a dam going up at Ipiranga," he said. "We had to relocate them."

"To Xavantina?" She couldn't think of anything down there except abandoned gold mines, maybe a rubber plantation or two. "Why can't you leave them with us?"

"Because they're . . . unique."

He was being so vague, so unforthcoming, she would have guessed that the entire tribe was going to be sold into gold-mining slavery, except something in his tone said that he really cared about what happened to them.

"Unique?" said Maria. "You mean linguistically? Culturally?"

He stuck his hands in his pockets. He licked his lips. After a while he said, "Genetically."

That was a first. "Oh yeah?" said Maria. "How's that?"

"Ipiranga's an extremely isolated valley. If it wasn't for the dam, these people might not have been discovered for another century. The other tribes in the area told us they were just a fairy tale." He glanced at her. "We don't think there's been any new blood in the Ipiranga population for five hundred years."

Maria let out a doubtful laugh. "They must be completely inbred. And sterile."

"You'd think so," said N'Lykli. "But they've been very careful."

A whole slew of genetic consequences rose up in her mind. Mutants. Family insanities and nightmarish physical defects passed down the generations. She knew them all. "They'd have to have written records to keep so-and-so's nephew from marrying his mother's grandniece."

"They have an oral tradition you wouldn't believe. Their children memorize family histories back two hundred generations. They *know* who they're not supposed to marry."

Maria blinked in the insect-laden night. "But they must have a few mistakes. Someone lies to their husband. Someone's got a girlfriend on the side—they can't be a hundred percent accurate."

"If they've made mistakes, none of them have survived. We haven't found any autism, or Down's." He finally gave her that three-armed sideshow freak look again. "Or Lucknow's."

Maria clenched her teeth, clenched her fists. "Excuse me?"

"Lucknow's Syndrome. Your albinism. That's what it is. Isn't it?"

She just stood there. She couldn't decide whether to sock him or start screaming. Not even Horace knew what *it* was called. No one was supposed to mention *it*. It was supposed to be as invisible as she was.

N'Lykli shifted uncomfortably. "If you have Lucknow's, your family must have originally been from the Ivory Coast. They were taken as slaves to South Carolina in the late 1700s and mixed with whites who were originally from County Cork in Ireland. That's the typical history for Lucknow's. It's a bad combination." He hesitated. "Unless you don't want children."

She stared at him. Her great-grandfather from South Carolina was "high yellow," as they said in those days to describe how dark he wasn't, referring not-so-subtly to the rapes of his grandmothers. His daughter's children turned out light skinned and light eyed, all crazy in their heads. Only one survived and that was Maria's mother, the least deranged, who finally went for gene testing and was told that her own freakishly albino daughter would bear monsters instead of grandchildren. That they would be squirming, mitten-handed imbeciles, white as maggots, dying as they exited the womb.

"Who the *hell* do you think you are?" whispered Maria.

"There's a cure," he said. "Or there will be." He made a vague gesture into the descending night, toward Intake. "International Pharmaceutical wants those people because their bloodlines are so carefully documented and so *clean*. There's a mutation in their genes—they all have it—it 'resets' the control regions in zygotic DNA. That means their genes can be used as templates to eliminate virtually any congenital illness—even aging. We've got an old lady who's a hundred years old and sharp as a whip. There's a twelve-year-old girl with the genes to wipe out leukemia." He moved closer. "We've got a guy who could be a source for a hundred new vaccines. He's incredible—the cure for everything. But we'll lose them all if your boss keeps them here. And he can. He has the authority."

"Get on the phone to International Pharmaceutical," she said and heard her voice shaking. "Get them to twist his arm."

"I can't," he said. "This isn't a public project. We're not even supposed to be here. We were supposed to pick them up and get them down to the southern facility. We wouldn't have stopped except we spent a day fixing the truck." He spread his hands, like the plagues of the world, not just Lucknow's, would be on her shoulders if she refused to lie for him. "Help us," he said. "Tell your boss everything's fine in Xavantina."

She couldn't make herself say anything. She couldn't make herself believe him.

He moved even closer. "You won't be sorry," he said in a low voice. "Do it, and I'll make sure you won't ever be sorry."

■

She took him back to Intake and told Horace that Hiller seemed to be a legit operation, that there was a receiving area at Xavantina and it had been approved according to *Plano de Desenvolvimento* standards. Horace grunted and smoked and made more irritated pronouncements about Xingu as a cheap motel on the highway to Brazil's industrial future. At about one in the morning, he stubbed out his cigarette and went to bed, leaving Maria to lock up.

Maria showed N'Lykli and the Mexican driver where they could sleep, and then she walked down to Area C, to have a better look at The Cure for Everything.

Xingu's compounds would never make it into Frommer's, but to fleeing tribes, the split greenwood shelters, clean water, and firepits were five-star accommodations. The only fences were to keep the compound areas separated. Intertribal conflicts could survive bulldozers and rifles like nothing else.

Maria passed the Xingu guard, who squinted at her, then waved her on. Closer to Area C she was surprised to run into a second guard. A short guy—the truck driver, she realized—built like a brick and too bulky for his Hiller jacket.

His eyes widened at the sight of Maria and he crossed himself. "You can't come in here."

"I work here," snapped Maria.

"Everybody's sleeping," said the guard, but Maria took another step toward him, letting him get a good look at her spirit-pale face, and his resolve seemed to evaporate. "Germs," he said weakly. "Don't give them your germs."

"I've had all my shots," she said, and kept walking.

■

They weren't asleep. It was too dark to make out details, but from her shadowy hiding place, Maria could see seven or eight people sitting by the nearest fire, talking to each other. No different than a hundred other intakes. Exhausted little kids had been bundled into the shelters. The adults would watch for unknown dangers until sunrise.

Maria crouched in the leaves, invisible, and listened. Five hundred years of isolation would mean an unfathomable dialect. She might be able to catch a word or two, but the proof of the Hiller Project would be in what she could hear and not comprehend. She had the rest of the night to decide if N'Lykli was lying, and if she decided he was, she would tell Horace everything in the morning. She would tell him the exact name for her ghostliness and what N'Lykli had promised her. Horace would understand.

She squinted into the haze of wood smoke. The tone of the conversation around the fire had risen, like an argument. One young man made wide, angry gestures. Something flashed in his ear, a brilliant ruby red, and Maria thought she caught the word for *prisoners* in Tupi-Guaraní.

Across from him, a remarkably old woman pounded a walking stick on the packed dirt. The fire showed her nearly-naked body— withered breasts and wiry muscles—striped here and there with yellow paint. And a scarlet glint in her ear.

The old woman pounded her walking stick even harder, raising puffs of dust. Flames leaped up, giving Maria a snapshot view of a half dozen elders with braided hair and feathers, the ruby glint in each earlobe. Their ancient faces focused on the young man's dissent. He shouted in a staccato burst of glottals and rising tones, closer to Chinese opera than any Amazon Basin language Maria had ever heard. The old woman made an unmistakably dismissive motion with both arms. Emphatic. The young man jumped to his feet and stalked off. The elders watched him go. The old woman glowered at the fire, and no one said another word.

In the dark, surrounded by mosquitoes and thick, damp heat, Maria eased out of her crouch. Bugs were crawling into her socks. Her left leg was cramping and she was holding her breath, but she could feel her body changing. She was becoming solid and brighter than she'd ever been before. Her life as a ghost was over. Right here. In this spot. Her invisibility and their isolation. Her scrupulously unconceived, mitten-handed mutant children, who had burrowed into her dreams for so many years, drifted around her, dispersing like smoke, and Maria felt the trees, the dirt, the insects and night birds—*everything*—hopeful and alive, and full of positive regeneration, for the first time in her life.

She got to her feet, wobbly with optimism, turned around and saw him.

He stared at her the way they all did. She stared back at his wide-set eyes and honest mouth. Yellow face paint and brilliant macaw feathers. His ruby earring wasn't jewelry at all, but a tiny digital sampler of some kind, ticking off combinations of numbers, pulsing as he breathed. She tried to tell herself he wasn't the one N'Lykli had told her about. That this wasn't the face and trim body of The Cure for Everything.

But it was.

My germs, she thought, and took an unsteady step backwards.

He moved toward her and spoke in halting Portuguese. "You see me speak. You hear me."

She nodded.

He took a breath through his teeth. "Please. Take me away, *Jamarikuma*."

Another word with ancient, Tupi-Guaranian roots. *Jamarikuma*: a grandmother of powerful female spirits.

She turned around and ran.

■

She went to see N'Lykli. Pounded on his door and woke him up.

"Where are you really taking them?" she said. "There's nothing in Xavantina but a couple of bankrupt rubber plantations."

He hunched on the edge of the cot, covering himself with the sheet. "International Pharmaceutical has a facility there."

"Do those people *know* you're—you're *milking* them?"

His face made a defensive twitch. "We've explained what we need from them and they've discussed it. They all understand about the dam. They know why they can't stay in Ipiranga."

"Why do they think they're going to be prisoners?"

N'Lykli sat up straight. "Look. They're not captives. There're a few who don't like the idea, but we're not taking them against their will. We've been in contact with them for almost a decade. We even explained about Xingu and your assimilation programs. They didn't want anything to do with it. They don't want to be separated."

"We don't separate families."

"Can you relocate an entire tribe—eight hundred and seventy-four people—to a nice neighborhood in Brasília?"

"But there's only—"

"This is the last group," he said. "We've been staging them into Xavantina for a month."

She sat down on the only chair in the room. "I can't even interview them to find out if any of what you're saying is true."

He shrugged again.

She took a breath. "So what am I supposed to do? Wait around until International Pharmaceutical announces a cure for Lucknow's?"

N'Lykli rubbed his chin. "You don't have to be cured of the syndrome to have normal children. You just need the right father."

Maria stared at him.

He looked down at the floor. "We don't just take blood samples. I can send you something in a couple of weeks. It'll be frozen and you'll have to use it right away. I'll send instructions . . ."

"You're going to send me *sperm?*"

"How else should I do it?" he said. "Would you rather make an appointment with him?"

"Oh, for *Christ's* sake!"

He watched her head for the door. "You're going to tell your boss what's going on?"

Maria stopped. Put her hands in her pockets and glared at him, the mosquito netting, the dank, bare room. *Jamarikuma.* Like hell.

"Goddamit," she said. "You'd better be out of here by daylight."

■

The Hiller Project truck pulled out at dawn, this time with the Jeep in the lead.

María stood out in full view, watching. N'Lykli gave her a

half-salute and looked around nervously, probably for Horace. The Mexican driver gunned the engine, going too fast over the ruts and holes of the unpaved road.

The truck followed, angling for the open gate. In the back, every face turned to stare at her.

The Cures for Alzheimer's, Lucknow's, and all kinds of cancer made small gestures against spirits, turned to each other to whisper, but they didn't look frightened. They didn't look resigned to their fates. They looked like tired travelers who were sick of cheap motels, ready to be wherever they were going. Except for one.

The Cure for Everything lunged against the railing. *"Jamarikuma!"* He shouted high in his throat. *"Jamarikuma!"* He shook the wooden side rails as the truck lurched through the gates and down the hill. She could hear him yelling over the diesel rumble even when the truck was well out of sight.

She stood there in the gray sunlight, taking deep breaths of churned earth and fumes, and felt her body go vague again. It was sudden and strange, like a wind had blown through her.

She knew she should go down to Intake and tell Horace everything, but she was afraid to. It seemed sickeningly obvious now that she should have made the Hiller people stay. Even if what N'Lykli had told her was true, she should have gone over to the Indians arguing around their campfires and made them talk to her. If The Cure for Everything could speak a little Portuguese, so could a few of the others.

Was she so desperate in her ghostliness that she would betray herself like this, give up her job, her life, her colleagues and friends—*everything* for a cure? For frozen *sperm?*

Yes, she was that desperate. Yes, she was.

She turned away from the gate and the diminishing sounds of the truck. *It's too late,* she told herself, and felt the lie in that as well.

■

She drove off with the Toyota Land Cruiser without telling anyone, before the diesel stink of the Hiller truck was gone. The Toyota was the newest of the Xingu vehicles and the only one with a full tank. She plunged it down the muddy hill after the Hiller truck. There weren't that many ways to get to Xavantina.

She caught up with the truck in less than half an hour, but stayed out of sight, a klick or so behind. Xingu's rutted jungle access turned to a graded lumber trail, and she dropped even further back. When the scraggly trees gave way to burned stumps and abandoned timber, she gave herself more distance, until the Hiller truck was a speck behind the speck of the Jeep, forging along the muddy curves in the ruined hillsides.

She followed them through grim little settlements of displaced Indians and rubber tappers who lived in squalor downstream from the local plantations, past islands of pristine jungle where monkeys screamed at her and brilliant parrots burst out of the trees in clouds of pure color.

Fourteen hours from Xingu, long after the moon went down, the truck turned off the half-paved local Xavantina highway onto a dirt road along a narrow river. In the pitch blackness, it made a sharp right and came to a stop.

Maria pulled into the last stand of trees. Doors slammed and there was a brief silence. Then a bank of floodlights came on overhead and she could see the truck sitting by the Jeep in a cleared area at the foot of a high chain-link fence. The Indians peered out of the back, pointing into the darkness while N'Lykli pulled the gates open and the vehicles drove through.

There were no signs to identify the place. Maria hunched over the Toyota's steering wheel, stiff in her shoulders, thick in her head, tired beyond even the desire for coffee. She lit her last cigarette and dragged deep for energy and ideas as N'Lykli swung the gates shut, locked them, tugged on them, and vanished into the dark.

In a minute, the floods went out, leaving Maria with the glowing tip of her cigarette. She waited a while longer, turned on the dome light and crawled into the back of the car where the tool box was. She dug until she found a heavy-duty pair of wire cutters.

■

Inside the gate, the road deteriorated into a wasteland of bulldozed ruts. Weeds and young trees grew to shoulder height. Small animals scurried away as Maria groped through the dark. Bloodthirsty insects found her bare neck, her ankles, and the backs of her hands.

Finally, she saw the glow of sulfur-colored floodlights, and at the top of the next rise, she got her first glimpse of the "facility."

A huddle of blocky, windowless buildings surrounded a fenced central courtyard. It had the look of an unfinished prison. Wire-topped fences glinted in the security floods.

She expected dogs, but didn't hear any. She made her way through the weeds expecting snakes, but decided that N'Lykli and his bloodsucking colleagues at Hiller had probably eliminated every poisonous thing for miles around—no accidental losses in their gene pool of cures. The whole idea made her furious—at *them* for such a blatant exploitation, and at herself for so badly needing what they'd found.

She circled the compound, trying to find an inconspicuous way to get into the inner courtyard, but the fences were new and some of them were electrified. When she had come almost all the way around to the front again, she found a lit row of barred windows on the ground floor of one of the blockhouses.

There was no one inside. The lights were dim, for security, not workers or visitors. Maria climbed up a hard dirt bank to the windowsill and hung on to the bars with both hands.

Inside, modern desks and new computers lined one side of a huge white room. At the other end, there was a small lab with racks of glassware and a centrifuge. Color-coded gene charts covered the walls. Yellow lines braided into red, producing orange offspring. Bright pink Post-it notes followed one line and dead-ended with a handwritten note and an arrow drawn in black marker. She could read the print without effort: *Autism?*

Mitten-handed mutants. Ghostly spirit children.

She let herself down from the windowsill and crept through brittle grass to the edge of the wire fence.

Inside, she could see one end of the compound and the lights of the blockhouse beyond. Dark human shapes were silhouetted against small fires and she realized she'd expected them to be treated as inmates, locked up for the night and under constant guard. Instead she could smell the wood smoke and hear their muffled voices. Women laughing. A baby squalling, then shushed. Hands pattered on a drum.

She touched the fence with the back of her hand, testing for current.

Nothing.

She listened, but there was no alarm that she could hear.

Someone chanted a verse of a song. A chorus of children sang in answer. For the first time, Maria saw the enormity of what she was about to do.

The Cure for Everything. Not just Lucknow's.

She pulled out the cutters and started working on the fence. The gene chart. *Autism.* The way *his* voice had sounded, shrieking *Jamarikuma!* None of this was right.

She crawled through the hole in the fence and they saw her right away. The singing and conversation stopped. She got to her feet, brushed off her knees and went near enough to the closest fire to be seen, but not close enough to be threatening. The Cure for Everything gave Maria a quick, urgent nod but he didn't stand up. Around him, a few heads cocked in recognition of her face, her skin.

The withered old woman Maria had seen at Xingu hobbled over from one of the other fires, leaning on her walking stick. She frowned at Maria and started speaking in accented Portuguese.

"We saw you at Xingu. You're the Jamarikuma. What are you doing here?"

"I'm here to help," said Maria.

"Help us do what?" said the old woman.

"You don't have to stay in this place," said Maria. "If you do, you and your children and your grandchildren's children won't ever be allowed to leave."

The old woman—and half a dozen other older members of the tribe—glanced at the Cure. Not in a particularly friendly way.

"What's this all about?" said the old woman to the Cure, still in Portuguese. "You've got a spirit arguing for you now?"

He replied in their own language. To Maria he sounded sulky.

"Do you understand why you're here?" said Maria. "These people . . ." She gestured at the looming buildings. "They want your blood, your . . ." *Genes* might mean *souls* to them. "You have a—a talent to cure diseases," said Maria. "That's why they want your blood."

Guarded eyes stared back from around the fire.

The old woman nodded. "What's so bad about that?"

"You won't ever be able to go back home," said Maria.

The old woman snorted. "At home they were trying to shoot us." She spat into the fire. "We're afraid to go back there."

"But *here* we're animals." The Cure pushed himself to his feet. "We're *prisoners!*"

"We've had this discussion," said the old woman sharply and turned to Maria. "We made a decision months ago. We said he didn't have to stay if he didn't want to, but he stayed anyway, and now he's bringing in spirits to make an argument that no one else agrees with. We're safer right here than we've been for years. No one's shooting at us. So we have to wear their ugly jewelry." She touched the ruby sampler in her ear. "So we lose a little blood now and then. It's just a scratch."

"But you're in a cage," said Maria.

"I don't like that part," said the old woman. "But you have to admit, it's a big cage, and mostly it keeps the bandits and murderers out."

The Cure jabbed a finger at Maria, making his point in harsh staccato tones. Maria only caught the word *Xingu*.

The old woman eyed Maria. "What would happen to us at Xingu?"

"We'd teach you how to be part of the world outside," said Maria. "We'd show you what you need to know to be farmers, or to live in the city if that's what you want."

"Are there guns in the world outside?"

It was a patronizing question. Maria felt sweat break out at the small of her back. "You know there are."

"Would we all be able to stay together, the entire tribe?" asked the old woman.

"We do the best we can," said Maria. "Sometimes it isn't possible to keep everyone together, but we try."

The old woman made a wide gesture into the dark. "We didn't lose one single person on the trip. You're saying you can't guarantee that for us at Xingu, though. Is that right?"

"Right," said Maria.

"But we'd be free."

Maria didn't say anything.

The old woman made a sharp gesture. "It's time for the Jamari-kuma spirit to leave. If that's what she actually is." She closed her eyes and began to hum, a spirit-dismissing song, Maria supposed, and she glanced at the Cure, who leaped to his feet.

"I am leaving. With the Jamarikuma."

The old woman nodded, still humming, as though she was glad he'd finally made up his mind.

The Cure took a step away from the fire. He walked—no, he sauntered around his silent friends, family, maybe even his wife. No one said anything and no one was shedding any tears. He came over to Maria and stood beside her.

"I will not come back," he said.

The old woman hummed a little louder, like she was covering his noise with hers.

■

When they got back to the Toyota, Maria unlocked the passenger side and let him in. He shut the door and she walked slowly around the back to give herself time to breathe. Her heart was pounding and her head felt empty and light, like she was dreaming. She leaned against the driver's side, just close enough to see his dim reflection in the side mirror. He was rubbing his sweaty face, hard, as though he could peel away his skin.

In that moment, she felt as though she could reach into the night, to just the right place and find an invisible door which would open into the next day. It was the results of a night with him that she wanted, she realized. He was like a prize she'd just won. For the first time, she wondered what his name was.

She pulled the driver's side open and got in beside him. She turned the key in the ignition and checked the rearview mirror as the dashboard lit up. All she could see of herself was a ghostly, in-distinct shape.

"Is something wrong?" he asked.

"Everything's fine." She said and let the truck blunder forward into the insect-laden night.

Later, when the access road evened out to pavement, he put his hot palm on her thigh. She kept driving, watching how the headlights cut only so far ahead into the darkness. She stopped just before the main road, and without looking at him, reached out to touch his fingers.

"Are we going to Xingu?" he asked, like a child.

"No," she said. "I can't go back."

"Neither can I," he said, and let her kiss him. Here. And there.

JACK WILLIAMSON

Jack Williamson is a marvel. There is simply no other word for him. The man has been delighting readers practically as long as science fiction has existed. When I first met Jack at a banquet in Lawrence, Kansas, I asked him about his earliest publication. He said, "Well, I published my first story in 1928. You were just a little girl." After I ran to the ladies' room to check in the mirror whether I'd really turned into my mother, I forgave him. I think Jack's sweetness and charm could get him forgiven anything.

Born in 1908, Jack lived in Mexico and West Texas before the family moved by covered wagon to a semidesert homestead in eastern New Mexico. He grew up there, escaping into his imagination via Jules Verne and other early SF. After three years of college, he dropped out to write science fiction, selling enough to keep himself alive until World War II. Back from service as a weather forecaster in the South Pacific, he wrote *The Humanoids*, worked as a newspaper editor, created the comic strip *Beyond Mars* for the *New York Sunday News*, earned a Ph.D. in English literature, and then taught at Eastern New Mexico University. Just your average normal life.

Jack still teaches one course a year while continuing to add to his oeuvre of fifty-odd novels. "The Ultimate Earth" is a section of his novel-in-progress, *Terraforming Earth*. The novella has earned him his first Nebula, which he says "was well worth the wait." "The Ultimate Earth" is so packed with ideas that it's difficult to imagine what will be left for the rest of the novel. But I have faith that Jack will find something.

THE ULTIMATE EARTH

Jack Williamson

1

We loved Uncle Pen. The name he gave us was too hard for us to say, and we made it Sandor Pen. As early as we could understand, the robots had told us that we were clones, created to watch the skies for danger and rescue Earth from any harm. They had kept us busy with our lessons and our chores and our workouts in the big centrifuge, but life in our little burrow left us little else to do. His visits were our best excitement.

He never told us when he was coming. We used to watch for him, looking from the high dome on the Tycho rim, down across the field of Moondust the digging machines had leveled. Standing huge on the edge of it, they were metal monsters out of space, casting long black shadows across the gray waste of rocks and dust and crater pits.

His visit on our seventh birthday was a wonderful surprise. Tanya saw him landing and called us up to the dome. His ship was a bright teardrop, shining in the black shadow of a gigantic metal insect. He jumped out of it in a sleek silvery suit that fitted like his skin. We waited inside the air lock to watch him peel it off. He was a small lean man, who looked graceful as a girl but still very strong. Even his body was exciting to see, though Dian ran and hid because he looked so strange.

Naked, his body had a light tan that darkened in the sunlit dome and faded fast when he went below. His face was a narrow heart-shape, his golden eyes enormous. Instead of hair like ours, his head was capped with sleek, red-brown fur. He needed no clothing, he told us, because his sex organs were internal.

He called Dian when he missed her, and she crept back to share the gifts he had brought from Earth. There were sweet fruits we had never tasted, strange toys, stranger games that he had to show us how to play. For Tanya and Dian there were dolls that sang strange songs in voices we couldn't understand and played loud music on tiny instruments we had never heard.

The best part was just the visit with him in the dome. Pepe and Casey had eager questions about life on the new Earth. Were there cities? Wild animals? Alien creatures? Did people live in houses, or underground in tunnels like ours? What did he do for a living? Did he have a wife? Children like us?

He wouldn't tell us much. Earth, he said, had changed since our parents knew it. It was now so different that he wouldn't know where to begin, but he let us take turns looking at it through the big telescope. Later, he promised, if he could find space gear to fit us, he would take us up to orbit the Moon and loop toward it for a closer look. Now, however, he was working to learn all he could about the old Earth, the way it had been ages ago, before the great impacts.

He showed it to us in the holo tanks and the brittle old paper books, the way it was with white ice caps over the poles and bare brown deserts on the continents. Terraformed, the new Earth had no deserts and no ice. Under the bright cloud spirals, the land was green where the sun struck it, all the way over the poles. It looked so wonderful that Casey and Pepe begged him to take us back with him to let us see it for ourselves.

"I'm sorry." He shook his neat, fur-crowned head. "Terribly sorry, but you can't even think of a trip to Earth."

We were looking from the dome. Earth stood high in the black north, where it always stood. Low in the west, the slow Sun blazed hot on the new mountains the machines had piled up around the spaceport, and filled the craters with ink.

Dian had learned by now to trust him. She sat on his knee, gazing up in adoration at his quirky face. Tanya stood behind him, playing a little game. She held her hand against his back to bleach the golden tan, and took it away to watch the Sun erase the print.

Looking hurt, Casey asked why we couldn't think of a trip to Earth.

"You aren't like me." That was very true. Casey has a wide black face with narrow Chinese eyes and straight black hair. "And you belong right here."

"I don't look like anybody." Casey shrugged. "Or belong to you."

"Of course you don't." Uncle Pen was gently patient. "But you do belong to the station and your great mission." He looked at me. "Remind him, Dunk."

My clone father was Duncan Yarrow. The master computer that runs the station often spoke with his holo voice. He had told us how we had been cloned again and again from the tissue cells left frozen in the cryostat.

"Sir, that's true." I felt a little afraid of Uncle Pen, but proud of all the station had done. "My holo father has told us how the big impacts killed Earth and killed it again. We have always brought it back to life." My throat felt dry. I had to gulp, but I went on. "If Earth's alive now, that's because of us."

"True. Very true." He nodded, with an odd little smile. "But perhaps you don't know that your little Moon has suffered a heavy impact of his own. If you are alive today, you owe your lives to me."

"To you?" We all stared at him, but Casey was nodding. "To you and the digging machines? I've watched them and wondered what they were digging for. When did that object hit the Moon?"

"¿Quién sabe?" He shrugged at Pepe, imitating the gesture and the voice Pepe had learned from his holo father. "It was long ago. Perhaps a hundred thousand years, perhaps a million. I haven't found a clue."

"The object?" Pepe frowned. "Something hit the station?"

"A narrow miss." Uncle Pen nodded at the great dark pit in the crater rim just west of us. "The ejecta smashed the dome and buried everything. The station was lost and almost forgotten. Only a myth till I happened on it."

"The diggers?" Casey turned to stare down at the landing field where Uncle Pen had left his flyer in the shadows of those great machines and the mountains they had built. "How did you know where to dig?"

"The power plant was still running," Uncle Pen said. "Keeping the computer alive. I was able to detect its metal shielding and then its radiation."

"We thank you." Pepe came gravely to shake his hand. "I'm glad to be alive."

"So am I," Casey said. "If I can get to Earth." He saw Uncle Pen beginning to shake his head, and went on quickly, "Tell us what you know about the Earth impacts and how we came down to terraform the Earth and terraform it again when it was killed again."

"I don't know what you did."

"You have showed us the difference we made," Casey said. "The land is all green now, with no deserts or ice."

"Certainly it has been transformed." Nodding, Uncle Pen stopped to smile at Tanya as she left her game with the Sun on his back and came to sit cross-legged at his feet. "Whatever you did was ages ago. Our historians are convinced that we've done more ourselves."

"You changed the Earth?" Casey was disappointed and a little doubtful. "How?"

"We removed undersea ledges and widened straits to reroute the ocean circulation and warm the poles. We diverted rivers to fill new lakes and bring rain to deserts. We engineered new life-forms that improved the whole biocosm."

"But still you owe us something. We put you there."

"Of course." Uncle Pen shrugged. "Excavating the station, I uncovered evidence that the last impact annihilated life on Earth. The planet had been reseeded sometime before the lunar impact occurred."

"We did it." Casey grinned. "You're lucky we were here."

■

"Your ship?" Pepe had gone to stand at the edge of the dome, looking down at the monster machines and Uncle Pen's neat little flyer, so different from the rocket spaceplanes we had seen in the old video holos. "Can it go to other planets?"

"It can." He nodded. "The planets of other suns."

Tanya's eyes went wide, and Pepe asked, "How does it fly in space with no rocket engines?"

"It doesn't," he said. "It's called a slider. It slides around space, not through it."

"To the stars?" Tanya whispered. "You've been to other stars?"

"To the planets of other stars." He nodded gravely. "I hope to go again when my work here is finished."

"Across the light-years?" Casey was awed. "How long does it take?"

"No time at all." He smiled at our wonderment. "Not in slider flight. Outside of space-time, there is no time. But there are laws of nature, and time plays tricks that may surprise you. I could fly across a hundred light-years to another star in an instant of my own time and come back in another instant, but two hundred years would pass here on Earth while I was away."

"I didn't know." Tanya's eyes went wider still. "Your friends would all be dead."

"We don't die."

She shrank away as if suddenly afraid of him. Pepe opened his mouth to ask something, and shut it without a word.

He chucked at our startlement. "We've engineered ourselves, you see, more than we've engineered the Earth."

Casey turned to look out across the shadowed craters at the huge globe of Earth, the green Americas blazing on the sunlit face, Europe and Africa only a shadow against the dark. He stood there a long time and came slowly back to stand in front of Uncle Pen.

"I'm going down to see the new Earth when I grow up." His face set stubbornly. "No matter what you say."

"Are you growing wings?" Uncle Pen laughed and reached a golden arm to pat him on the head. "If you didn't know, the impact smashed all your old rocket craft to junk."

He drew quickly back.

"Really, my boy, you do belong here." Seeing his hurt, Uncle Pen spoke more gently. "You were cloned for your work here at the station. A job that ought to make you proud."

Casey made an angry swipe across his eyes with the back of his hand and swallowed hard, but he kept his voice even.

"Maybe so. But where's any danger now?"

Uncle Pen had an odd look. He took a long moment to answer.

"We are not aware of any actual threat from another impacting bolide. All the asteroids that used to approach Earth's orbit have been diverted, most of them steered into the Sun."

"So?" Casey's dark chin had a defiant jut. "Why did you want to dig us up?"

"For history." Uncle Pen looked away from us, up at the huge, far-off Earth. "I hope you try to understand what that means. The resurfaced Earth had lost nearly every trace of our beginning. Historians were trying to prove that we had evolved on some other planet and migrated here. Tycho Station is proof that Earth is the actual mother world. I've found our roots here under the rubble."

"I guess you can be proud of that," Casey said, "but who needs the station now?"

"Nobody, really." He shrugged, with an odd little twist of his golden lips, and I thought he felt sorry for Casey. "If another disaster did strike the Earth, which isn't likely at all, it could be repeopled by the colonies."

"So you dug us up for nothing?"

"If you knew what I have done," Pen leaned and reached as if to hug him, but he shrank farther away. "It wasn't easy! We've had to invent and improvise. We had to test the tissue cells still preserved in the cryostat, and build new equipment in the maternity lab. A complex system. It had to be tested." He smiled down into Tanya's beaming devotion. "The tests have turned out well."

"So we are just an experiment?"

"Aren't you glad to be alive?"

"Maybe," Casey muttered bitterly. "If I can get off the Moon. I don't want to sit here till I die, waiting for nothing at all."

Looking uncomfortable, Pen just reached down to lift Tanya up in his arms.

"We were meant for more than that," Casey told him. "I want a life."

"Please, my dear boy, you must try to understand." Patiently, Uncle Pen shook his furry head. "The station is a precious historic monument, our sole surviving relic of the early Earth and early man. You are part of it. I'm sorry if you take that for a misfortune, but there is certainly no place for you on Earth."

2

Sandor Pen kept coming to the Moon as we grew up, though not so often. He brought tantalizing gifts. Exotic fruits that had to be eaten before they spoiled. New games and difficult puzzles. Little holo cubes that had held living pictures of us, caught us year after year as we grew up from babies in the maternity lab. He was always genial and kind, though I thought he came to care less for us as we grew older.

His main concern was clearly the station itself. He cleared junk and debris out of the deepest tunnels, which had been used for workshops and storage, and stocked them again with new tools and spare parts that the robots could use to repair themselves and maintain the station.

Most of his time on the visits was spent in the library and museum with Dian and her holo mother. He studied the old books and holos and paintings and sculptures, carried them away to be restored, and brought identical copies back to replace them. For a time he had the digging machines busy again, removing rubble from around the station and grinding it up to make concrete for a massive new retaining wall that they poured to reinforce the station foundation.

For our twenty-first birthday, he had the robots measure us for space suits like his own. Sleek and mirror-bright, they fitted like our skins and let us feel at home outside the dome. We wore them down to see one of our old rocket spaceplanes, standing on the field beside his little slipship. His robots had dug it out of a smashed hangar, and he now had them rebuilding it with new parts from Earth.

One of the great digging machines had extended a leverlike arm to hold it upright. A robot was replacing a broken landing strut, fusing it smoothly in place with some process that made no glow of heat. Casey spoke to the robot, but it ignored him. He climbed up to knock on the door. It responded with a brittle computer voice that was only a rattle in our helmets.

"Open up," he told it. "Let us in."

"Admission denied." Its hard machine voice had Pen's accent.

"By what authority?"

"By the authority of Director Sandor Pen, Lunar Research Site."

"Ask the director to let us in."

"Admission denied."

"So you think." Casey shook his head, his words a sardonic whisper in my helmet. "If you know how to think."

■

Back inside the air lock, Pen had waited to help us shuck off the mirror suits. Casey thanked him for the gift and asked if the old spaceplane would be left here on the Moon.

"Forget what you're thinking." He gave Casey a penetrating glance. "We're taking it down to Earth."

"I wish I could come."

"I'm sorry you can't." His face was firmly set, but a flush of pleasure turned it a richer gold. "It's to stand at the center of our new historic memorial, located on the Australian subcontinent. It presents our reconstruction of the prehistoric past. The whole story of the pre-impact planet and pre-impact man."

He paused to smile at Tanya. Flushed pink, she smiled back at him.

"It's really magnificent! Finding the lunar site was my great good fortune, and working it has been my life for many years. It has filled a gap in human history. Answered questions that scholars had fought over for ages. You yourselves have a place there, with a holographic diorama of your childhood."

Casey asked again why we couldn't see it. "Because you belong here." Impatience edged his voice. "And because of the charter that allowed us to work the site. We agreed to restore the station to its original state, and to import no genetic materials from it that might contaminate the Earth. We are to leave the site exactly as it was before the impact, protected and secured from any future trespass."

■

We all felt sick with loss on the day he told us his work at the site was done. As a farewell gift, he took us two by two to orbit the Moon. Casey and I went up together, sitting behind him in his tiny slipship. We had seen space and Earth from the dome all our lives, but the flight was still an exciting adventure.

The mirror hull was invisible from inside, so that our seats seemed to float free in open space. The Moon's gray desolation spread wider beneath us, and dwindled again to a bright bubble floating in a gulf of darkness. Though Pen touched nothing I saw, the stars blazed suddenly brighter, the Milky Way a broad belt of gem-strewn splendor all around us. The Sun was dimmed and hugely magnified to let us see the dark spots across its face.

Still he touched nothing and I felt no new motion, but now Australia expanded. The deserts were gone. A long new sea lay across the center of the continent, crescent-shaped and vividly blue.

"The memorial." He pointed to a broad tongue of green land thrust into the crescent. "If you ever get to Earth—which I don't expect—you could meet your doubles there in the Tycho exhibit."

Casey asked, "Is Mona there?"

Mona Lisa Live was the professional name of the woman Casey's father brought with him when he forced his way aboard the escape plane just ahead of the first impact. We knew them only from their holo images, he with the name "El Chino" and the crossed flags of Mexico and China tattooed across his black chest, she with the Leonardo painting on her belly.

Those ancient images had been enough to let us all catch the daring spirit and desperate devotion that had brought them finally to the Moon from the Medellin nightclub where he found her. From his first glimpse of her holo, Casey had loved her and dreamed of a day when they might be together again. I'd heard him ask my holo father why she had not been cloned with us.

"Ask the computer." He shrugged in the fatalistic way he had when his voice had its dry computer undertone. "It could have been done. Her tissue specimens are still preserved in the cryostat."

"Do you know why she wasn't cloned?"

"The computer seldom explains." He shrugged again. "If you

want my own guess, she and Kell reached the Moon as unexpected intruders. The maternity lab was not prepared to care for them or their clones."

"Intruders?" Casey's dark face turned darker. "At least DeFort thought their genes were worth preserving. If I'm worth cloning, Mona ought to be. Someday she will be."

∎

Back in the station dome, Pen made his final farewell. We thanked him for that exciting glimpse of the far-off Earth, for the space suits and all his gifts, for restoring us to life. A trifling repayment, he said, for all he had found at the station. He shook our hands, kissed Tanya and Dian, and got into his silvery suit. We followed him down to the air lock. Tanya must have loved him more than I knew. She broke into tears and ran off to her room as the rest of us watched his bright little teardrop float away toward Earth.

"We put them down there," Casey muttered. "We have a right to see what we have done."

∎

When the robots left the restored spaceplane standing on its own landing gear, the digging machine crept away to join the others. Busy again, they were digging a row of deep pits. We watched them bury themselves under the rubble, leaving only a row of new craters that might become a puzzle, I thought, to later astronomers. Casey called us back to the dome to watch a tank truck crawling out of the underground hangar dug into the crater rim.

"We're off to Earth!" He slid his arm around Pepe. "Who's with us?"

Arne scowled at him. "Didn't you hear Sandor?"

"Sandor's gone." He grinned at Pepe. "We have a plan of our own."

They hadn't talked about it, but I had heard their whispers and seen them busy in the shops. Though the spacebending science of the slipship was still a mystery to us, I knew the robots had taught them astronautics and electronics. I knew they had made holos of Pen, begging him to say more about the new Earth than he ever would.

"I don't know your plan." Arne made a guttural grunt. "But I have seen the reports of people who went down to evaluate our terraforming. They've never found anything they liked, and never got back to the Moon."

"*¿Qué importa?*" Pepe shrugged. "Better that than wasting our lives waiting *por nada.*"

"We belong here." Stubbornly, Arne echoed what Pen had said. "Our mission is just to keep the station alive. Certainly not to throw ourselves away on insane adventures. I'm staying here."

Dian chose to stay with him, though I don't think they were in love. Her love was the station itself, with all its relics of the old Earth. Even as a little child, she had always wanted to work with her holo mother, recording everything that Pen took away to be copied and returned.

Tanya had set her heart on Sandor Pen. I think she had always dreamed that someday he would take her with him back to Earth. She was desolate and bitter when he left without her, her pride in herself deeply hurt.

"He did love us when we were little," she sobbed when Pepe begged her to join him and Casey. "But just because we were children. Or just interesting pets. Interesting because we aren't his kind of human, and people that live forever don't have children."

Pepe begged again, I think because he loved her. Whatever they found on Earth, it would be bigger than our tunnels, and surely more exciting. She cried and kissed him and chose to stay. The new Earth had no place for her. Sandor wouldn't want her, even if she found him. She promised to listen for their radio and pray they came back safe.

I had always been the station historian. Earth was where history was happening. I shook hands with Pepe and Casey and agreed to go with them.

"You won't belong," Tanya warned us. "You'll have to look out for yourselves."

She found water canteens and ration packs for us, and reminded us to pack safari garments to wear when we got out of our space gear. We took turns in the dome, watching the tank truck till it reached the plane and the robots began pumping fuel.

"Time." Casey wore a grin of eager expectation. "Time to say good-bye."

Dian and Arne shook our hands, wearing very solemn faces. Tanya clung a long time to Pepe and kissed me and Casey, her face so tearstained and drawn that I ached with pity for her. We got into our shining suits, went out to the plane, climbed the landing stair. Again the door refused to open.

Casey stepped back to speak on his helmet radio.

"Priority message from Director Sandor Pen." His crackling voice was almost Pen's. "Special orders for restored spaceplane SP2469."

The door responded with a clatter of speech that was alien to me.

"Orders effective now," Casey snapped. "Tycho Station personnel K. C. Kell, Pedro Navarro, and Duncan Yare are authorized to board for immediate passage to Earth."

Silently, the door swung open.

I had expected to find a robot at the controls, but we found ourselves alone in the nose cone, the pilot seat empty. Awed by whatever the plane had become, we watched it operate itself. The door swung shut. Air seals hissed. The engines snorted and roared. The ship trembled, and we lifted off the Moon.

Looking back for the station, all I found was the dome, a bright little eye peering into space from the rugged gray peaks of the crater rim. It shrank till I lost it in the great lake of black shadow and the bright black peak at the center of the Tycho crater. The Moon dwindled till we saw it whole, gray and impact-battered, dropping behind us into a black and bottomless pit.

Pen's flight in the slipship may have taken an hour or an instant. In the old rocket ship, we had time to watch three full rotations of the slowly swelling planet ahead. The jets were silent through most of the flight, with only an occasional whisper to correct our course. We floated in free fall, careful not to blunder against the controls. Taking turns belted in the seats, we tried to sleep but seldom did. Most of the time we spent searching Earth with binoculars, searching for signs of civilization.

"Nothing," Casey muttered again and again. "Nothing that

looks like a city, a railway, a canal, a dam. Nothing but green. Only forest, jungle, grassland. Have they let the planet return to nature?"

"*Tal vez.*" Pepe always shrugged. "*Pero o no.* We are still too high to tell."

At last the jets came back to life, steering us down into air-breaking orbit. Twice around the puzzling planet, and Australia exploded ahead. The jets thundered. We fell again, toward the wide tongue of green land between the narrow cusps of that long crescent lake.

3

Looking from the windows, we found the spaceplane standing on an elevated pad at the center of a long quadrangle covered with tended lawns, shrubs and banks of brilliant flowers. Wide avenues all around it were walled with buildings that awed and amazed me.

"Sandor's Tycho Memorial!" Pepe jogged my ribs. "There's the old monument at the American capital! I know it from Dian's videos."

"Ancient history." Casey shrugged as if it hardly mattered. "I want to see Earth today."

Pepe opened the door. In our safari suits, we went out on the landing for a better view. The door shut. I heard it hiss behind us, sealing itself. He turned to stare again. The monument stood at the end of the quadrangle, towering above its image in a long reflecting pool, flanked on one side by a Stonehenge in gleaming silver, on the other by a sandbanked Sphinx with the nose restored.

We stood goggling at the old American capital at the other end of the mall, the British Houses of Parliament to its right, and Big Ben tolling the time. The Kremlin adjoined them, gilded onion domes gleaming above the grim redbrick walls. The Parthenon, roofed and new and magnificent as ever, stood beyond them on a rocky hill.

Across the quadrangle I found the splendid domes of the Taj Mahal, Saint Peter's Basilica, the Hagia Sophia from ancient Istanbul. On higher ground in the distance, I recognized the Chrysler

Building from old New York, the Eiffel Tower from Paris, a Chinese pagoda, the Great Pyramid clad once again in smooth white marble. Farther off, I found a gray mountain ridge that copied the familiar curve of Tycho's rim, topped with the shine of our own native dome.

"We got here!" Elated, Pepe slapped Casey's back. "Now what?"

"They owe us." Casey turned to look again. "We put them here, whenever it was. This ought to remind them how they got here and what we've given them."

"If they care." Pepe turned back to the door. "Let's see if we can call Sandor."

"Facility closed." We heard the door's toneless robot voice. "Admission denied by order of Tycho Authority."

"Let us in!" Casey shouted. "We want the stuff we left aboard. Clothing, backpacks, canteens. Open the door so we can get them."

"Admission denied."

He hit the door with his fist and kissed his bruised knuckles.

"Admission denied."

"We're here, anyhow."

Pepe shrugged and started down the landing stair. A strange bellow stopped him, rolling back from the walls around. It took us a moment to see that it came from a locomotive chuffing slowly past the Washington Monument, puffing white steam. Hauling a train of open cars filled with seated passengers, it crept around the quadrangle, stopping often to let riders off and on.

The Sun was high, and we shaded our eyes to study them. All as lean and trim as Sandor, and often nude, they had the same nut-brown skins. Many carried bags or backpacks. A few scattered across the lawns and gardens, most waited at the corners for signal lights to let them cross the avenue.

"Tourists, maybe?" I guessed. "Here to see Sandor's recovered history?"

"But I see no children." Casey shook his head. "You'd think they'd bring the children."

"They're people, anyhow." Pepe grinned hopefully. "We'll find somebody to tell us more than Sandor did."

■

We climbed down the stairs, on down a wide flight of steps to a walk that curved through banks of strange and fragrant blooms. Ahead of us a couple had stopped. The woman looked a little odd, I thought, with her head of short ginger-hued fur instead of hair, yet as lovely as Mona had looked in the holos made when she and El Chino reached the Moon. The man was youthful and handsome as Sandor. I thought they were in love.

Laughing at something he had said, she ran a little way ahead and turned to pose for his camera, framed between the monument and the Sphinx. She had worn a scarlet shawl around her shoulders. At a word from him, she whipped it off and smiled for his lens. Her daintily nippled breasts had been pale beneath the shawl, and he waited for the sun to color them.

We watched till he had snapped the camera. Laughing again, she ran back to toss the shawl around his shoulders and throw her arms around him. They clung together for a long kiss. We had stopped a dozen yards away. Casey spoke hopefully when they turned to face us.

"Hello?"

They stared blankly at us. Casey managed an uncertain smile, but a nervous sweat had filmed his dark Oriental face.

"Forgive us, please. Do you speak English? *Français? ¿Español?*"

They frowned at him, and the man answered with a stream of vowels that were almost music and a rattle of consonants I knew I could never learn to imitate. I caught a hint of Sandor's odd accent but nothing like our English. They moved closer. The man pulled the little camera out of his bag, clicked it at Casey, stepped nearer to get his head. Laughing at him, the woman came to pose again beside Casey, slipping a golden arm around him for a final shot.

"We came in that machine. Down from the Moon!" Desperation on his face, he gestured at the spaceplane behind us, turned to point toward the Moon's pale disk in the sky above the Parthenon, waved to show our flight from it to the pedestal. "We've just landed from Tycho Station. If you understand—"

Laughing at him, they caught hands and ran on toward the Sphinx.

"What the hell!" Staring after them, he shook his head. "What the bloody hell!"

"They don't know we're real." Pepe chuckled bitterly. "They take us for dummies. Part of the show."

■

We followed a path that led toward the Parthenon and stopped at the curb to watch the traffic flowing around the quadrangle. Cars, buses, vans, occasional trucks; they reminded me of street scenes in pre-impact videos. A Yellow Cab pulled up beside us. A woman sprang out. Slim and golden-skinned, she was almost a twin of the tourist who had posed with Casey.

The driver, however, might have been an unlikely survivor from the old Earth. Heavy, swarthy, wheezing for his breath, he wore dark glasses and a grimy leather jacket. Lighting a cigarette, he hauled himself out of the cab, waddled around to open the trunk, handed the woman a folded tripod, and grunted sullenly when she tipped him.

Casey walked up to him as he was climbing back into the cab.

"Sir!" He seemed not to hear, and Casey called louder. "Sir!"

Ignoring us, he got into the cab and pulled away. Casey turned with a baffled frown to Pepe and me.

"Did you see his face? It was dead! Some stiff plastic. His eyes are blind, behind those glasses. He's some kind of robot, no more alive than our robots on the Moon."

Keeping a cautious distance, we followed the woman with the tripod. Ignoring us, she stopped to set it up to support a flat round plate of some black stuff. As she stepped away, a big transparent bubble swelled out of the plate, clouded, turned to silver. She leaned to peer into it.

Venturing closer, I saw that the bubble had become a circular window that framed the Washington Monument, the Statue of Liberty, and the Sphinx. They seemed oddly changed, magnified and brighter, suddenly in motion. Everything shook. The monument leaned and toppled, crushing the statue. The Sphinx looked down across the fragments, intact and forever enigmatic.

I must have come too close. The woman turned with an irritated frown to brush me away as if I had been an annoying fly. Retreating, I looked again. As she bent again to the window, the sky in it changed. The Sun exploded into a huge, dull-red ball that turned the whole scene pink. Close beside it was a tiny, bright-blue star. Our spaceplane took shape in the foreground, the motors firing and white flame washing the pedestal, as if it were taking off to escape catastrophe.

Awed into silence, Casey gestured us away.

"An artist!" Pepe whispered. "An artist at work."

We walked on past the Parthenon and waited at the corner to cross the avenue. Pepe nodded at the blue-clad cop standing out on the pavement with a whistle and a white baton, directing traffic. "Watch him. He's mechanical."

So were most of the drivers. The passengers, however, riding in the taxis and buses or arriving on the train, looked entirely human, as live as Sandor himself, eager as the tourists of the pre-impact Earth to see these monumental restorations of their forgotten past.

They flocked the sidewalks, climbed the Capital steps to photograph the quadrangle and one another, wandered around the corner and on down the avenue. We fell in with them. They seldom noticed Pepe or me, but sometimes stopped to stare at Casey or take his picture.

"One more robot!" he muttered. "That's what they take me for."

■

We spent the rest of the day wandering replicated streets, passing banks, broker's offices, shops, bars, hairdressers, restaurants, police stations. A robot driver had parked his van in front of a bookstore to unload cartons stamped *Encyclopaedia Britannica*. A robot beggar was rattling coins in a tin cup. A robot cop was pounding in pursuit of a red-spattered robot fugitive. We saw slim gold-skinned people, gracefully alive, entering restaurants and bars, trooping into shops, emerging with their purchases.

Footsore and hungry before the day was over, we followed a tantalizing aroma that led us to a line of golden folk waiting under a sign that read:

STEAK PLUS!
PRIME ANGUS BEEF
DONE TO YOUR ORDER

Pepe fretted that we had no money for a meal.

"We'll eat before we tell them," Casey said.

"They're human, anyhow." Pepe grasped for some crumb of comfort. "They like food."

"I hope they're human."

Standing in line, I watched and listened to those ahead of us, hoping for any link of human contact, finding none at all. A few turned to give us puzzled glances. One man stared at Casey till I saw his fists clenching. Their speech sometimes had rhythm and pitch that made an eerie music, but I never caught a hint of anything familiar.

A robot at the door was admitting people a few at a time. His bright-lensed eyes looked behind us when we reached him. Finding nobody, he shut the door.

Limping under Earth gravity, growing hungrier and thirstier, we drifted on until the avenue ended at a high wall of something clear as glass, which cut the memorial off like a slicing blade. Beyond the wall lay an open landscape that recalled Dian's travel videos of tropical Africa. A line of trees marked a watercourse that wound down a shallow valley. Zebras and antelope grazed near us, unalarmed by a dark-maned lion watching sleepily from a little hill.

"There's water we could drink." Pepe nodded at the stream. "If we can get past the wall."

We walked on till it stopped us. Seamless, hard and slick, too tall for us to climb, it ran on in both directions as far as we could see. Too tired to go farther, we sat there on the curb watching the freedom of the creatures beyond till dusk and a chill in the air drove us back to look for shelter. What we found was a stack of empty cartons behind a discount furniture outlet. We flattened a few of them to make a bed, ripped up the largest to cover us, and tried to sleep.

"You can't blame Sandor," Pepe muttered as we lay there shivering under our cardboard. "He told us we'd never belong."

4

We dozed on our cardboard pallet, aching under the heavy drag of Earth's gravity through a never-ending night, and woke stiff and cold and desperate. I almost wished we were back on the Moon.

"There has to be a hole in the fence," Casey tried to cheer us. "To let the tourists in."

The train had come from the north. Back at the wall, we limped north along a narrow road inside it, our spirits lifting a little as exercise warmed us. Beyond a bend, the railway ran out of a tunnel, across a long steel bridge over a cliff-rimmed gorge the stream had cut, and into our prison through a narrow archway in the barrier.

"We'd have to walk the bridge." Pepe stopped uneasily to shake his head at the ribbon of water on the canyon's rocky floor, far below. "A train could catch us on the track."

"We'll just wait for it to pass," Casey said.

We waited, lying hidden in a drainage ditch beside the track till the engine burst out of the tunnel, steam whistle howling. The cars rattled past us, riders leaning to stare at Sandor's restorations ahead. We clambered out of the ditch and sprinted across the bridge. Jumping off the track at the tunnel mouth, we rolled down a grass slope, got our breath, and tramped southwest away from the wall and into country that looked open.

The memorial sank behind a wooded ridge until all we could see was Sandor's replica of our own lookout dome on his replica of Tycho's rugged rim. We came out across a wide valley floor, scattered with clumps of trees and grazing animals I recognized; wildebeest, gazelles, and a little herd of graceful impala.

"Thanks to old Calvin DeFort. Another Noah saving Earth from a different deluge." Casey shaded his eyes to watch a pair of ostriches running from us across the empty land. "But where are the people?"

"Where's any water?" Pepe muttered. "No deluge, please. Just water we can drink."

We plodded on through tall green grass till I saw elephants marching out of a stand of trees off to our right. A magnificent bull with great white tusks, half a dozen others behind him, a baby with its mother. They came straight toward us. I wanted to run, but Casey simply beckoned for us to move aside. They ambled past us to drink from a pool we hadn't seen. Waiting till they had moved on, we turned toward the pool. Pepe pushed ahead and bent to scoop water up in his cupped hands.

"Don't!" a child's voice called behind us. "Unclean water might harm you."

A small girl came running toward us from the trees where the elephants had been. The first child we had seen, she was daintily lovely in a white blouse and a short blue skirt, her fair face half hidden under a wide-brimmed hat tied under her chin with a bright red ribbon.

"Hello." She stopped a few yards away, her blue eyes wide with wonder. "You are the Moon men?"

"And strangers here." Casey gave her our names. "Strangers in trouble."

"You deceived the ancient spaceship," she accused us soberly. "You should not be here on Earth."

We gaped at her. "How did you know?"

"The ship informed my father."

We stood silent, lost in wonder of our own. A charming picture of childish innocence, but she had shaken me with a chill of terror. Pepe stepped warily back from her, but after a moment Casey caught his breath to ask, "Who is your father?"

"You called him your uncle when you knew him on the Moon." Pride lit her face. "He is a very great and famous man. He discovered the lunar site and recovered the lost history of humankind. He rebuilt the ancient structures you saw around you where the ship came down."

"I get it." Casey nodded, looking crestfallen and dazed. "I think I begin to get it."

"We can't be sorry." Blinking at her, Pepe caught a long breath. "We'd had too much of the Moon. But now we're lost here, in a world I don't begin to understand. Do you know what will happen to us?"

"My father isn't sure." She looked away toward the replicated

Tycho dome. "I used to beg him to take me with him to the Moon. He said the station had no place for me." She turned to study us again. "You are interesting to see. My name is—"

She uttered a string of rhythmic consonants and singing vowels, and smiled at Pepe's failure when he tried to imitate them.

"Just call me Tling," she said. "That will be easier for you to say." She turned to Pepe. "If you want water, come with me."

We followed her back to a little circle of square stones in the shade of the nearest tree. Beckoning us to sit, she opened a basket, found a bottle of water, and filled a cup for Pepe. Amused at the eager way he drained it, she filled it again for him, and then for Casey and me.

"I came out to visit the elephants," she told us. "I love elephants. I am very grateful to you Moon people for preserving the tissue specimens that have kept so many ancient creatures alive."

I had caught a tantalizing fragrance when she opened the basket. She saw Pepe's eyes still on it.

"I brought food for some of my forest friends," she said. "If you are hungry."

Pepe said we were starving. She spread a white napkin on one of the stones and began laying out what she had brought. Fruits I thought were peachlike and grapelike and pearlike, but wonderfully sweet and different. Small brown cakes with aromas that that wet my mouth. We devoured them so avidly that she seemed amused.

"Where are the people?" Casey waved his arm at the empty landscape. "Don't you have cities?"

"We do," she said. "Though my father says they are smaller than those you built on the prehistoric Earth." She gestured toward the elephants. "We share the planet with other beings. He says you damaged it when you let your own biology run out of control."

"Maybe we did, but that's not what brought the impactor." Casey frowned again. "You are the only child we have seen."

"There's not much room for us. You see, we don't die."

I was listening, desperately hoping for something that might help us find or make a place for ourselves, but everything I heard was making our new world stranger. Casey gazed at her.

"Why don't you die?"

"If I can explain—" She paused as if looking for an answer we might understand. "My father says I should tell you that we have changed ourselves since the clones came back to colonize the dead Earth. We have altered the genes and invented the nanorobs."

"Nanorobs?"

She paused again, staring at the far-off elephants.

"My father calls them artificial symbiotes. They are tiny things that live like bacteria in our bodies but do good instead of harm. They are partly organic, partly diamond, partly gold. They move in the blood to repair or replace injured cells, or regrow a missing organ. They assist our nerves and our brain cells."

The food forgotten, we were staring at her. A picture of innocent simplicity in the simple skirt and blouse and floppy hat, she was suddenly so frightening that I trembled. She reached to put her small hand on mine before she went on.

"My father says I should say they are tiny robots, half-machine and half-alive. They are electronic. They can be programmed to store digital information. They pulse in unison, making their own waves in the brain and turning the whole body into a radio antenna. Sitting here speaking to you, I can also speak to my father."

She looked up to smile at me, her small hand closing on my fingers.

"Mr. Dunk, please don't be afraid of me. I know we seem different. I know I seem strange to you, but I would never harm you."

She was so charming that I wanted to take her in my arms, but my awe had grown to dread. We all shrank from her and sat wordless till hunger drove us to attack the fruit and cakes again. Pepe began asking questions as we ate.

Where did she live?

"On that hill." She nodded toward the west, but I couldn't tell which hill she meant. "My father selected a place where he could look out across the memorial."

Did she go to school?

"School?" The word seemed to puzzle her for a moment, and then she shook her head. "We do not require the schools my father says you had in the prehistoric world. He says your schools existed

to program the brains of young people. Our nanocoms can be programmed and reprogrammed instantly, with no trouble at all, to load
whatever information we need. That is how I learned your English
when I needed it."

She smiled at his dazed face and selected a plump purple berry
for herself.

"Our bodies, however, do need training." Delicately, she wiped
her lips on a white napkin. "We form social groups to play games
or practice skills. We fly our sliders all around the Earth. I love to
ski on high mountains where snow falls. I've dived off coral reefs
to observe sea things. I like music, art, drama, games of creation."

"That should be fun." Pepe's eyes were wide. "More fun than
life in our tunnels on the Moon." His face went suddenly dark. "I
hope your father doesn't send us back there."

"He can't, even if he wanted to." She laughed at his alarm.
"He's finally done with the excavation. The charter site is closed
and protected for future ages. All intrusion prohibited."

"So what will he do with us?"

"Does he have to do anything?" Seeming faintly vexed, she
looked off toward the station dome on the crater ridge. "He says
he has no place ready for you, but there are humanoid replicates
playing your roles there in the Tycho simulation. I suppose you
could replace them, if that would make you happy."

"Pretending we were back on the Moon?" Casey turned grim.
"I don't think so."

"If you don't want that—"

She stopped, tipped her head as if to listen, and began gathering the water bottle and the rest of the fruit into the basket. Anxiously, Pepe asked if something was wrong.

"My mother." Frowning, she shook her head. "She's calling
me home."

"Please!" Casey begged her. "Can't you stay a little longer?
You are the only friend we've found. I don't know what we can
do without you."

"I wish I could help you, but my mother is afraid for me."

"I wondered if you weren't in danger." He glanced out across
the valley. "We saw a lion. Your really shouldn't be out here alone."

"It's not the lion." She shook her head. "I know him. A wonderful friend, so fast and strong and fierce." Her eyes shone at the recollection. "And I know a Bengal tiger. He was hiding in the brush because he was afraid of people. I taught him that we would never hurt him. Once he let me ride him when he chased a gazelle. It was wonderfully exciting."

Her voice grew solemn.

"I'm glad the gazelle got away, though the tiger was hungry and very disappointed. I try to forgive him, because I know he has to kill for food, like all the lions and leopards. They must kill, to stay alive. My mother says it is the way of nature, and entirely necessary. Too many grazing things would destroy the grass and finally starve themselves."

We stared again, wondering at her.

"How did you tame the tiger?"

"I think the nanorobs help me reach his mind, the way I touch yours. He learned that I respect him. We are good friends. He would fight to protect me, even from you."

"Is your mother afraid of us?"

She picked up the basket and stood shifting on her feet, frowning at us uncertainly.

"The nanorobs—" She hesitated. "I trust you, but the nanorobs—"

She stopped again.

"I thought you said nanorobs were good."

"That's the problem." She hesitated, trouble on her face. "My mother says you have none. She can't reach your minds. You do not hear when she speaks to you. She says you don't belong, because you are not one of us. What she fears—what she fears is you."

Speechless, Casey blinked at her sadly.

"I am sorry to go so soon." With a solemn little bow for each of us, she shook our hands. "Sorry you have no nanorobs. Sorry my mother is so anxious. Sorry to say good-bye."

"Please tell your father—" Casey began.

"He knows," she said. "He is sorry you came here."

Walking away with her basket, she turned to wave her hand at us, her face framed for a moment by the wide-brimmed hat. I thought she was going to speak, but in a moment she was gone.

"Beautiful!" Casey whispered. "She'll grow up to be another Mona."

Looking back toward the copied monuments of the old Earth, the copied station dome shining on the copied Tycho rim, I saw a dark-maned lion striding across the valley toward the pool where the elephants had drunk. Three smaller females followed. None of them our friends. I shivered.

5

We wandered on up the valley after Tling left us, keeping clear of the trees and trying to stay alert for danger or any hint of help.

"If Sandor lives out here," Casey said, "there must be others. People, I hope, who won't take us for robots."

We stopped to watch impala drinking at a water hole. They simply raised their heads to look at us, but fled when a cheetah burst out of a thicket. The smallest was too slow. The cheetah knocked it down and carried it back into the brush.

"No nanorobs for them," Pepe muttered. "Or us."

We tramped on, finding no sign of anything human. By mid-afternoon, hungry and thirsty again, with nothing human in view ahead, we sat down to rest on an outcropping of rock. Pepe dug a little holo of Tanya out of his breast pocket and passed it to show us her dark-eyed smile.

"If we hadn't lost the radio—" He caught himself, with a stiff little grin. "Still, I guess we wouldn't call. I'd love to hear her voice. I know she's anxious, but I wouldn't want her to know the fix we're in—"

He stopped when a shadow flickered across the holo. Looking up, we found a silvery slider craft dropping to the grass a few yards from us. An oval door dilated in the side of it. Tling jumped out.

"We found you!" she cried. "Even with no nanorobs. Here is my mother."

A slender woman came out behind her, laughing at Pepe when he tried to repeat the name she gave us.

"She says you can just call her Lo."

Tling still wore the blouse and skirt, with her wide-brimmed hat, but Lo was nude except for a gauzy blue sash worn over her shoulder. As graceful and trim, and nearly as sexless as Sandor, she had the same cream-colored skin, already darkening where the sun struck it, but she had a thick crown of bright red-brown curls instead of Sandor's cap of sleek fur.

"Dr. Yare." Tling spoke carefully to let us hear. "Mr. Navarro. Mr. Kell, who is also called El Chino. They were cloned at Tycho Station from prehistoric tissue specimens."

"You were cloned for duty there." Lo eyed us severely. "How did you get here?"

"We lied to the ship." Casey straightened wryly to face her. "We did it because we didn't want to live out our lives in that pit on the Moon. I won't say I'm sorry, but now we are in trouble. I don't want to die."

"You will die," she told him bluntly. "Like all your kind. You carry no nanorobs."

"I guess." He shrugged. "But first we want a chance to live."

"Mother, please!" Tling caught her hand. "With no nanorobs, they are in immediate danger here. Can we help them stay alive?"

"That depends on your father."

"I tried to ask him," Tling said. "He didn't answer."

We watched Lo's solemn frown, saw Tling's deepening trouble.

"I wish you had nanorobs." She turned at last to translate for us. "My father has gone out to meet an interstellar ship that has just come back after eight hundred years away. The officers are telling him a very strange story."

She looked up at her mother, as if listening.

"It carried colonists for the planets of the star Enthel, which is four hundred light-years toward the galactic core. They had taken off with no warning of trouble. The destination planet had been surveyed and opened for settlement. It had rich natural resources, with no native life to be protected. Navigation algorithms for the flight had been tested, occupation priorities secured."

She stared up at the sky, in baffled dismay.

"Now the ship has returned, two thousand colonists still aboard."

Casey asked what had gone wrong. We waited, watching their anxious frowns.

"My father is inquiring." Tling turned back to us. "He's afraid of something dreadful."

"It must have been dreadful," Pepe whispered. "Imagine eight hundred years on a ship in space!"

"Only instants for them." Tling shook her head, smiling at him. "Time stops, remember, at the speed of light. By their own time, they left only yesterday. Yet their situation is still hard enough. Their friends are scattered away. Their whole world is gone. They feel lost and desperate."

She turned to her mother. "Why couldn't they land?"

Her mother listened again. Far out across the valley I saw a little herd of zebras running. I couldn't see what had frightened them.

"My father is asking," she told us at last. "The passengers were not told why the ship had to turn back. The officers have promised a statement, but my father says they can't agree on what to say. They aren't sure what they found on the destination planet. He believes they're afraid to say what they believe."

The running zebras veered aside. I saw the tawny flash of a lion charging to meet them, saw a limping zebra go down. My own ankle was aching from a stone that had turned under my foot, and I felt as helpless as the zebra.

"Don't worry, Mr. Dunk." Tling reached to touch my arm. "My father is very busy with the ship. I don't know what he can do with you, but I don't want the animals to kill you. I think we can keep you safe till he comes home. Can't we, mother?"

Her lips pressed tight, Lo shrugged as if she had forgotten us.

"Please, mother. I know they are primitives, but they would never harm me. I can understand them the way I understand the animals. They are hungry and afraid, with nowhere else to go."

Lo stood motionless for a moment, frowning at us.

"Get in."

She beckoned us into the flyer and lifted her face again as if listening to the sky.

■

We soared toward a rocky hill and landed on a level ledge near the summit. Climbing out, we looked down across the grassy valley and over the ridge to Sandor's memorial just beyond. Closer than I expected, I found the bright metal glint of the rebuilt spaceplane on the mall, the Capitol dome and the Washington obelisk, the white marble sheen of the Egyptian pyramid looming out of green forest beyond.

"My father picked this spot." Tling nodded toward the cliff. "He wanted to watch the memorial built."

While her mother stood listening intently at the sky, Tling inspected our mudstained safari suits.

"You need a bath," she decided, "before you eat."

Running ahead, she took us down an arched tunnel into the hill and showed me into a room far larger than my cell below the station dome. Warm water sprayed me when I stepped into the shower, warm air dried me. A human-shaped robot handed me my clothing when I came out, clean and neatly folded. It guided me to a room where Tling was already sitting with Pepe and Casey at a table set with plates around a pyramid of fragrant fruit.

"Mr. Chino asked about my mother." She looked up to smile at me. "You saw that she's different, with different nanorobs. She comes from the Garenkrake system, three hundred light-years away. Its people had forgotten where they came from. She wanted to know. When her search for the mother planet brought her here, she found my father already digging at the Tycho site. They've worked together ever since."

Pepe and Casey were already eating. Casey turned to Tling, who was nibbling delicately at something that looked like a huge purple orchid.

"What do you think will happen to us?"

"I'll ask my father when I can." She glanced toward the ceiling. "He is still busy with the ship's officers. I'm sorry you're afraid of my mother. She doesn't hate you, not really. If she seems cool to you, it's just because she has worked so long at the site, digging up relics of the first world. She thinks you seem so—so primitive."

She shook her head at our uneasy frowns.

"You told her you lied to the ship." She looked at Casey. "That bothers her, because the nanorobs do not transmit untruths or let people hurt each other. She feels sorry for you."

Pepe winced. "We feel sorry for ourselves."

∎

Tling sat for a minute, silently, frowning, and turned back to us.

"The ship is big trouble for my father," she told us. "It leaves him no time for you. He says you should have stayed on the Moon."

"I know." Casey shrugged. "But we're here. We can't go back. We want to stay alive."

"I feel your fear." She gave us an uneasy smile. "My father's too busy to talk to you, but if you'll come to my room, there is news about the ship."

The room must have been her nursery. In one corner was a child's bed piled with dolls and toys, a cradle on the floor beside it. The wall above was alive with a scenic holo. Long-legged birds flew away from a water hole when a tiger came out of tall grass to drink. A zebra stallion ventured warily close, snuffing at us. A prowling leopard froze and ran from a bull elephant. She gestured at the wall.

"I was a baby here, learning to love the animals."

That green landscape was suddenly gone. The wall had become a wide window that showed us great spacecraft drifting though empty blackness. Blinding highlights glared where the Sun struck it. The rest was lost in shadow, but I made out a thick bright metal disk, slowly turning. Tiny-looking sliders clung around a bulging dome at its center.

"It's in parking orbit, waiting for anywhere to go," Tling said. "Let's look inside."

She gave us glimpses of the curving floors where the spin created a false gravity. People sat in rows of seats like those in holos of ancient aircraft. More stood crowded in aisles and corridors. I heard scraps of hushed and anxious talk.

". . . home on a Pacific island."

The camera caught a woman with a crown of what looked like bright golden feathers instead of hair. Holding a whimpering baby in one arm, the other around a grim-faced man, she was answering questions from someone we didn't see. The voice we heard was Tling's.

"It's hard for us." Her lips were not moving, but the voice went sharp with her distress. "We had a good life there. Mark's an imagineer. I was earning a good living as a genetic artist, designing ornamentals to special order. We are not the pioneer type, but we did want a baby." An ironic wry smile twisted her lips. "A dream come true!"

She lifted the infant to kiss its gold-capped head.

"Look at us now." She smiled sadly at the child. "We spent our savings for a vision of paradise on Fendris Four. A tropical beach-front between the surf and a bamboo forest, snow on a volcanic cone behind it. A hundred families of us, all friends forever."

She sighed and rocked the baby.

"They didn't let us off the ship. Or even tell us why. We're desperate, with our money gone and baby to care for. Now they say there's nowhere else we can go."

■

The wall flickered and the holos came back with monkeys chattering in jungle treetops.

"That's the problem," Tling said. "Two thousand people like them, stuck on the ship with nowhere to live. My father's problem now, since the council voted to put him in charge."

Casey asked, "Why can't they leave the ship?"

"If you don't understand—" She was silent for a moment. "My mother says it's the way of the nanorobs. They won't let people overrun the planet and use it up like my mother says the primitives did, back before the impacts. Births must be balanced by migration. Those unlucky people lost their space when they left Earth."

"Eight hundred years ago?"

"Eight hundred of our time." She shrugged. "A day or so of theirs."

"What can your father do for them?"

"My mother says he's still searching for a safe destination."

"If he can't find one—" Casey frowned. "And they can't come home. It seems terribly unfair. Do you let the nanorobs rule you?"

"Rule us?" Puzzled, she turned her head to listen and nodded at the wall. "You don't understand. They do unite us, but there is no conflict. They live in all of us, acting to keep us alive and well, guiding us to stay free and happy, but moving us only by our own consent. My mother says they are part of what you used to call the unconscious."

"Those people on the ship?" Doubtfully, Casey frowned. "Still alive, I guess, but not free to get off or happy at all."

"They are troubled." Nodding soberly, she listened again. "But my mother says I should explain the nanorob way. She says the old primitives lived in what she calls the way of the jungle genes, back when survival required traits of selfish aggression. The nanorobs have let us change our genes to escape the greed and jealousy and, violence that led to so much crime and war and pain on the ancient Earth. They guide us toward what is best for all. My mother says the people on the ship will be content to follow the nanorob way when my father has helped them find it."

She turned her head. "I heard my mother call."

I hadn't heard a thing, but she ran out of the room. In the holo wall, high-shouldered wildebeest were leaping off a cliff to swim across a river. One stumbled, toppled, vanished under the rapid water. We watched in dismal silence till Casey turned to frown at Pepe and me.

"I don't think I like the nanorob way."

We had begun to understand why Sandor had no place on Earth for us.

6

"Dear sirs, I must beg you to excuse us."

Tling made a careful little bow and explained that her mother was taking her to dance and music practice, then going on to a meeting about the people on the stranded ship. We were left alone with the robots. They were man-shaped, ivory-colored, blank-faced. Lacking nanorobs, they were voice-controlled.

Casey tried to question them about the population, cities, and industries of the new Earth, but they had been programmed only for domestic service, with no English or information about any-thing else. Defeated by their blank-lensed stares, we sat out on the terrace, looking down across the memorial and contemplating our own uncertain future, till they called us in for dinner.

The dishes they served us were strange, but Pepe urged us to eat while we could.

"*¿Mañana?*" He shook his head uneasily. "*¿Quién sabe?*"

Night was falling before we got back to the terrace. A thin Moon was setting in the west. In the east, a locomotive headlight flashed across the memorial. The mall was lit for evening tours, the Taj Mahal a glowing gem, the Great Pyramid an ivory island in the creeping dusk. The robots had our beds ready when the light went out. They had served wine with dinner, and I slept without a dream.

Awake early next morning, rested again and lifted with unreasonable hope, I found Tling standing outside at the end of the terrace, looking down across the valley. She had hair like her mother's, not feathers or fur, but blonde and cropped short. Despite the awesome power of her nanorobs, I thought she looked very small and vulnerable. She started when I spoke.

"Good morning, Mr. Dunk." She wiped at her face with the back of her hand and tried to smile. I saw that her eyes were puffy and red. "How is your ankle?"

"Better."

"I was worried." She found a pale smile. "Because you have no symbiotes to help repair such injuries."

I asked if she had heard from her father and the emigrant ship. She turned silently to look again across the sunlit valley and the memorial. I saw the far plume of steam from an early train crawling over the bridge toward the Sphinx.

"I watched a baby giraffe." Her voice was slow and faint, almost as if she was speaking to herself. "I saw it born. I watched it learning to stand, nuzzling its mother, learning to suck. It finally followed her away, wobbling on its legs. It was beautiful—"

Her voice failed. Her hand darted to her lips. She stood trembling, staring at me, her eyes wide and dark with pain.

"My father!" Her voice came suddenly sharp and thin, almost a scream. "He's going away. I'll never see him again."

She ran back inside.

When the robots called us to breakfast, we found her sitting between her parents. She had washed her tear-streaked face, but the food on her plate had not been touched. Here out of the Sun, Sandor's face had gone pale and grim. He seemed not to see us till Tling turned to frown at him. He rose then, and came around the table to shake our hands.

"Good morning, Dr. Pen." Casey gave him a wry smile. "I see why you didn't want us here, but I can't apologize. We'll never be sorry we came."

"Sit down." He spoke shortly. "Let's eat."

We sat. The robots brought us plates loaded with foods we had never tasted. Saying no more to us, Sandor signaled a robot to refill his cup of the bitter black tea and bent over a bowl of crimson berries. Tling sat looking up at him in anguished devotion till Casey spoke.

"Sir, we heard about your problem with the stranded colonists. Can you tell us why their ship came back?"

"Nothing anybody understands." He shook his head and gave Tling a tender smile before he pushed the berries aside and turned gravely back to us. His voice was quick and crisp. "The initial survey expedition had found their destination planet quite habitable and seeded it with terran-type life. Expeditions had followed to settle the three major continents. This group was to find room on the third.

"They arrived safe but got no answer when they called the planet from orbit. The atmosphere was hazed with dust that obscured the surface, but a search in the infrared found relics of a very successful occupation. Pavements, bridges, masonry, steel skeletons that had been buildings. All half buried under dunes of red, windblown dust. No green life anywhere. A derelict craft from one of the pioneer expeditions was still in orbit, but dead as the planet.

"They never learned what killed the planet. No news of the disaster seems to have reached any other world, which suggests that it struck unexpectedly and spread fast. The medical officers believe the killer may have been some unknown organism that attacks organic life, but the captain refused to allow any attempt to land or investigate. She elected to turn back at once, without contact. A choice that probably saved their lives."

He picked up his spoon and bent again to his bowl of berries.

I tried one of them. It was tart, sweet, with a heady tang I can't describe.

"Sir," Casey spoke again, "we saw those people. They're desperate. What will happen to them now?"

"A dilemma." Sandor looked at Tling, with a sad little shrug. She turned her head to hide a sob. "Habitable planets are relatively rare. The few we find must be surveyed, terraformed, approved for settlement. As events came out, these people have been fortunate. We were able to get an emergency waiver that will allow them to settle on an open planet, five hundred light-years in toward the core. Fuel and fresh supplies are being loaded now."

"And my father—" Tling looked up at me, her voice almost a wail. "He has to go with them. All because of me."

He put his arm around her and bent his face to hers. Whatever he said was silent. She climbed into his arms. He hugged her, rocking her back and forth like a baby, till her weeping ceased. With a smile that broke my heart, she kissed him and slid out of his arms.

"Excuse us, please." Her voice quivering, she caught his hand. "We must say good-bye."

She led him out of the room.

■

Lo stared silently after them till Pepe tapped his bowl to signal the robots for a second serving of the crimson berries.

"It's true." With a long sigh, she turned back to us. "A painful thing for Tling. For all three of us. This is not what we planned."

Absently, she took a little brown cake from a tray the robot was passing and laid it on her plate, untasted.

"¿Que tienes?" Pepe gave her a puzzled look.

"We hoped to stay together," she said. "Sandor and I have worked here for most of the century, excavating the site and restoring what we could. With that finished, I wanted to see my homeworld again. We were going back there together, Tling with us. Taking the history we had learned, we were planning to replicate the memorial there."

Bleakly, she shook her head.

"This changes everything. Sandor feels a duty to help the colonists find a home. Tling begged him to take us with him, but—" She shrugged in resignation, her lips drawn tight. "He's afraid of whatever killed Enthel Two. And there's something else. His brother—"

She looked away for a moment.

"He has a twin brother. His father had to emigrate when they were born. He took the twin. His mother had a career in nanorob genetics she couldn't leave. Sandor stayed here with her, longing for his twin. He left when he was grown, searched a dozen worlds, never found him. He did find me. That's the happy side."

Her brief smile faded.

"A hopeless quest, I've told him. There are too many worlds, too many light-years. Slider flights may seem quick, but they take too long. Yet he can't give up the dream."

■

"Can we—" Casey checked himself to look at Pepe and me. We nodded, and he turned anxiously back to Lo. "If Sandor does go out on the emigrant ship, would he take us with him?"

She shook her head and sat staring at nothing till Pepe asked, "*¿Por qué no?*"

"Reasons enough." Frowning, she picked up the little brown cake, broke it in half, dropped the fragments back on her plate. "First of all, the danger. Whatever killed that planet could kill another. He got the waiver, in fact, because others were afraid to go. The colonists had no choice, but he doesn't want to kill you."

"It's our choice." Casey shrugged. "When you have to jump across hundreds of years of space and time, don't you always take a risk?"

"Not like this one." She shrugged unhappily. "Enthel Two is toward the galactic core. So is this new one. If the killer is coming from the core—"

Pale face set, she shook her fair-haired head.

"We'll take the risk." Casey glanced again at us and gave her a stiff little grin. "You might remind him that we weren't cloned to live forever. He has more at stake than we do."

Her body stiffened, fading slowly white.

"Tling and I have begged him." Her voice was faint. "But he feels commanded."

"By his nanorobs? Can't he think of you and Tling?"

Her answer took a long time to come.

"You don't understand them." She seemed composed again; I wondered if her own nanorobs had eased her pain. "You may see them as micromachines, but they don't make us mechanical. We've kept all the feelings and impulses the primitives had. The nanorobs simply make us better humans. Sandor is going not just for the colonists, but for me and Tling, for people everywhere."

"If the odds are as bad as they look—" Casey squinted doubtfully. "What can one man hope to do?"

"Nothing, perhaps." She made a bleak little shrug. "But he has an idea. Long ago, before he ever left Earth to search for his brother, he worked with his mother on her nanorob research. He has reprogrammed himself with the science. If the killer is some kind of virulent organism, he thinks the nanorobs might be modified into a shield against it."

"Speak to him," Casey begged her. "Get him to take us with him. We'll help him any way we can."

"You?" Astonishment widened her eyes. "How?"

"We put you here on Earth," he told her. "Even with no nanorobs at all."

"So you did." Golden color flushed her skin. "I'll speak to him." Silent for a moment, she shook her head. "Impossible. He says every seat on the ship is filled."

She paused, frowning at the ceiling. The robot was moving around the table, offering a bowl of huge flesh-colored mushrooms that had a tempting scent of frying ham.

"We are trying to plan a future for Tling." Her face was suddenly tight, her voice hushed with feeling. "A thousand years will pass before he gets back. He grieves to leave Tling."

"I saw her this morning," I said. "She's terribly hurt."

"We are trying to make it up. I've promised that she will see him again."

Pepe looked startled. "How can that happen?"

She took a mushroom, sniffed it with a nod of approval, and laid it on her plate.

"We must plan the time," she told him. "Tling and I will travel. I want to see what the centuries have done to my own homeworld.

It will take careful calculation and the right star flights, but we'll meet him back here on the date of his return."

"If—"

Casey swallowed his voice. Her face went pale, but after a moment she gave us a stiff little smile and had the robot offer the mushrooms again. They had a name I never learned, and a flavor more like bittersweet chocolate than ham. The meal ended. She left us there alone with the robots, with nowhere to go, no future in sight.

"A thousand years!" Pepe muttered. "I wish we had nanorobs."

"Or else—"

Casey turned to the door.

"News for you." Lo stood there, smiling at us. "News from the emigrant ship. Uneasy passengers have arranged for new destinations, leaving empty places. Sandor has found seats for you."

7

Sandor took us to our seats on the emigrant ship. Wheel-shaped and slowly spinning, it held us to the floors with a force weaker than Earth's gravity, stronger than the Moon's. A blue light flashed to warn us of the space-time slide. Restraints folded around us. I felt a gut-wrenching tug. The restraints released us. With no sense of any other change, we sat uneasily waiting.

The big cabin was hushed. Watching faces, I saw eager expectation give way to disappointment and distress. I heard a baby crying, someone shouting at a robot attendant, then a rising clamor of voices at the brink of panic. Sandor sat looking gravely away till I asked him what was wrong.

"We don't know." He grinned at our dazed wonderment. "At least we've made the skip to orbit. Five hundred light-years. You're old men now."

He let us follow him to the lounge, where a tall ceiling dome imaged a new sky. The Milky Way looked familiar. I found the Orion Nebula, but all the nearer stars had shifted beyond recognition. I felt nothing from the ship's rotation; the whole sky seemed to turn around us. Two suns rose, set close together. One was yellow, smaller and paler than our own, the brighter a hot blue dazzle. The planet climbed behind them, a huge round blot on the field of unfamiliar stars, edged with the blue sun's glare. Looking for the glow of cities, all I saw was darkness.

Anxious passengers were clustering around crew members uniformed in the ship's blue-and-gold caps and sashes. Most of their questions were in the silent language of the nanorobs, but their faces revealed dismay. I heard voices rising higher, cries of shock and dread.

We turned to Sandor.

"The telescopes pick up no artificial lights." His lean face was bleakly set. "Radio calls get no answer. The electronic signal spectrum appears dead." He shook his head, with a heavy sigh. "I was thinking of my brother. I'd hoped to find him here."

With gestures of apology to us, uneasy people pushed to surround him. He looked away to listen, frowning at the planet's dark shadow, and turned forlornly to go. He spoke his final words for us.

"We'll be looking for survivors."

We watched that crescent of blue-and-orange fire widen with each passage across the ceiling dome till at last we saw the planet's globe. Swirls and streamers of high cloud shone brilliantly beneath the blue sun's light, but thick red dust dulled everything under them.

One hemisphere was all ocean, except for the gray dot of an isolated island. A single huge continent covered most of the other, extending far south of the equator and north across the pole. Mountain ranges walled the long west coast. A single giant river system drained the vast valley eastward. From arctic ice to polar sea it was all rust-red, nothing green anywhere.

"A rich world it must have been." Sandor made a dismal shrug. "But now—?"

He turned to nod at a woman marching into the room. A woman so flat-chested, masculine, and strange that I had to look twice. Gleaming red-black scales covered her angular body, even her hairless head. Her face was a narrow triangle, her chin sharply pointed, her eyes huge and green. We stared as she sprang to a circular platform in the center of the room.

"Captain Vlix," he murmured. "She's older than I am, born back in the days when nanorobs were new and body forms experimental. I sailed with her once. She remembered my brother asking if she knew me. That was Earth centuries ago. She had no clues to give me."

Heads were turning in attention. I saw uneasy expectation give way to bitter disappointment. Sandor stood frozen, widened eyes fixed on her, till she turned to meet another officer joining her on the platform. They conferred in silence.

"What is it?" Casey whispered. Sandor seemed deaf till Casey touched his arm and asked again, "What did she say?"

"Nothing good." Sandor turned to us, his voice hushed and hurried. "She was summing up a preliminary report from the science staff. This dead planet is the second they have reached. The other was two hundred light-years away. The implications—"

He hunched his shoulders, his skin gone pale.

"Yes? What are they?"

With a painful smile, he tried to gather himself.

"At this point, only speculation. The killer has reached two worlds. How many more? Its nature is not yet known. The science chief suggests that it could possibly be a malignant nanorob, designed to attack all organic life. It certainly seems aggressive, advancing on an interstellar front from the direction of the galactic core."

"What can we do?"

"Nothing, unless we come to understand it." He glanced at the captain and spread his empty hands. "Nanorobs are designed to survive and reproduce themselves. They are complex, half alive, half machine, more efficient than either. The early experimenters worked in terror of accident, of creating something malignant that might escape the laboratory. This could be a mutation. It could be a weapon, reprogrammed by some madman—though his own nanorobs should have prevented that."

He looked again at the captain, and slowly shook his head.

"The officers are doing what they can. A robotic drone is being prepared to attempt a low-level survey of surface damage. A search has already begun for any spacecraft that might remain in orbit. And—"

He broke off to watch a thin man with a gray cap and sash who darted out of the crowd and jumped to join the officers on the platform.

"That's Benkar Rokehut." He made a wry face. "A fellow Earthman, born in my own century. A noted entrepreneur, or perhaps I should say gambler. Noted for taking unlikely chances. He has opened half a dozen worlds, made and lost a dozen fortunes. He funded the initial surveys and settlements here. He has a fortune at stake."

His golden shoulders tossed to an ironic shrug.

"He may love wild chances, but he doesn't want to die."

Rokehut faced the captain for a moment, and turned silently to address the room. Gesturing at the planet, pointing at features on the surface, he kept turning to follow as it crept overhead, kept on talking. When Captain Vlix moved as if to stop him, he burst suddenly into speech, shouting vehemently at her, his pale skin flushing redder than the planet.

"His emotions have overcome his nanorobs." Sandor frowned and drew us closer. "All he sees is danger. Though that first lost planet is two hundred light-years from this one, they both lie toward the Core from Earth. He believes the killer pathogen is spreading from somewhere toward the Core, possibly carried by refugees. He wants us to head out for the frontier stars toward the Rim."

The officers moved to confront him. What they said was silent, but I saw Rokehut's face fade almost to the gray of his cap and sash. He snatched them off, threw them off the platform, waved his fists and shouted. Yielding at last, he shuffled aside and stood glaring at Captain Vlix, his fists still clenched with a purely human fury.

She turned silently back to face the room, speaking with a calm control.

"The officers agree that we do seem to face an interstellar invasion." Sandor spoke softly. "But blind flight can only spread the contagion, if panicky refugees carry it. In the end, unless we get some better break—"

With a sad little shrug, he paused to look hard at us.

"Tycho Station could become the last human hope. It is sealed, shielded, well concealed. The Moon has no surface life to attract or sustain any kind of pathogen." His lips twisted to a quirk of bitter humor. "Even if it wins, there's hope for humanity. It should die when no hosts are left to carry it. You clones may have another book to write before your epic ends."

■

Captain Vlix left the room, Rokehut and his people close behind her. The robot attendants were circulating with trays of hard brown biscuits and plastic bubbles of fruit juice.

"The best we can do," Sandor said. "With zero times in transit, the ship carries no supplies or provisions for any prolonged stay aboard. We must move on with no long delay, yet the officers agree that we must wait for whatever information we can get from the drone."

■

It descended over the glaciers that fringed the polar cap and flew south along the rugged west coast. Its cameras projected their images on the dome and the edge of the floor. Standing there, I could feel that I was riding in its nose. It must have flown high and fast, but the images were processed to make it seem that we hovered low and motionless over a deserted seaport or the ruin of a city and climbed to soar on to the next.

All we saw was dust and desolation. Broken walls of stone or brick, where roofs had fallen in. Tangles of twisted steel where towers had stood. Concrete seawalls around empty harbors. And everywhere, wind-drifted dunes of dead red dust and wind-whipped clouds of rust-colored dust, sometimes so dense it hid the ground.

The drone turned east near the equator, climbing over mountain peaks capped with snows dyed the color of drying blood. It paused over broken dams in high mountain canyons and crossed a network of dust-choked irrigation canals.

"I've dreamed of my brother." Sandor made a solemn face. "Dreamed I might find him here." He stopped to sigh and gaze across an endless sea of wave-shaped dunes. "Dreams! All of us dreaming we had endless life and time for everything. And now—"

■

The drone had reached the dead east coast and flown on across the empty ocean. The lounge was silent again, disheartened people drifting away. Casey asked if we were turning back.

"Not quite yet." Sandor tipped his head, listening. "Captain

Vlix reports that the search team has found something in low polar orbit. Maybe a ship. Maybe just a rock. Maybe something else entirely. She's launching a pilot pod to inspect it."

■

Music had lifted back in the lounge, its unfamiliar trills and runs and strains broken by long gaps of nothing I could sense. A woman with a baby in her arms was swaying to a rhythm I couldn't hear. Silent people were dozing or wandering the aisles. A silent group had gathered around Rokehut at the end of the room, frowning and gesticulating.

"He still wants us to run for our lives," Sandor said. "For a star two thousand light-years out toward the Rim. An idiot's dream! To complete the slide he'd have to calculate the exact relative position of the star two thousand years from now. He has no data for it."

The attendants came back with juice and little white wafers. Rokehut and his group refused them, with angry gestures, and trooped away to confront the captain again.

"A mild sedative." Sandor waved the robot away. "If you need to relax."

I accepted a wafer. It had a vinegar taste and it hit me with a sudden fatigue. I slept in my seat till Casey shook my arm.

"The pod has reached that object in orbit," Sandor told us. "The pilot identifies it as the craft that brought the last colonists. His attempts at contact get no response. Rokehut has offered him a fortune to go aboard. Permission has been granted, with the warning that he won't be allowed back on our ship. He reports that his service robot is now cutting the security bolts to let him into the air lock."

I watched the people around us, silently listening, frowning intently, expectantly nodding, frowning again.

"He's inside." Head tipped aside, eyes fixed on something far away, Sandor spoke at last. "The pathogen got there ahead of him. He has found red dust on the decks, but he hopes for protection from his space gear. He believes the killer was already on the planet before the ship arrived. The cargo was never unloaded. All organics have crumbled, but metal remains unchanged.

"He's pushing on—"

Sandor stopped to listen and shake his head.

"The pilot was on his way to the control room, searching for records or clues. He never got there." He leaned his head and nodded. "The science chief is summing up what evidence he has. It points to something airborne, fast-acting, totally lethal. It must have killed everybody who ever knew what it is."

■

Captain Vlix allowed Rokehut and his partisans to poll the passengers. Overwhelmingly, they voted to turn back toward Earth at once. The lounge became a bedlam of angry protest when departure was delayed, hushed a little when Captain Vlix came back to the platform.

"She says Earth is out," Sandor told us, "for two sufficient reasons. We might find that the pathogen is already there. Even if we found it safe, she says we would certainly be regarded as a suspected carrier, warned away and subject to attack if we tried to make any contact."

"That recalls a legend of the old Earth." Casey nodded bleakly. "The legend of a ghost ship called the Flying Dutchman, that sailed forever and never reached a port."

■

The strange constellations flickered out of the ceiling dome, and the drone's images returned. The limitless ocean beneath it looked blue as Earth's when we glimpsed it through rifts in the clouds, but the sky was yellow, the larger sun a sullen red, the blue one now a hot pink point.

"The island's somewhere ahead." Sandor stood with us in the lounge, frowning at the horizon. "If we ever get there. It's losing altitude. Losing speed. Probably damaged by the dust."

White-capped waves rose closer as it glided down through scattered puffs of cumulus.

"There it is!" Sandor whispered before I had seen it. "Just to the right."

I strained to see. The image dimmed and flickered as the drone bored through a tuft of pink-tinted cloud. Something blurred the far horizon. At first a faint dark streak, it faded and came back as we searched it for color.

"Green?" A sharp cry from Casey. "Isn't it green?"

"It was," Sandor said. "We're going down."

A foam-capped mountain of blue-green water climbed ahead of the drone. It crashed with an impact I almost felt, but I thought I had caught a flash of green.

8

The ceiling dome had gone dark when the drone broke up. After a moment it was spangled again with those new constellations. The dead ship, immense and high overhead, was a fire-edged silhouette against the Milky Way.

"You saw it!" Casey shouted at Sandor. "Something green. Something alive!"

Frowning, Sandor shook his head.

"I saw a brief greenish flash. Probably from some malfunction as the drone went down."

"It was green," Casey insisted. "Aren't they landing anybody to take a look?"

"No time for that."

"But if the island is alive—"

"How could that be?" He was sharply impatient. "We've seen the whole planet dead. Whatever killed it killed the drone before it ever touched the surface. The captain isn't going to risk any sort of contact."

"If she would let us land—" Casey waited for Pepe and me to nod. "We could radio a report."

"Send you down to die?" Sandor's eyes went wide. "She cares too much for life. She would never consider it."

"Don't think we care for life? Tell her we were cloned to keep the Earth and humankind alive. But tell her we were also cloned to die. If we must, I don't know a better way."

Sandor took us to meet Captain Vlix, and translated for us. Our visit was brief, but still enough to let me glimpse a spark of humanity beneath her gleaming crimson scales. I don't know what he told her, but it caught her interest. She had him question us about Tycho Station and our lives there.

"You like it?" Her huge green eyes probed us with a disturbing intensity. "Life without nanorobs? Knowing you must die?"

"We know." Casey nodded. "I don't dwell on it."

"I must admire your idealism." A frown creased her crimson scales. "But the science staff reports no credible evidence of life on the planet. I can't waste your lives."

"We saw evidence we believe," Casey said. "In that last second as the drone went down. Considering the stakes, we're ready to take the risk."

"The stakes are great." Her eyes on Sandor, she frowned and finally nodded her red-scaled head. "You may go."

There were no space suits to fit us. That didn't matter, Casey said; space gear had not saved the pilot who boarded the derelict. With Sandor translating, the service robots showed Pepe how to operate the flight pod, a streamlined bubble much like the slider that had brought Sandor to the Moon. He shook our hands and wished us well.

"Make it quick," he told us. "Captain Vlix expects no good news from you. No news at all, in fact, after you touch down. Our next destination is still under debate. None looks safe, or satisfies everybody, but we can't delay."

Pepe made it quick, and we found the island green.

Rising out of the haze of dust as we dived, the shallow sea around it faded from the blue of open water through a hundred shades of jade and turquoise to the vivid green of life. The island was bowl-shaped, the great caldera left by an ancient volcanic explosion. Low hills rimmed a circular valley with a small blue lake at the center. A line of green trees showed the course of a stream that ran through a gap in the hills from the lake down to the sea.

"Kell?" Sandor's voice crackled from the radio before we touched the ground. "Navarro? Yare? Answer if you can."

"Tell him!" Casey grinned at Pepe as he dropped our slider pod to a wide white beach that looked like coral sand. "It looks a lot better than our pits in the Moon. No matter what."

Pepe echoed him, "No matter what."

"Tell him we're opening the air lock," Casey said. "If we can breathe the air, we're heading inland."

Pepe opened the air lock. I held my breath till I had to inhale. The air was fresh and cool, but I caught a faint acrid bite. In a moment my eyes were burning. Pepe sneezed and clapped a handkerchief over his nose. Casey smothered a cough and peered at us sharply.

"Can you report?" Sandor's anxious voice. "Can you breathe?"

Casey coughed and blew his nose.

"Breathing," he gasped. "Still breathing."

I thought we were inhaling the pathogen. I hadn't known the pilot who died on the derelict, or the millions or billions it had killed. I felt no personal pain for them, but Pepe and Casey were almost part of me. I put my arms around them. We huddled there together, sneezing and wheezing, till Pepe laughed and pulled away.

"If this is death, it ain't so bad." He jogged me in the ribs. "Let's get out and take a closer look."

We stumbled out of the lock and stood there on the hard wet sand beside the pod, breathing hard and peering around us. The sky was a dusty pink, the suns a tiny red moon eye and a bright pink spark. The beach sloped up to low green hills. Perhaps half a mile south along the beach, green jungle covered the delta at the mouth of the little river. Pepe picked up a scrap of seaweed the waves had left.

"Still green." He studied it, sniffed it. "It smells alive."

My lungs were burning. Every breath, I thought, might be my last, yet I always stayed able to struggle for another. Pepe dropped the handkerchief and climbed back in the slider to move it higher on the beach, farther from the water. He returned with a portable radio. Casey blew his nose again, and started south along the beach, toward the delta. We followed him, breathing easier as we went.

The little river had cut its way between two great black basaltic cliffs. Casey stopped before we reached them, frowning up at the nearest. I looked and caught a deeper breath. The summit had been carved into a face. The unfinished head of a giant struggling out of the stone.

"Sandor!" Casey walked closer, staring up at the great dark face. "It's Sandor."

"It is." Shading his eyes, Pepe whispered huskily. "Unless we're crazy."

I had to sneeze again, and wondered what the dust was doing to us.

Sandor called again from the ship, but Pepe seemed too stunned to speak. A rope ladder hung across the face, down to the beach. Black and gigantic, gazing out at the sky, lips curved in a puckish smile, the head was certainly Sandor's.

"We're okay." Rasping hoarsely into the phone, Pepe answered at last. "Still breathing."

Walking closer to the cliff, we found a narrow cave. A jutting ledge sheltered a long workbench hewn from an untrimmed log, a forge with a pedal to work the bellows, a basket of charcoal, a heavy anvil, a long shelf cluttered with roughly-made hammers and chisels and drills.

"The sculptor's workshop." Casey stepped back across a reef of glassy black chips on the sand, litter fallen from the chisel. "Who is the sculptor?"

He touched his lips at Pepe when Sandor called again.

"Tell him to hold the ship. Tell him we're alive and pushing inland. Tell him we've found human life, or strong evidence for it. But not a word about the face. Not till we have something Captain Vlix might believe."

▪

We hiked inland, following a smooth-worn footpath along the riverbank. The valley widened. We came out between two rows of trees, neatly spaced, bearing bright red fruit.

"¡Cerezas!" Pepe cried. "Cherries! A cherry orchard."

He picked a handful and shared them, tart, sweet, hard to believe. We came to an apple orchard, to rows of peach and pear trees, all laden with unripe fruit. We found a garden farther on, watered by a narrow ditch that diverted water from the river. Tomato vines, yams, squash, beans, tall green corn.

Casey caught his breath and stopped. I stared past him at a man—a man who might have been Sandor's double—who came striding up the path to meet us.

"Sandor?" His eager voice was almost Sandor's, though the accent made it strange. "Sandor?"

We waited, hardly breathing, while he came on to us. The image of Sandor, bronzed dark from the sun, he had the same trim frame, the same sleek brown fur crowning his head, the same pixie face and golden eyes. He stopped to scan us with evident disappointment, and pointed suddenly when he saw Pepe's radio.

Pepe let him have it. Eagerly, hands shaking, he made a call. The other Sandor answered with a quick and breathless voice. Their excited words meant nothing to me, no more than their silent communion after they fell silent, but I could read the flow of feeling on the stranger's weathered face. Wonder, fear, hope, tears of joy.

At last the Sandor on the ship had a moment for us.

"You've found my brother. Call him Corath if you need a name. Captain Vlix is ready for a jump toward the Rim. She is slow to believe what you're saying, with her ship at risk but Rokehut is demanding a chance for confirmation and I must see my brother. She's letting me come down. . . ."

■

Corath beckoned. We followed him down the path till we could see the distant lake and a ruined building on a hill. Once it must have been impressive, but the stone walls were roofless now, windows and doorways black and gaping. He stopped us at his very simple residence, a thatched roof over a bare wooden floor with a small stone-walled enclosure at the rear. Waiting for Sandor, we sat at a table under the thatch. He poured cherry wine for us from a black ceramic jug and stood waiting, staring away at the sky.

Sandor landed his silvery flight pod on the grass in front of the dwelling. Corath ran to meet him. They stopped to gaze at each other, to touch each other, to grip each other's hands. They hugged and stepped apart and stood a long time face to face without a word I could hear, laughing and crying, hugging again, until at last Sandor rubbed his wet eyes and turned to us.

"I saw—saw the head." Breathing hard, he stopped to clear his throat and peer again into Corath's face as if to verify that he was real. "It was meant to be my own, though at first I thought it was his. He has been here almost two hundred years, marooned by the pathogen. With no way to search for me, he says, except inside the mountain."

A spasm of coughing bent him over. Corath held his arm till he drew himself upright and turned soberly back to us.

"We were coughing," Pepe said. "Sneezing. Wheezing. We thought we had the killer pathogen."

"Something kin to it, my brother says. But benign. He says it saved your lives."

We had to hold our questions. They forgot us, standing together a long time in silence before they laughed and embraced again. Sandor wiped at his tears at last and turned back to us.

"The pathogen got here two hundred years ago. Corath knows no more than we do about its origin or history. It caught him here on the island, at work on the same sort of nanorob research I once hoped to undertake. He was testing immunities and looking for quantum effects that might extend the contact range. The range effect is still not fully tested, but his new nanorob did make him immune. Too late to save the rest of the planet, it did wipe the pathogen off the island. . . ."

Captain Vlix was still a stubborn skeptic, terrified of contamination. She refused to let Sandor bring his brother aboard, or even to come back himself. Yet, with Rokehut and some of the other passengers still at odds over a new destination, she let the second officer bring a little group of desperate volunteers down to see the live island for themselves.

They came off the pod jittery and pale. Fits of coughing and sneezing turned them whiter still, until Corath and his news of their new immunity brought their color back. To make his own survival sure, the officer drew a drop of Corath's blood and scratched it into his arm with a needle. Still breathing, but not yet entirely certain, he wanted to see the research station.

Corath took us to tour the ruin on the hill. The pathogen had destroyed wood and plastic, leaving only bare stone and naked steel. A quake had toppled one roofless wall, but the isolation chamber was still intact. An enormous windowless concrete box, it had heavy steel doors with an air lock between them.

Black with rust, the doors yawned open now, darkness beyond them. He struck fire with flint, steel, and tinder, lit a torch, led us inside. The chamber was empty, except for the clutter of abandoned equipment on the workbenches and a thick carpet of harmless gray dust on the floor.

We found nothing to reveal the structure of his new nanorob, nothing to explain how its wind-borne spores had set us to sneezing and made us safe. Corath answered with only a noncommittal shrug when Pepe dared to ask if the infection had made us immortal.

"At least the dust hasn't killed us," Casey said. "Good enough for me."

The officer went back to the ship with a bottle of Corath's healing blood. Captain Vlix agreed to hold the ship in orbit. Rokehut brought his engineers to survey the island and stake out a settlement site on the plateau beyond the lake. Passengers came down with their luggage and crates of freight, ready now to stake their futures on the island and Corath's promise that the red dust could make fertile soil.

He decided to stay there with them.

Sandor took us with him back aboard. Convinced at last, Captain Vlix was waiting to greet us at the airlock, embracing him almost as tearfully as his brother had. When she had finally wiped her eyes and turned away, he spoke to us.

"Our job now is to fight the pathogen with Corath's nanorob. Volunteers in flight pods are setting out to carry it to all the nearest worlds. I am taking it to Lo and Tling back on Earth. Do you want to come?"

We did.

BETTY BALLANTINE APPRECIATION

Every so often, SFWA gives a special award to a person who has made an outstanding contribution to the field as a whole. In Kansas City, SFWA honored Betty Ballantine, that gracious lady who, with her late husband Ian Ballantine, changed SF publishing forever. Before the award presentation, a special appreciation was offered by Shelly Shapiro, editorial director of Del Rey Books, who works with such diverse authors as Anne McCaffrey, Arthur C. Clarke, Greg Bear, and the writers of the *Star Wars* publishing program.

SHELLY SHAPIRO

Ballantine Books could hardly let this opportunity go by without saying a few words of appreciation to Betty Ballantine.

Ian and Betty were some of the first and strongest supporters of science fiction in the book publishing industry. Among their very first hardcovers, back in the early 1950s, were books like *The October Country* and *The Space Merchants*. Betty Ballantine edited Ballantine's SF before bringing Judy-Lynn del Rey aboard, and was behind Ballantine's early acquisition of such notable luminaries as Arthur C. Clarke, Anne McCaffrey, Larry Niven, James Blish, Katherine Kurtz, and Fred Pohl. Not to mention Tolkien—at one point, Ballantine published the only authorized edition of *The Lord of the Rings* in the U.S.

It's really thanks to Betty and Ian Ballantine that Judy-Lynn and Lester had such a strong backlist foundation on which to build their new imprint. In fact, I think it's safe to say that without Betty Ballantine, there might not have been a Del Rey Books at all. So, to Betty, a special and heartfelt thank-you from all of us at Del Rey Books and Ballantine Books.

KELLY LINK

Kelly Link is a quiet, unassuming woman with a wicked sense of humor. We first met when she attended Clarion, the eminent workshop for aspiring science fiction writers. It was clear to everyone how talented she was but not how quickly she would develop her talent. Less than a decade later, Peter Straub would call her "the most impressive writer of her generation." A lot goes on behind those quiet brown eyes.

Kelly's story "Travels with the Snow Queen" won the Tiptree Award in 1997, and "The Specialist's Hat" took the 1999 World Fantasy Award. Her first collection, *Stranger Things Happen*, came out in 2001, to much praise. She coedits the zine *Lady Churchill's Rosebud Wristlet*. Currently Kelly, who lives in Brooklyn with husband Gavin J. Grant, is working on her first novel.

"Louise's Ghost" is a poignant look at the things we cherish, the things we misinterpret, and the things we don't value enough until it's too late. It marks Kelly's first Nebula but not, I suspect, her last.

LOUISE'S GHOST

Kelly Link

Two women and a small child meet in a restaurant. The restaurant is nice—there are windows everywhere. The women have been here before. It's all that light that makes the food taste so good. The small child—a girl dressed all in green, hairy green sweater, green T-shirt, green corduroys, and dirty sneakers with green-black laces—sniffs. She's a small child but she has a big nose. She might be smelling the food that people are eating. She might be smelling the warm light that lies on top of everything.

None of her greens match except of course they are all green.

"Louise," one woman says to the other.

"Louise," the other woman says.

They kiss.

The maitre d' comes up to them. He says to the first woman, "Louise, how nice to see you. And look at Anna! You're so big. Last time I saw you, you were so small. This small." He holds his index finger and his thumb together as if pinching salt. He looks at the other woman.

Louise says, "This is my friend, Louise. My best friend. Since Girl Scout camp. Louise."

The maitre d' smiles. "Yes, Louise. Of course. How could I forget?"

■

Louise sits across from Louise. Anna sits between them. She has a notebook full of green paper and a green crayon. She's drawing something, only it's difficult to see what, exactly. Maybe it's a house.

Louise says, "Sorry about you-know-who. Teacher's day. The sitter canceled at the last minute. And I had such a lot to tell you, too! About you know, number eight. Oh boy, I think I'm in love. Well, not in love."

She is sitting opposite a window, and all that rich soft light falls on her. She looks creamy with happiness, as if she's carved out of butter. The light loves Louise, the other Louise thinks. Of course it loves Louise. Who doesn't?

◼

This is one thing about Louise. She doesn't like to sleep alone. She says that her bed is too big. There's too much space. She needs someone to roll up against, or she just rolls around all night. Some mornings she wakes up on the floor. Mostly she wakes up with other people.

When Anna was younger, she slept in the same bed as Louise. But now she has her own room, her own bed. Her walls are painted green. Her sheets are green. Green sheets of paper with green drawings are hung up on the wall. There's a green teddy bear on the green bed and a green duck. She has a green light in a green shade. Louise has been in that room. She helped Louise paint it. She wore sunglasses while she painted. This passion for greenness, Louise thinks, this longing for everything to be a variation on a theme, it might be hereditary.

This is the second thing about Louise. Louise likes cellists. For about four years, she has been sleeping with a cellist. Not the same cellist. Different cellists. Not all at once, of course. Consecutive cellists. Number eight is Louise's newest cellist. Numbers one through seven were cellists as well, although Anna's father was not. That was before the cellists. BC. In any case, according to Louise, cellists generally have low sperm counts.

Louise meets Louise for lunch every week. They go to nice restaurants. Louise knows all the maitre d's. Louise tells Louise about the cellists. Cellists are mysterious. Louise hasn't figured them out yet. It's something about the way they sit, with their legs open and their arms curled around, all hunched over their cellos. She says they look solid but inviting. Like a door. It opens and you walk in.

Doors are sexy. Wood is sexy, and bows strung with real hair. Also cellos don't have spit valves. Louise says that spit valves aren't sexy.

Louise is in public relations. She's a fund-raiser for the symphony—she's good at what she does. It's hard to say no to Louise. She takes rich people out to dinner. She knows what kinds of wine they like to drink. She plans charity auctions and masquerades. She brings sponsors to the symphony to sit on stage and watch rehearsals. She takes the cellists home afterwards.

Louise looks a little bit like a cello herself. She's brown and curvy and tall. She has a long neck and her shiny hair stays pinned up during the day. Louise thinks that the cellists must take it down at night—Louise's hair—slowly, happily, gently.

At camp Louise used to brush Louise's hair.

Louise isn't perfect. Louise would never claim that her friend was perfect. Louise is a bit bowlegged and she has tiny little feet. She wears long, tight silky skirts. Never pants, never anything floral. She has a way of turning her head to look at you, very slowly. It doesn't matter that she's bowlegged.

The cellists want to sleep with Louise because she wants them to. The cellists don't fall in love with her, because Louise doesn't want them to fall in love with her. Louise always gets what she wants.

Louise doesn't know what she wants. Louise doesn't want to want things.

Louise and Louise have been friends since Girl Scout camp. How old were they? Too young to be away from home for so long. They were so small that some of their teeth weren't there yet. They were so young they wet the bed out of homesickness. Loneliness. Louise slept in the bunk bed above Louise. Girl Scout camp smelled like pee. Summer camp is how Louise knows Louise is bowlegged. At summer camp they wore each other's clothes.

Here is something else about Louise, a secret. Louise is the only one who knows. Not even the cellists know. Not even Anna.

Louise is tone-deaf. Louise likes to watch Louise at concerts. She has this way of looking at the musicians. Her eyes get wide and she doesn't blink. There's this smile on her face as if she's being introduced to someone whose name she didn't quite catch. Louise thinks that's really why Louise ends up sleeping with them, with the cellists. It's because she doesn't know what else they're good for. Louise hates for things to go to waste.

■

A woman comes to their table to take their order. Louise orders the grilled chicken and a house salad and Louise orders salmon with lemon butter. The woman asks Anna what she would like. Anna looks at her mother.

Louise says, "She'll eat anything as long as it's green. Broccoli is good. Peas, lima beans, iceberg lettuce. Lime sherbet. Bread rolls. Mashed potatoes."

The woman looks down at Anna. "I'll see what we can do," she says.

Anna says, "Potatoes aren't green."

Louise says, "Wait and see."

Louise says, "If I had a kid—"

Louise says, "But you don't have a kid." She doesn't say this meanly. Louise is never mean, although sometimes she is not kind.

Louise and Anna glare at each other. They've never liked each other. They are polite in front of Louise. It is humiliating, Louise thinks, to hate someone so much younger. The child of a friend. I should feel sorry for her instead. She doesn't have a father. And soon enough, she'll grow up. Breasts. Zits. Boys. She'll see old pictures of herself and be embarrassed. She's short and she dresses like a Keebler elf. She can't even read yet!

Louise says, "In any case, it's easier than the last thing. When she only ate dog food."

Anna says, "When I was a dog—"

Louise says, hating herself, "You were never a dog."

Anna says, "How do you know?"

Louise says, "I was there when you were born. When your mother was pregnant. I've known you since you were this big." She pinches her fingers together, the way the maitre d' pinched his, only harder.

Anna says, "It was before that. When I was a dog."

Louise says, "Stop fighting, you two. Louise, when Anna was a dog, that was when you were away. In Paris. Remember?"

"Right," Louise says. "When Anna was a dog, I was in Paris."

Louise is a travel agent. She organizes package tours for senior citizens. Trips for old women. To Las Vegas, Rome, Belize, cruises to the Caribbean. She travels frequently herself and stays in three-star hotels. She tries to imagine herself as an old woman. What she would want.

Most of these women's husbands are in care or dead or living with younger women. The old women sleep two to a room. They like hotels with buffet lunches and saunas, clean pillows that smell good, chocolates on the pillows, firm mattresses. Louise can see herself wanting these things. Sometimes Louise imagines being old, waking up in the mornings, in unfamiliar countries, strange weather, foreign beds. Louise asleep in the bed beside her.

Last night Louise woke up. It was three in the morning. There was a man lying on the floor beside the bed. He was naked. He lay on his back, staring up at the ceiling, his eyes open, his mouth open, nothing coming out. He was bald. He had no eyelashes, no hair on his arms or legs. He was large, not fat but solid. Yes, he was solid. It was hard to tell how old he was. It was dark, but Louise doesn't think he was circumcised. "What are you doing here?" she said loudly.

The man wasn't there anymore. She turned on the lights. She looked under the bed. She found him in her bathroom, above the bathtub, flattened up against the ceiling, staring down, his hands and feet pressed along the ceiling, his penis drooping down, apparently the only part of him that obeyed the laws of gravity. He seemed smaller now. Deflated. She wasn't frightened. She was angry.

"What are you doing?" she said. He didn't answer. Fine, she thought. She went to the kitchen to get a broom. When she came back, he was gone. She looked under the bed again, but he was really gone this time. She looked in every room, checked to make sure that the front door was locked. It was.

Her arms creeped. She was freezing. She filled up her hot water bottle and got in bed. She left the light on and fell asleep sitting up. When she woke up in the morning, it might have been a dream, except she was holding the broom.

■

The woman brings their food. Anna gets a little dish of peas, Brussels sprouts, and collard greens. Mashed potatoes and bread. The plate is green. Louise takes a vial of green food coloring out of her purse. She adds three drops to the mashed potatoes. "Stir it," she tells Anna.

Anna stirs the mashed potatoes until they are a waxy green. Louise mixes more green food coloring into a pat of butter and spreads it on the dinner roll.

"When I was a dog," Anna says, "I lived in a house with a swimming pool. And there was a tree in the living room. It grew right through the ceiling. I slept in the tree. But I wasn't allowed to swim in the pool. I was too hairy."

"I have a ghost," Louise says. She wasn't sure that she was going to say this. But if Anna can reminisce about her former life as a dog, then surely she, Louise, is allowed to mention her ghost. "I think it's a ghost. It was in my bedroom."

Anna says, "When I was a dog I bit ghosts."

Louise says, "Anna, be quiet for a minute. Eat your green food before it gets cold. Louise, what do you mean? I thought you had ladybugs."

"That was a while ago," Louise says. Last month she woke up because people were whispering in the corners of her room. Dead leaves were crawling on her face. The walls of her bedroom were alive. They heaved and dripped red. "What?" she said, and a lady-bug walked into her mouth, bitter like soap. The floor crackled when she walked on it, like red cellophane. She opened up her windows. She swept ladybugs out with her broom. She vacuumed them up. More flew in the windows, down the chimney. She moved out for three days. When she came back, the ladybugs were gone—mostly gone—she still finds them tucked into her shoes, in the folds of her underwear, in her cereal bowls and her wineglasses, and between the pages of her books.

Before that it was moths. Before the moths, a possum. It shat on her bed and hissed at her when she cornered it in the pantry. She called an animal shelter and a man wearing a denim jacket and heavy gloves came and shot it with a tranquilizer dart. The possum sneezed and shut its eyes. The man picked it up by the tail. He posed like that for a moment. Maybe she was supposed to take a picture. Man with possum. She sniffed. He wasn't married. All she smelled was possum.

"How did it get in here?" Louise said.

"How long have you been living here?" the man asked. Boxes of Louise's dishes and books were still stacked up against the walls of the rooms downstairs. She still hadn't put the legs on her mother's dining room table. It lay flat on its back on the floor, amputated.

"Two months," Louise said.

"Well, he's probably been living here longer than that," the man from the shelter said. He cradled the possum like a baby. "In the walls or the attic. Maybe in the chimney. Santa claws. Huh." He laughed at his own joke. "Get it?"

"Get that thing out of my house," Louise said.

"Your house!" the man said. He held out the possum to her, as if she might want to reconsider. "You know what he thought? He thought this was his house."

"It's my house now," Louise said.

■

Louise says, "A ghost? Louise, it is someone you know? Is your mother okay?"

"My mother?" Louise says. "It wasn't my mother. It was a naked man. I'd never seen him before in my life."

"How naked?" Anna says. "A little naked or a lot?"

"None of your beeswax," Louise says.

"Was it green?" Anna says.

"Maybe it was someone that you went out with in high school," Louise says. "An old lover. Maybe he just killed himself, or was in a horrible car accident. Was he covered in blood? Did he say anything? Maybe he wants to warn you about something."

"He didn't say anything," Louise says. "And then he vanished. First he got smaller and then he vanished."

Louise shivers and then so does Louise. For the first time she feels frightened. The ghost of a naked man was levitating in her bathtub. He could be anywhere. Maybe while she was sleeping, he was floating above her bed. Right above her nose, watching her sleep. She'll have to sleep with the broom from now on.

"Maybe he won't come back," Louise says, and Louise nods. What if he does? Who can she call? The rude man with the heavy gloves?

The woman comes to their table again. "Any dessert?" she wants to know. "Coffee?"

"If you had a ghost," Louise says, "how would you get rid of it?" Louise kicks Louise under the table.

The woman thinks for a minute. "I'd go see a psychiatrist," she says. "Get some kind of prescription. Coffee?"

But Anna has to go to her tumble class. She's learning how to stand on her head. How to fall down and not be hurt. Louise gets the woman to put the leftover mashed green potatoes in a container, and she wraps up the dinner rolls in a napkin and bundles them into her purse along with a few packets of sugar.

They walk out of the restaurant together, Louise first. Behind her, Anna whispers something to Louise. "Louise?" Louise says.

"What?" Louise says, turning back.

"You need to walk behind me," Anna says. "You can't be first."

"Come back and talk to me," Louise says, patting the air. "Say thank you, Anna."

Anna doesn't say anything. She walks before them, slowly, so that they have to walk slowly as well.

"So what should I do?" Louise says.

"About the ghost? I don't know. Is he cute? Maybe he'll creep in bed with you. Maybe he's your demon lover."

"Oh, please," Louise says. "Yuck."

Louise says, "Sorry. You should call your mother."

"When I had the problem with the ladybugs," Louise says, "she said they would go away if I sang them that nursery rhyme. 'Ladybug, ladybug, fly away home.'"

"Well," Louise says, "they did go away, didn't they?"

"Not until I went away first," Louise says.

"Maybe it's someone who used to live in the house before you moved in. Maybe he's buried under the floor of your bedroom or in the wall or something."

"Just like the possum," Louise says. "Maybe it's Santa Claus."

■

Louise's mother lives in a retirement community two states away. Louise cleaned out her mother's basement and garage, put her mother's furniture in storage, sold her mother's house. Her mother wanted this. She gave Louise the money from the sale of the house so that Louise could buy her own house. But she won't come visit Louise in her new house. She won't let Louise send her on a package vacation. Sometimes she pretends not to recognize Louise when Louise calls. Or maybe she really doesn't recognize her. Maybe this is why Louise's clients travel. Settle down in one place and you get lazy. You don't bother to remember things like taking baths, or your daughter's name.

When you travel, everything's always new. If you don't speak the language, it isn't a big deal. Nobody expects you to understand everything they say. You can wear the same clothes every day and the other travelers will be impressed with your careful packing. When you wake up and you're not sure where you are. There's a perfectly good reason for that.

"Hello, Mom," Louise says when her mother picks up the phone.

"Who is this?" her mother says.

"Louise," Louise says.

"Oh yes," her mother says. "Louise, how nice to speak to you."

There is an awkward pause and then her mother says, "If you're calling because it's your birthday, I'm sorry. I forgot."

"It isn't my birthday," Louise says. "Mom, remember the ladybugs?"

"Oh yes," her mother says. "You sent pictures. They were lovely."

"I have a ghost," Louise says, "and I was hoping that you would know how to get rid of it."

"A ghost!" her mother says. "It isn't your father, is it?"

"No!" Louise says. "This ghost doesn't have any clothes on, Mom. It's naked and I saw it for a minute and then it disappeared and then I saw it again in my bathtub. Well, sort of."

"Are you sure it's a ghost?" her mother says.

"Yes, positive." Louise says.

"And it isn't your father?"

"No, it's not Dad. It doesn't look like anyone I've ever seen before."

Her mother says, "Lucy—you don't know her—Mrs. Peterson's husband died two nights ago. Is it a short fat man with an ugly moustache? Dark complected?"

"It isn't Mr. Peterson," Louise says.

"Have you asked what it wants?"

"Mom, I don't care what it wants," Louise says. "I just want it to go away."

"Well," her mother says, "try hot water and salt. Scrub all the floors. You should polish them with lemon oil afterwards so they don't get streaky. Wash the windows, too. Wash all the bed linens and beat all the rugs. And put the sheets back on the bed inside out. And turn all your clothes on the hangers inside out. Clean the bathroom."

"Inside out," Louise says.

"Inside out," her mother says. "Confuses them."

"I think it's pretty confused already. About clothes, anyway. Are you sure this works?"

"Positive," her mother says. "We're always having supernatural infestations around here. Sometimes it gets hard to tell who's alive and who's dead. If cleaning the house doesn't work, try hanging garlic up on strings. Ghosts hate garlic. Or they like it. It's either one or the other, love it, hate it. So what else is happening? When are you coming to visit?"

"I had lunch today with Louise," Louise says.

"Aren't you too old to have an imaginary friend?" her mother says.

"Mom, you know Louise. Remember? Girl Scouts? College? She has the little girl, Anna? Louise?"

"Of course I remember Louise," her mother says. "My own daughter. You're a very rude person." She hangs up.

Salt, Louise thinks. Salt and hot water. She should write these things down. Maybe she could send her mother a tape recorder. She sits down on the kitchen floor and cries. That's one kind of salt water. Then she scrubs floors, beats rugs, washes her sheets and her blankets. She washes her clothes and hangs them back up, inside out. While she works, the ghost lies half under the bed, feet and genitalia pointed at her accusingly. She scrubs around it. Him. It.

She is being squeamish, Louise thinks. Afraid to touch it. And that makes her angry, so she picks up her broom. Pokes at the fleshy thighs, and the ghost hisses under the bed like an angry cat. She jumps back and then it isn't there anymore. But she sleeps on the living room sofa. She keeps all the lights on in all the rooms of the house.

■

"Well?" Louise says.

"It isn't gone," Louise says. She's just come home from work. "I just don't know *where* it is. Maybe it's up in the attic. It might be standing behind me, for all I know, while I'm talking to you on the phone and every time I turn around, it vanishes. Jumps back in the mirror or wherever it is that it goes. You may hear me scream. By the time you get here, it will be too late."

"Sweetie," Louise says, "I'm sure it can't hurt you."

"It hissed at me," Louise says.

"Did it just hiss, or did you do something first?" Louise says. "Kettles hiss. It just means the water's boiling."

"What about snakes?" Louise says. "I'm thinking it's more like a snake than a pot of tea."

"You could ask a priest to exorcise it. If you were Catholic. Or you could go to the library. They might have a book. *Exorcism for Dummies.* Can you come to the symphony tonight? I have extra tickets."

"You've always got extra tickets," Louise says.

"Yes, but it will be good for you," Louise says. "Besides, I haven't seen you for two days."

"Can't do it tonight," Louise says. "What about tomorrow night?"

"Well, okay," Louise says. "Have you tried reading the Bible to it?"

"What part of the Bible would I read?"

"How about the begetting part? That's official sounding," Louise says.

"What if it thinks I'm flirting? The guy at the gas station today said I should spit on the floor when I see it and say, 'In the name of God, what do you want?'"

"Have you tried that?"

"I don't know about spitting on the floor," Louise says. "I just cleaned it. What if it wants something gross, like my eyes? What if it wants me to kill someone?"

"Well," Louise says, "that would depend on who it wanted you to kill."

■

Louise goes to dinner with her married lover. After dinner, they will go to a motel and fuck. Then he'll take a shower and go home, and she'll spend the night at the motel. This is a *Louise*-style economy. It makes Louise feel slightly more virtuous. The ghost will have the house to himself.

Louise doesn't talk to Louise about her lover. He belongs to her, and to his wife, of course. There isn't enough left over to share. She met him at work. Before him she had another lover, another married man. She would like to believe that this is a charming quirk, like being bowlegged or sleeping with cellists. But perhaps it's a character defect instead, like being tone-deaf or refusing to eat food that isn't green.

Here is what Louise would tell Louise, if she told her. I'm just borrowing him—I don't want him to leave his wife. I'm glad he's married. Let someone else take care of him. It's the way he smells—the way married men smell. I can smell when a happily married man comes into a room, and they can smell me, too, I think. So can the wives—that's why he has to take a shower when he leaves me.

But Louise doesn't tell Louise about her lovers. She doesn't want to sound as if she's competing with the cellists.

"What are you thinking about?" her lover says. The wine has made his teeth red.

It's the guiltiness that cracks them wide open. The guilt makes them taste so sweet, Louise thinks. "Do you believe in ghosts?" she says.

Her lover laughs. "Of course not."

If he were her husband, they would sleep in the same bed every night. And if she woke up and saw the ghost, she would wake up her husband. They would both see the ghost. They would share responsibility. It would be a piece of their marriage, part of the things they don't have (can't have) now, like breakfast or ski vacations or fights about toothpaste. Or maybe he would blame her.

If she tells him now that she saw a naked man in her bedroom, he might say that it's her fault.

"Neither do I," Louise says. "But if you did believe in ghosts. Because you saw one. What would you do? How would you get rid of it?"

Her lover thinks for a minute. "I wouldn't get rid of it," he says. "I'd charge admission. I'd become famous. I'd be on *Oprah*. They would make a movie. Everyone wants to see a ghost."

"But what if there's a problem?" Louise says. "Such as. What if the ghost is naked?"

Her lover says, "Well, that would be a problem. Unless you were the ghost. Then I would want you to be naked all the time."

■

But Louise can't fall asleep in the motel room. Her lover has gone home to his home which isn't haunted, to his wife who doesn't know about Louise. Louise is as unreal to her as a ghost. Louise lies awake and thinks about her ghost. The dark is not dark, she thinks, and there is something in the motel room with her. Something her lover has left behind. Something touches her face. There's something bitter in her mouth. In the room next door someone is walking up and down. A baby is crying somewhere, or a cat.

She gets dressed and drives home. She needs to know if the ghost is still there or if her mother's recipe worked. She wishes she'd tried to take a picture.

She looks all over the house. She takes her clothes off the hangers in the closet and hangs them back right-side out. The ghost isn't anywhere. She can't find him. She even sticks her face up the chimney.

She finds the ghost curled up in her underwear drawer. He lies facedown, hands open and loose. He's naked and downy all over like a baby monkey.

Louise spits on the floor, feeling relieved. "In God's name," she says, "what do you want?"

The ghost doesn't say anything. He lies there, small and hairy and forlorn, facedown in her underwear. Maybe he doesn't know what he wants any more than she does. "Clothes?" Louise says.

"Do you want me to get you some clothes? It would be easier if you stayed the same size."

The ghost doesn't say anything. "Well," Louise says. "You think about it. Let me know." She closes the drawer.

■

Anna is in her green bed. The green light is on. Louise and the baby-sitter sit in the living room while Louise and Anna talk. "When I was a dog," Anna says, "I ate roses and raw meat and borscht. I wore silk dresses."

"When you were a dog," Louise hears Louise say, "you had big silky ears and four big feet and a long silky tail and you wore a collar made out of silk and a silk dress with a hole cut in it for your tail."

"A green dress," Anna says. "I could see in the dark."

"Good night, my green girl," Louise says, "good night, good night."

Louise comes into the living room. "Doesn't Louise look beautiful," she says, leaning against Louise's chair and looking in the mirror. "The two of us. Louise and Louise and Louise and Louise. All four of us."

"Mirror, mirror, on the wall," the baby-sitter says, "who is the fairest Louise of all?" Patrick the baby-sitter doesn't let Louise pay him. He takes symphony tickets instead. He plays classical guitar and composes music himself. Louise and Louise would like to hear his compositions, but he's too shy to play for them. He brings his guitar sometimes, to play for Anna. He's teaching her the simple chords.

"How is your ghost?" Louise says. "Louise has a ghost," she tells Patrick.

"Smaller," Louise says. "Hairier." Louise doesn't really like Patrick. He's in love with Louise for one thing. It embarrasses Louise, the hopeless way he looks at Louise. He probably writes love songs for her. He's friendly with Anna. As if that will get him anywhere.

"You tried garlic?" Louise says. "Spitting? Holy water? The library?"

"Yes," Louise says, lying.

"How about country music?" Patrick says. "Johnny Cash, Patsy Cline, Hank Williams?"

"Country music?" Louise says. "Is that like holy water?"

"I read something about it," Patrick says. "In *New Scientist,* or *Guitar* magazine, or maybe it was *Martha Stewart Living.* It was something about the pitch, the frequencies. Yodeling is supposed to be effective. Makes sense when you think about it."

"I was thinking about summer camp," Louise says to Louise. "Remember how the counselors used to tell us ghost stories?"

"Yeah," Louise says. "They did that thing with the flashlight. You made me go to the bathroom with you in the middle of the night. You were afraid to go by yourself."

"I wasn't afraid," Louise says. "You were afraid."

■

At the symphony, Louise watches the cellists and Louise watches Louise. The cellists watch the conductor and every now and then they look past him, over at Louise. Louise can feel them staring at Louise. Music goes everywhere, like light and, like light, music loves Louise. Louise doesn't know how she knows this—she can just feel the music, wrapping itself around Louise, insinuating itself into her beautiful ears, between her lips, collecting in her hair and in the little scoop between her legs. And what good does it do Louise, Louise thinks? The cellists might as well be playing jackhammers and spoons.

Well, maybe that isn't entirely true. Louise may be tone-deaf, but she's explained to Louise that it doesn't mean she doesn't like music. She feels it in her bones and back behind her jaw. It scratches itches. It's like a crossword puzzle. Louise is trying to figure it out, and right next to her, Louise is trying to figure out Louise.

The music stops and starts and stops again. Louise and Louise clap at the intermission and then the lights come up and Louise says, "I've been thinking a lot. About something. I want another baby."

"What do you mean?" Louise says, stunned. "You mean like Anna?"

"I don't know," Louise says. "Just another one. You should

have a baby, too. We could go to Lamaze classes together. You could name yours Louise after me and I could name mine Louise after you. Wouldn't that be funny?"

"Anna would be jealous," Louise says.

"I think it would make me happy," Louise says. "I was so happy when Anna was a baby. Everything just tasted good, even the air. I even liked being pregnant."

Louise says, "Aren't you happy now?"

Louise says, "Of course I'm happy. But don't you know what I mean? Being happy like that?"

"Kind of," Louise says. "Like when we were kids. You mean like Girl Scout camp."

"Yeah," Louise says. "Like that. You would have to get rid of your ghost first. I don't think ghosts are very hygienic. I could introduce you to a very nice man. A cellist. Maybe not the highest sperm count, but very nice."

"Which number is he?" Louise says.

"I don't want to prejudice you," Louise says. "You haven't met him. I'm not sure you should think of him as a number. I'll point him out. Oh, and number eight, too. You have to meet my beautiful boy, number eight. We have to go out to lunch so I can tell you about him. He's smitten. I've smited him."

Louise goes to the bathroom and Louise stays in her seat. She thinks of her ghost. Why can't she have a ghost and a baby? Why is she always supposed to give up something? Why can't other people share?

Why does Louise want to have another baby anyway? What if this new baby hates Louise as much as Anna does? What if it used to be a dog? What if her own baby hates Louise?

When the musicians are back on stage, Louise leans over and whispers to Louise, "There he is. The one with big hands, over on the right."

It isn't clear to Louise which cellist Louise means. They all have big hands. And which cellist is she supposed to be looking for? The nice cellist she shouldn't be thinking of as a number? Number eight? She takes a closer look. All of the cellists are handsome from where Louise is sitting. How fragile they look, she thinks, in their serious black clothes, letting the music run down their strings like that and pour through their open fingers. It's careless of them. You have to hold on to things.

There are six cellists on stage. Perhaps Louise has slept with all of them. Louise thinks, if I went to bed with them, with any of them, I would recognize the way they tasted, the things they liked, and the ways they liked them. I would know which number they were. But they wouldn't know me.

■

The ghost is bigger again. He's prickly all over. He bristles with hair. The hair is reddish brown and sharp-looking. Louise doesn't think it would be a good idea to touch the ghost now. All night he moves back and forth in front of her bed, sliding on his belly like a snake. His fingers dig into the floorboards and he pushes himself forward with his toes. His mouth stays open as if he's eating air.

Louise goes to the kitchen. She opens a can of beans, a can of pears, hearts of palm. She puts the different things on a plate and places the plate in front of the ghost. He moves around it. Maybe he's like Anna—picky. Louise doesn't know what he wants. Louise refuses to sleep in the living room again. It's her bedroom after all. She lies awake and listens to the ghost press himself against her clean floor, moving backwards and forwards before the foot of the bed all night long.

In the morning the ghost is in the closet, upside down against the wall. Enough, she thinks, and she goes to the mall and buys a stack of CDs. Patsy Cline, Emmylou Harris, Hank Williams, Johnny Cash, Lyle Lovett. She asks the clerk if he can recommend anything with yodeling on it, but he's young and not very helpful.

"Never mind," she says. "I'll just take these."

While he's running her credit card, she says, "Wait. Have you ever seen a ghost?"

"None of your business, lady," he says. "But if I had, I'd make it show me where it buried its treasure. And then I'd dig up the treasure and I'd be rich and then I wouldn't be selling you this stupid country shit. Unless the treasure had a curse on it."

"What if there wasn't any treasure?" Louise says.

"Then I'd stick the ghost in a bottle and sell it to a museum," the kid says. "A real live ghost. That's got to be worth something.

I'd buy a hog and ride it to California. I'd go make my own music, and there wouldn't be any fucking yodeling."

The ghost seems to like Patsy Cline. It isn't that he says anything. But he doesn't disappear. He comes out of the closet. He lies on the floor so that Louise has to walk around him. He's thicker now, more solid. Maybe he was a Patsy Cline fan when he was alive. The hair stands up all over his body, and it moves gently, as if a breeze is blowing through it.

They both like Johnny Cash. Louise is pleased—they have something in common now.

"I'm on to Jackson," Louise sings. "You big-talkin' man."

The phone rings in the middle of the night. Louise sits straight up in bed. "What?" she says. "Did you say something?" Is she in a hotel room? She orients herself quickly. The ghost is under the bed again, one hand sticking out as if flagging down a bedroom taxi. Louise picks up the phone.

"Number eight just told me the strangest thing," Louise says. "Did you try the country music?"

"Yes," Louise says. "But it didn't work. I think he liked it."

"That's a relief," Louise says. "What are you doing on Friday?"

"Working," Louise says. "And then I don't know. I was going to rent a video or something. Want to come over and see the ghost?"

"I'd like to bring over a few people," Louise says. "After rehearsal. The cellists want to see the ghost, too. They want to play for it, actually. It's kind of complicated. Maybe you could fix dinner. Spaghetti's fine. Maybe some salad, some garlic bread. I'll bring wine."

"How many cellists?" Louise says.

"Eight," Louise says. "And Patrick's busy. I might have to bring Anna. It could be educational. Is the ghost still naked?"

"Yes," Louise says. "But it's okay. He got furry. You can tell her he's a dog. So what's going to happen?"

"That depends on the ghost," Louise says. "If he likes the cellists, he might leave with one of them. You know, go into one of the cellos. Apparently it's very good for the music. And it's good for the ghost, too. Sort of like those little fish that live on the big fishes. Remoras. Number eight is explaining it to me. He said that haunted instruments aren't just instruments. It's like they have a soul. The musician doesn't play the instrument anymore. He or she plays the ghost."

"I don't know if he'd fit," Louise says. "He's largish. At least part of the time."

Louise says, "Apparently cellos are a lot bigger on the inside than they look on the outside. Besides, it's not like you're using him for anything."

"I guess not," Louise says.

"If word gets out, you'll have musicians knocking on your door day and night, night and day," Louise says. "Trying to steal him. Don't tell anyone."

■

Gloria and Mary come to see Louise at work. They leave with a group in a week for Greece. They're going to all the islands. They've been working with Louise to organize the hotels, the tours, the passports, and the buses. They're fond of Louise. They tell her about their sons, show her pictures. They think she should get married and have a baby.

Louise says, "Have either of you ever seen a ghost?"

Gloria shakes her head. Mary says, "Oh, honey, all the time when I was growing up. It runs in families sometimes, ghosts and stuff like that. Not as much now, of course. My eyesight isn't so good now."

"What do you do with them?" Louise says.

"Not much," Mary says. "You can't eat them and you can't talk to most of them and they aren't worth much."

"I played with a Ouija board once," Gloria says. "With some other girls. We asked it who we would marry, and it told us some names. I forget. I don't recall that it was accurate. Then we got scared. We asked it who we were talking to, and it spelled out Z-E-U-S. Then it was just a bunch of letters. Gibberish."

"What about music?" Louise says.

"I like music," Gloria says. "It makes me cry sometimes when I hear a pretty song. I saw Frank Sinatra sing once. He wasn't so special."

"It will bother a ghost," Mary says. "Some kinds of music will stir it up. Some kinds of music will lay a ghost. We used to catch ghosts in my brother's fiddle. Like fishing, or catching fireflies in a jar. But my mother always said to leave them be."

"I have a ghost," Louise confesses.

"Would you ask it something?" Gloria says. "Ask it what it's like being dead. I like to know about a place before I get there. I don't mind going someplace new, but I like to know what it's going to be like. I like to have some idea."

■

Louise asks the ghost but he doesn't say anything. Maybe he can't remember what it was like to be alive. Maybe he's forgotten the language. He just lies on the bedroom floor, flat on his back, legs open, looking up at her like she's something special. Or maybe he's thinking of England.

■

Louise makes spaghetti. Louise is on the phone talking to caterers. "So you don't think we have enough champagne," she says. "I know it's a gala, but I don't want them falling over. Just happy. Happy signs checks. Falling over doesn't do me any good. How much more do you think we need?"

Anna sits on the kitchen floor and watches Louise cutting up tomatoes. "You'll have to make me something green," she says.

"Why don't you just eat your crayon?" Louise says. "Your mother isn't going to have time to make you green food when she has another baby. You'll have to eat plain food like everybody else, or else eat grass like cows do."

"I'll make my own green food," Anna says.

"You're going to have a little brother or a little sister," Louise says. "You'll have to behave. You'll have to be responsible. You'll have to share your room and your toys—not just the regular ones, the green ones, too."

"I'm not going to have a sister," Anna says. "I'm going to have a dog."

"You know how it works, right?" Louise says, pushing the drippy tomatoes into the saucepan. "A man and a woman fall in love and they kiss and then the woman has a baby. First she gets fat and then she goes to the hospital. She comes home with a baby."

"You're lying," Anna says. "The man and the woman go to the pound. They pick out a dog. They bring the dog home and they feed it baby food. And then one day all the dog's hair falls out and it's pink. And it learns how to talk, and it has to wear clothes. And they give it a new name, not a dog name. They give it a baby name and it has to give the dog name back."

"Whatever," Louise says. "I'm going to have a baby, too. And it will have the same name as your mother and the same name as me. Louise. Louise will be the name of your mother's baby, too. The only person named Anna will be you."

"My dog name was Louise," Anna says. "But you're not allowed to call me that."

Louise comes in the kitchen. "So much for the caterers," she says. "So where is it?"

"Where's what?" Louise says.

"The you-know-what," Louise says, "you know."

"I haven't seen it today," Louise says. "Maybe this won't work. Maybe it would rather live here." All day long she's had the radio turned on, tuned to the country station. Maybe the ghost will take the hint and hide out somewhere until everyone leaves.

The cellists arrive. Seven men and a woman. Louise doesn't bother to remember their names. The woman is tall and thin. She has long arms and a long nose. She eats three plates of spaghetti. The cellists talk to each other. They don't talk about the ghost. They talk about music. They complain about acoustics. They tell Louise that her spaghetti is delicious. Louise just smiles. She stares at the woman cellist, sees Louise watching her. Louise shrugs, nods. She holds up five fingers.

Louise and the cellists seem comfortable. They tease each other. They tell stories. Do they know? Do they talk about Louise? Do they brag? Compare notes? How could they know Louise better than Louise knows her? Suddenly Louise feels as if this isn't her house after all. It belongs to Louise and the cellists. It's their ghost, not hers. They live here. After dinner they'll stay and she'll leave.

Number five is the one who likes foreign films, Louise remembers. The one with the goldfish. Louise said number five had a great sense of humor.

Louise gets up and goes to the kitchen to get more wine, leaving Louise alone with the cellists. The one sitting next to Louise says, "You have the prettiest eyes. Have I seen you in the audience sometimes?"

"It's possible," Louise says.

"Louise talks about you all the time," the cellist says. He's young, maybe twenty-four or twenty-five. Louise wonders if he's the one with the big hands. He has pretty eyes, too. She tells him that.

"Louise doesn't know everything about me," she says, flirting.

Anna is hiding under the table. She growls and pretends to bite the cellists. The cellists know Anna. They're used to her. They probably think she's cute. They pass her bits of broccoli, lettuce.

The living room is full of cellos in black cases the cellists brought in, like sarcophaguses on little wheels. Sarcophabuses. Dead baby carriages. After dinner the cellists take their chairs into the living room. They take out their cellos and tune them. Anna insinuates herself between cellos, hanging on the backs of chairs. The house is full of sound.

Louise and Louise sit on chairs in the hall and look in. They can't talk. It's too loud. Louise reaches into her purse, pulls out a packet of earplugs. She gives two to Anna, two to Louise, keeps two for herself. Louise puts her earplugs in. Now the cellists sound as if they are underground, down in some underground lake, or in a cave. Louise fidgets.

The cellists play for almost an hour. When they take a break Louise feels tender, as if the cellists have been throwing things at her. Tiny lumps of sound. She almost expects to see bruises on her arms.

The cellists go outside to smoke cigarettes. Louise takes Louise aside. "You should tell me now if there isn't a ghost," she says. "I'll tell them to go home. I promise I won't be angry."

"There is a ghost," Louise says. "Really." But she doesn't try to sound too convincing. What she doesn't tell Louise is that she's stuck a Walkman in her closet. She's got the Patsy Cline CD on repeat with the volume turned way down.

Louise says, "So he was talking to you during dinner. What do you think?"

"Who?" Louise says. "Him? He was pretty nice."

Louise sighs. "Yeah. I think he's pretty nice, too."

The cellists come back inside. The young cellist with the glasses and the big hands looks over at both of them and smiles a big blissed smile. Maybe it wasn't cigarettes that they were smoking.

Anna has fallen asleep inside a cello case, like a fat green pea in a coffin.

Louise tries to imagine the cellists without their clothes. She tries to picture them naked and fucking Louise. No, *fucking* Louise, fucking her instead. Which one is number four? The one with the beard? Number four, she remembers, likes Louise to sit on top and bounce up and down. She does all the work while he waves his hand. He conducts her. Louise thinks it's funny.

Louise pictures all of the cellists, naked and in the same bed. She's in the bed. The one with the beard first. Lie on your back, she tells him. Close your eyes. Don't move. I'm in charge. I'm conducting this affair. The one with the skinny legs and the poochy stomach. The young one with curly black hair, bent over his cello as if he might fall in. Who was flirting with her. Do this, she tells a cellist. Do this, she tells another one. She can't figure out what to do with the woman. Number five. She can't even figure out how to take off number five's clothes. Number five sits on the edge of the bed, hands tucked under her buttocks. She's still in her bra and underwear.

Louise thinks about the underwear for a minute. It has little flowers on it. Periwinkles. Number five waits for Louise to tell her what to do. But Louise is having a hard enough time figuring out where everyone else goes. A mouth has fastened itself on her breast. Someone is tugging at her hair. She is holding on to someone's penis with both hands, someone else's penis is rubbing against her cunt. There are penises everywhere. Wait your turn, Louise thinks. Be patient.

Number five has pulled a cello out of her underwear. She's

playing a sad little tune on it. It's distracting. It's not sexy at all. Another cellist stands up on the bed, jumps up and down. Soon they're all doing it. The bed creaks and groans, and the woman plays faster and faster on her fiddle. Stop it, Louise thinks, you'll wake the ghost.

"Shit!" Louise says—she's yanked Louise's earplug out, drops it in Louise's lap. "There he is under your chair. Look. Louise, you really do have a ghost."

The cellists don't look. Butter wouldn't melt in their mouths. They are fucking their cellos with their fingers, stroking music out, promising the ghost yodels and Patsy Cline and funeral marches and whole cities of music and music to eat and music to drink and music to put on and wear like clothes. It isn't music Louise has ever heard before. It sounds like a lullaby, and then it sounds like a pack of wolves, and then it sounds like a slaughterhouse, and then it sounds like a motel room and a married man saying I love you and the shower is running at the same time. It makes her teeth ache and her heart rattle.

It sounds like the color green. Anna wakes up. She's sitting in the cello case, hands over her ears.

This is too loud, Louise thinks. The neighbors will complain. She bends over and sees the ghost, small and unobjectionable as a lapdog, lying under her chair. Oh, my poor baby, she thinks. Don't be fooled. Don't fall for the song. They don't mean it.

But something is happening to the ghost. He shivers and twists and gapes. He comes out from under the chair. He leaves all his fur behind, under the chair in a neat little pile. He drags himself along the floor with his strong beautiful hands, scissoring with his legs along the floor like a swimmer. He's planning to change, to leave her and go away. Louise pulls out her other earplug. She's going to give them to the ghost. "Stay here," she says out loud, "stay here with me and the real Patsy Cline. Don't go." She can't hear herself speak. The cellos roar like lions in cages and licks of fire. Louise opens her mouth to say it louder, but the ghost is going. Fine, okay, go comb your hair. See if I care.

Louise and Louise and Anna watch as the ghost climbs into a cello. He pulls himself up, shakes the air off like drops of water. He gets smaller. He gets fainter. He melts into the cello like spilled milk. All the other cellists pause. The cellist who has caught Louise's ghost plays a scale. "Well," he says. It doesn't sound any different to Louise but all the other cellists sigh.

It's the bearded cellist who's caught the ghost. He holds on to his cello as if it might grow legs and run away if he let go. He looks like he's discovered America. He plays something else. Something old-fashioned, Louise thinks, a pretty old-fashioned tune, and she wants to cry. She puts her earplugs back in again. The cellist looks up at Louise as he plays and he smiles. You owe me, she thinks.

But it's the youngest cellist, the one who thinks Louise has pretty eyes, who stays. Louise isn't sure how this happens. She isn't sure that she has the right cellist. She isn't sure that the ghost went into the right cello. But the cellists pack up their cellos and they thank her and they drive away, leaving the dishes piled in the sink for Louise to wash.

The youngest cellist is still sitting in her living room. "I thought I had it," he says. "I thought for sure I could play that ghost."

"I'm leaving," Louise says. But she doesn't leave.

"Good night," Louise says.

"Do you want a ride?" Louise says to the cellist.

He says, "I thought I might hang around. See if there's another ghost in here. If that's okay with Louise."

Louise shrugs. "Good night," she says to Louise.

"Well," Louise says, "good night." She picks up Anna, who has fallen asleep on the couch. Anna was not impressed with the ghost. He wasn't a dog and he wasn't green.

"Good night," the cellist says, and the door slams shut behind Louise and Anna.

Louise inhales. He's not married, it isn't that smell. But it reminds her of something.

"What's your name?" she says, but before he can answer her, she puts her earplugs back in again. They fuck in the closet and then in the bathtub and then he lies down on the bedroom floor and Louise sits on top of him. To exorcise the ghost, she thinks. Hotter in a chilly sprout.

The cellist's mouth moves when he comes. It looks like he's saying, "Louise, Louise," but she gives him the benefit of the doubt. He might be saying her name.

She nods encouragingly. "That's right," she says. "Louise."

The cellist falls asleep on the floor. Louise throws a blanket over him. She watches him breathe. It's been a while since she's watched a man sleep. She takes a shower and she does the dishes. She puts the chairs in the living room away. She gets an envelope and she picks up a handful of the ghost's hair. She puts it in the envelope and she sweeps the rest away. She takes her earplugs out but she doesn't throw them away.

In the morning, the cellist makes her pancakes. He sits down at the table and she stands up. She walks over and sniffs his neck. She recognizes that smell now. He smells like Louise. Burnt sugar and orange juice and talcum powder. She realizes that she's made a horrible mistake.

Louise is furious. Louise didn't know Louise knew how to be angry. Louise hangs up when Louise calls. Louise drives over to Louise's house and no one comes to the door. But Louise can see Anna looking out the window.

Louise writes a letter to Louise. "I'm so sorry," she writes. "I should have known. Why didn't you tell me? He doesn't love me. He was just drunk. Maybe he got confused. Please, please forgive me. You don't have to forgive me immediately. Tell me what I should do."

At the bottom she writes, "P.S. I'm not pregnant."

Three weeks later, Louise is walking a group of symphony patrons across the stage. They've all just eaten lunch. They drank wine. She is pointing out architectural details, rows of expensive spotlights. She is standing with her back to the theater. She is talking, she points up, she takes a step back into air. She falls off the stage.

A man—a lawyer—calls Louise at work. At first she thinks it must be her mother who has fallen. The lawyer explains. Louise is the one who is dead. She broke her neck.

While Louise is busy understanding this, the lawyer, Mr. Bostick, says something else. Louise is Anna's guardian now.

"Wait, wait," Louise says. "What do you mean? Louise is in the hospital? I have to take care of Anna for a while?"

No, Mr. Bostick says. Louise is dead.

"In the event of her death, Louise wanted you to adopt her daughter, Anna Geary. I had assumed that my client Louise Geary had discussed this with you. She has no living family. Louise told me that you were her family."

"But I slept with her cellist," Louise said. "I didn't mean to. I didn't realize which number he was. I didn't know his name. I still don't. Louise is so angry with me."

But Louise isn't angry with Louise anymore. Or maybe now she will always be angry with Louise.

Louise picks Anna up at school. Anna is sitting on a chair in the school office. She doesn't look up when Louise opens the door. Louise goes and stands in front of her. She looks down at Anna and thinks, This is all that's left of Louise. This is all I've got now. A little girl who only likes things that are green, who used to be a dog. "Come on, Anna," Louise says. "You're going to come live with me."

■

Louise and Anna live together for a week. At work, Louise avoids her married lover. She doesn't know how to explain things. First a ghost and now a little girl. That's the end of the motel rooms.

Louise and Anna go to Louise's funeral and throw dirt at Louise's coffin. Anna throws her dirt hard, like she's aiming for something. Louise holds on to her handful too tightly. When she lets go, there's dirt under her fingernails. She sticks a finger in her mouth.

All the cellists are there. They look amputated without their cellos, smaller, childlike. Anna, in her funereal green, looks older than they do. She holds Louise's hand grudgingly. Louise has promised that Anna can have a dog. No more motels for sure. She'll have to buy a bigger house, Louise thinks, with a yard. She'll sell her house and Louise's house and put the money in a trust for Anna. She did this for her mother—this is what you have to do for family.

While the minister is still speaking, number eight lies down on the ground beside the grave. The cellists on either side each take an arm and pull him back up again. Louise sees that his nose is running. He doesn't look at her, and he doesn't wipe his nose, either. When the two cellists walk him away, there's grave dirt on the seat of his pants.

Patrick is there. His eyes are red. He waves his fingers at Anna, but he stays where he is. Loss is contagious—he's keeping a safe distance.

The woman cellist, number five, comes up to Louise after the funeral. She embraces Louise, Anna. She tells them that a special memorial concert has been arranged. Funds will be raised. One of the smaller concert halls will be named the Louise Geary Memorial Hall. Louise agrees that Louise would have been pleased. She and Anna leave before the other cellists can tell them how sorry they are, how much they will miss Louise.

In the evening Louise calls her mother and tells her that Louise is dead.

"Oh, sweetie," her mother says. "I'm so sorry. She was such a pretty girl. I always liked to hear her laugh."

"She was angry with me," Louise says. "Her daughter Anna is staying with me now."

"What about Anna's father?" her mother says. "Did you get rid of that ghost? I'm not sure it's a good idea having a ghost in the same house as a small girl."

"The ghost is gone," Louise says.

There is a click on the line. "Someone's listening in," her mother says. "Don't say anything—they might be recording us. Call me back from a different phone."

Anna has come into the room. She stands behind Louise. She says, "I want to go live with my father."

"It's time to go to sleep," Louise says. She wants to take off her funeral clothes and go to bed. "We can talk about this in the morning."

Anna brushes her teeth and puts on her green pajamas. She does not want Louise to read to her. She does not want a glass of water. Louise says, "When I was a dog . . ."

Anna says, "You were never a dog—" and pulls the blanket, which is not green, up over her head and will not say anything else.

■

Mr. Bostick knows who Anna's father is. "He doesn't know about Anna," he tells Louise. "His name is George Candle and he lives in Oregon. He's married and has two kids. He has his own company—something to do with organic produce, I think, or maybe it was construction."

"I think it would be better for Anna if she were to live with a real parent," Louise says. "Easier. Someone who knows something about kids. I'm not cut out for this."

Mr. Bostick agrees to contact Anna's father. "He may not even admit he knew Louise," he says. "He may not be okay about this."

"Tell him she's a fantastic kid," Louise says. "Tell him she looks just like Louise."

■

In the end George Candle comes and collects Anna. Louise arranges his airline tickets and his hotel room. She books two return tickets out to Portland for Anna and her father and makes sure Anna has a window seat. "You'll like Oregon," she tells Anna. "It's green."

"You think you're smarter than me," Anna says. "You think you know all about me. When I was a dog, I was ten times smarter than you. I knew who my friends were because of how they smelled. I know things you don't."

But she doesn't say what they are. Louise doesn't ask.

George Candle cries when he meets his daughter. He's almost as hairy as the ghost. Louise can smell his marriage. She wonders what Anna smells.

"I loved your mother very much," George Candle says to Anna. "She was a very special person. She had a beautiful soul."

They go to see Louise's gravestone. The grass on her grave is greener than the other grass. You can see where it's been tipped in, like a bookplate. Louise briefly fantasizes her own funeral, her own gravestone, her own married lover standing beside her gravestone.

She knows he would go straight home after the funeral to take a shower. If he went to the funeral.

The house without Anna is emptier than Louise is used to. Louise didn't expect to miss Anna. Now she has no best friend, no ghost, no adopted former dog. Her lover is home with his wife, sulking, and now George Candle is flying home to his wife. What will she think of Anna? Maybe Anna will miss Louise just a little.

That night Louise dreams of Louise endlessly falling off the stage. She falls and falls and falls. As Louise falls she slowly comes apart. Little bits of her fly away. She is made up of ladybugs.

Anna comes and sits on Louise's bed. She is a lot furrier than she was when she lived with Louise. "You're not a dog," Louise says.

Anna grins her possum teeth at Louise. She's holding a piece of okra. "The supernatural world has certain characteristics," Anna says. "You can recognize it by its color, which is green, and by its texture, which is hirsute. Those are its outside qualities. Inside the supernatural world things get sticky but you never get inside things, Louise. Did you know that George Candle is a werewolf? Look out for hairy men, Louise. Or do I mean married men? The other aspects of the green world include music and smell."

Anna pulls her pants down and squats. She pees on the bed, a long acrid stream that makes Louise's eyes water.

Louise wakes up sobbing. "Louise," Louise whispers. "Please come and lie on my floor. Please come haunt me. I'll play Patsy Cline for you and comb your hair. Please don't go away."

She keeps a vigil for three nights. She plays Patsy Cline. She sits by the phone because maybe Louise could call. Louise has never not called, not for so long. If Louise doesn't forgive her, then she can come and be an angry ghost. She can make dishes break or make blood come out of the faucets. She can give Louise bad dreams. Louise will be grateful for broken things and blood and bad dreams. All of Louise's clothes are up on their hangers, hung right-side out. Louise puts little dishes of flowers out, plates with candles and candy. She calls her mother to ask how to make a ghost appear but her mother refuses to tell her. The line may be tapped. Louise will have to come down, she says, and she'll explain in person.

■

Louise wears the same dress she wore to the funeral. She sits up in the balcony. There are enormous pictures of Louise up on the stage. Influential people go up on the stage and tell funny stories about Louise. Members of the orchestra speak about Louise. Her charm, her beauty, her love of music. Louise looks through her opera glasses at the cellists. There is the young one, number eight, who caused all the trouble. There is the bearded cellist who caught the ghost. She stares through her glasses at his cello. Her ghost runs up and down the neck of his cello, frisky. It coils around the strings, hangs upside-down from a peg.

She examines number five's face for a long time. Why you? Louise thinks. If she wanted to sleep with a woman, why did she sleep with you? Did you tell her funny jokes? Did you go shopping together for clothes? When you saw her naked, did you see that she was bowlegged? Did you think that she was beautiful?

The cellist next to number five is holding his cello very carefully. He runs his fingers down the strings as if they were tangled and he were combing them. Louise stares through her opera glasses. There is something in his cello. Something small and bleached is looking back at her through the strings. Louise looks at Louise and then she slips back through the f hole, like a fish.

■

They are in the woods. The fire is low. It's night. All the little girls are in their sleeping bags. They've brushed their teeth and spit, they've washed their faces with water from the kettle, they've zipped up the zippers of their sleeping bags.

A counselor named Charlie is saying, "I am the ghost with the one black eye, I am the ghost with the one black eye."

Charlie holds her flashlight under her chin. Her eyes are two black holes in her face. Her mouth yawns open, the light shining through her teeth. Her shadow eats up the trunk of the tree she sits under.

During the daytime Charlie teaches horseback riding. She isn't much older than Louise or Louise. She's pretty and she lets them ride the horses bareback sometimes. But that's daytime Charlie.

Nighttime Charlie is the one sitting next to the fire. Nighttime Charlie is the one who tells stories.

"Are you afraid?" Louise says.

"No," Louise says.

They hold hands. They don't look at each other. They keep their eyes on Charlie.

Louise says, "Are *you* afraid?"

"No," Louise says. "Not as long as you're here."

I have known Jim Kelly my whole life—at least, my whole writing life. We met when he and John Kessel sent me a postcard about a story I had written. At that time Jim, John, and I were SF neophytes, each having published a few stories. I thought he was charming, smart, and handsome. I still do. He is also one of the best workshop critics I have ever seen: Story Doctor Kelly.

There has been a lot of printer toner under the bridge since then. Jim has developed astonishing versatility, writing novels, short stories, essays, stage and audioplays, and planetarium shows. His books include *Strange but Not a Stranger*, *Think Like a Dinosaur and Other Stories*, *Wildlife*, and *Look into the Sun*. He has won two Hugos, for "Think Like a Dinosaur" (1996) and "Ten to the Sixteenth to One" (2000). He writes a column about the Internet for *Asimov's*. Jim also serves as a governor-appointed councilor on the New Hampshire State Council on the Arts. He bats right, thinks left, has "too many hobbies," and still finds time to write wonderful stories like "Undone."

You may have wondered what *you* would do if you were ever stranded in time. Or not. What Mada does is both shocking and very human.

James Patrick Kelly

panic attack

The ship screamed. Its screens showed Mada that she was surrounded in threespace. A swarm of Utopian asteroids was closing on her, brain clans and mining DIs living in hollowed-out chunks of carbonaceous chondrite, any one of which could have mustered enough votes to abolish Mada in all ten dimensions.

"I'm going to die," the ship cried, "I'm going to die, I'm going to . . ."

"I'm not." Mada waved the speaker off impatiently and scanned downwhen. She saw that the Utopians had planted an identity mine five minutes into the past that would boil her memory to vapor if she tried to go back in time to undo this trap. Upwhen, then. The future was clear, at least as far as she could see, which wasn't much beyond next week. Of course, that was the direction they wanted her to skip. They'd be happiest making her their great-great-great-grandchildren's problem.

The Utopians fired another spread of panic bolts. The ship tried to absorb them, but its buffers were already overflowing. Mada felt her throat tighten. Suddenly she couldn't remember how to spell *luck,* and she believed that she could feel her sanity oozing out of her ears.

"So let's skip upwhen," she said.

"You s-sure?" said the ship. "I don't know if . . . how far?"

"Far enough so that all of these drones will be fossils."

"I can't just . . . I need a number, Mada."

A needle of fear pricked Mada hard enough to make her reflexes kick. "Skip!" Her panic did not allow for the luxury of numbers. "Skip now!" Her voice was tight as a fist. "Do it!"

Time shivered as the ship surged into the empty dimensions. In threespace, Mada went all wavy. Eons passed in a nanosecond, then she washed back into the strong dimensions and solidified.

She merged briefly with the ship to assess damage. "What have you done?" The gain in entropy was an ache in her bones.

"I–I'm sorry, you said to skip so . . ." The ship was still jittery.

Even though she wanted to kick its sensorium in, she bit down hard on her anger. They had both made enough mistakes that day. "That's all right," she said, "we can always go back. We just have to figure out when we are. Run the star charts."

two-tenths of a spin

The ship took almost three minutes to get its charts to agree with its navigation screens—a bad sign. Reconciling the data showed that it had skipped forward in time about two-tenths of a galactic spin. Almost twenty million years had passed on Mada's home-world of Trueborn, time enough for its crust to fold and buckle into new mountain ranges, for the Green Sea to bloom, for the glaciers to march and melt. More than enough time for everything and everyone Mada had ever loved—or hated—to die, turn to dust and blow away.

Whiskers trembling, she checked downwhen. What she saw made her lose her perch and float aimlessly away from the command mod's screens. There had to be something wrong with the ship's air. It settled like dead, wet leaves in her lungs. She ordered the ship to check the mix.

The ship's deck flowed into an enormous plastic hand, warm as blood. It cupped Mada gently in its palm and raised her up so that she could see its screens straight on.

"Nominal, Mada. Everything is as it should be."

That couldn't be right. She could breathe ship-nominal atmosphere. "Check it again," she said.

"Mada, I'm sorry," said the ship.

The identity mine had skipped with them and was still dogging her, five infuriating minutes into the past. There was no getting around it, no way to undo their leap into the future. She was trapped two-tenths of a spin upwhen. The knowledge was like a sucking hole in her chest, much worse than any wound the Utopian psychological war machine could have inflicted on her.

"What do we do now?" asked the ship.

Mada wondered what she should say to it. Scan for hostiles? Open a pleasure sim? Cook a nice, hot stew? Orders twisted in her mind, bit their tails and swallowed themselves.

She considered—briefly—telling it to open all the air locks to the vacuum. Would it obey this order? She thought it probably would, although she would as soon chew her own tongue off as utter such cowardly words. Had not she and her sibling batch voted to carry the revolution into all ten dimensions? Pledged themselves to fight for the Three Universal Rights, no matter what the cost the Utopian brain clans extracted from them in blood and anguish?

But that had been two-tenths of a spin ago.

bean thoughts

"Where are you going?" said the ship.

Mada floated through the door bubble of the command mod. She wrapped her toes around the perch outside to steady herself.

"Mada, wait! I need a mission, a course, some line of inquiry."

She launched down the companionway.

"I'm a Dependent Intelligence, Mada." Its speaker buzzed with self-righteousness. "I have the right to proper and timely guidance."

The ship flowed a veil across her trajectory; as she approached, it went taut. That was DI thinking: the ship was sure that it could just bounce her back into its world. Mada flicked her claws and slashed at it, shredding holes half a meter long.

"And I have the right to be an individual," she said. "Leave me alone."

She caught another perch and pivoted off it toward the green-house blister. She grabbed the perch by the door bubble and paused to flow new alveoli into her lungs to make up for the oxygen-depleted, carbon-dioxide-enriched air mix in the green-house. The bubble shivered as she popped through it and she breathed deeply. The smells of life helped ground her whenever operation of the ship overwhelmed her. It was always so needy and there was only one of her.

It would have been different if they had been designed to go out in teams. She would have had her sibling Thiras at her side; to-gether they might have been strong enough to withstand the Utopian's panic . . . *no!* Mada shook him out of her head. Thiras was gone; they were all gone. There was no sense in looking for comfort, downwhen or up. All she had was the moment, the tick of the relentless present, filled now with the moist, bittersweet breath of the dirt, the sticky savor of running sap, the bloom of perfume on the flowers. As she drifted through the greenhouse, leaves brushed her skin like caresses. She settled at the potting bench, opened a bin and picked out a single bean seed.

Mada cupped it between her two hands and blew on it, letting her body's warmth coax the seed out of dormancy. She tried to merge her mind with its blissful unconsciousness. Cotyledons stirred and began to absorb nutrients from the endosperm. A bean cared nothing about proclaiming the Three Universal Rights: the right of all independent sentients to remain individual, the right to manipulate their physical structures and the right to access the timelines. Mada slowed her metabolism to the steady and deliber-ate rhythm of the bean—what Utopian could do that? They held that individuality bred chaos, that function alone must determine form and that undoing the past was sacrilege. Being Utopians, they could hardly destroy Trueborn and its handful of colonies. Instead they had tried to put the Rights under quarantine.

Mada stimulated the sweat glands in the palms of her hands. The moisture wicking across her skin called to the embryonic root in the bean seed. The tip pushed against the seed coat. Mada's sib-ling batch on Trueborn had pushed hard against the Utopian blockade, to bring the Rights to the rest of the galaxy.

Only a handful had made it to open space. The brain clans had hunted them down and brought most of them back in disgrace to Trueborn. But not Mada. No, not wily Mada, Mada the fearless, Mada whose heart now beat but once a minute.

The bean embryo swelled and its root cracked the seed coat. It curled into her hand, branching and rebranching like the timelines. The roots tickled her.

Mada manipulated the chemistry of her sweat by forcing her sweat ducts to reabsorb most of the sodium and chlorine. She parted her hands slightly and raised them up to the grow lights. The cotyledons emerged and chloroplasts oriented themselves to the light. Mada was thinking only bean thoughts as her cupped hands filled with roots and the first true leaves unfolded. More leaves budded from the nodes of her stem, her petioles arched and twisted to the light, *the light*. It was only the light—violet-blue and orange-red—that mattered, the incredible shower of photons that excited her chlorophyll, passing electrons down carrier molecules to form adenosine diphosphate and nicotinamide adenine dinucleo . . .

"Mada," said the ship. "The order to leave you alone is now superseded by primary programming."

"What?" The word caught in her throat like a bone.

"You entered the greenhouse forty days ago."

Without quite realizing what she was doing, Mada clenched her hands, crushing the young plant.

"I am directed to keep you from harm, Mada," said the ship. "It's time to eat."

She glanced down at the dead thing in her hands. "Yes, all right." She dropped it onto the potting bench. "I've got something to clean up first but I'll be there in a minute." She wiped the corner of her eye. "Meanwhile, calculate a course for home."

natural background

Not until the ship scanned the quarantine zone at the edge of the Trueborn system did Mada begin to worry. In her time the zone had swarmed with the battle asteroids of the brain clans. Now the

Utopians were gone. Of course, that was to be expected after all this time. But as the ship re-entered the home system, dumping excess velocity into the empty dimensions, Mada felt a chill that had nothing to do with the temperature in the command mod.

Trueborn orbited a spectral type G3V star, which had been known to the discoverers as HR3538. Scans showed that the Green Sea had become a climax forest of deciduous hardwood. There were indeed new mountains—knife edges slicing through evergreen sheets—that had upthrust some eighty kilometers off the Fire Coast, leaving Port Henoch landlocked. A rain forest choked the plain where the city of Blair's Landing had once sprawled.

The ship scanned life in abundance. The seas teemed and flocks of Trueborn's flyers darkened the skies like storm clouds: kippies and bluewings and warblers and migrating stilts. Animals had re-taken all three continents, lowland and upland, marsh and tundra. Mada could see the dust kicked up by the herds of herbivorous aram from low orbit. The forest echoed with the clatter of shindies and the shriek of blowhards. Big hunters like kar and divil padded across the plains. There were new species as well, mostly invertebrates but also a number of lizards and something like a great, mossy rat that built mounds five meters tall.

None of the introduced species had survived: dogs or turkeys or llamas. The ship could find no cities, towns, buildings—not even ruins. There were neither tubeways nor roads, only the occasional animal track. The ship looked across the entire electromagnetic spectrum and saw nothing but the natural background.

There was nobody home on Trueborn. And as far as they could tell, there never had been.

"Speculate," said Mada.

"I can't," said the ship. "There isn't enough data."

"There's your data." Mada could hear the anger in her voice. "Trueborn, as it would have been had we never even existed."

"Two-tenths of a spin is a long time, Mada."

She shook her head. "They ripped out the foundations, even picked up the dumps. There's nothing, *nothing* of us left." Mada was gripping the command perch so hard that the knuckles of her toes were white. "Hypothesis," she said, "the Utopians got tired of our troublemaking and wiped us out. Speculate."

"Possible, but that's contrary to their core beliefs." Most DIs had terrible imaginations. They couldn't tell jokes, but then they couldn't commit crimes, either.

"Hypothesis: they deported the entire population, scattered us to prison colonies. Speculate."

"Possible, but a logistical nightmare. The Utopians prize the elegant solution."

She swiped the image of her home planet off the screen, as if to erase its unnerving impossibility. "Hypothesis: there are no Utopians anymore because the revolution succeeded. Speculate."

"Possible, but then where did everyone go? And why did they return the planet to its pristine state?"

She snorted in disgust. "What if," she tapped a finger to her forehead, "maybe we *don't* exist. What if we've skipped to another timeline? One in which the discovery of Trueborn never happened? Maybe there has been no Utopian Empire in this timeline, no Great Expansion, no Space Age, maybe no human civilization at all."

"One does not just skip to another timeline at random." The ship sounded huffy at the suggestion. "I've monitored all our dimensional reinsertions quite carefully, and I can assure you that all these events occurred in the timeline we currently occupy."

"You're saying there's no chance?"

"If you want to write a story, why bother asking my opinion?"

Mada's laugh was brittle. "All right then. We need more data." For the first time since she had been stranded upwhen, she felt a tickle stir the dead weight she was carrying inside her. "Let's start with the nearest Utopian system."

chasing shadows

The HR683 system was abandoned and all signs of human habitation had been obliterated. Mada could not be certain that everything had been restored to its pre-Expansion state because the ship's database on Utopian resources was spotty. HR4523 was similarly deserted. HR509, also known as Tau Ceti, was only 11.9

light-years from Earth and had been the first outpost of the Great Expansion.

Its planetary system was also devoid of intelligent life and human artifacts—with one striking exception.

Nuevo LA was spread along the shores of the Sterling Sea like a half-eaten picnic lunch. Something had bitten the roofs off its buildings and chewed its walls. Metal skeletons rotted on its docks, transports were melting into brown and gold stains. Once-proud boulevards crumbled in the orange light; the only traffic was wind-blown litter chasing shadows.

Mada was happy to survey the ruin from low orbit. A closer inspection would have spooked her. "Was it war?"

"There may have been a war," said the ship, "but that's not what caused this. I think it's deliberate deconstruction." In extreme magnification, the screen showed a concrete wall pock-marked with tiny holes, from which dust puffed intermittently. "The composition of that dust is limestone, sand, and aluminum silicate. The buildings are crawling with nanobots and they're eating the concrete."

"How long has this been going on?"

"At a guess, a hundred years, but that could be off by an order of magnitude."

"Who did this?" said Mada. "Why? Speculate."

"If this is the outcome of a war, then it would seem that the victors wanted to obliterate all traces of the vanquished. But it doesn't seem to have been fought over resources. I suppose we could imagine some deep ideological antagonism between the two sides that led to this, but such an extreme of cultural psychopathology seems unlikely."

"I hope you're right." She shivered. "So they did it themselves, then? Maybe they were done with this place and wanted to leave it as they found it?"

"Possible," said the ship.

Mada decided that she was done with Nuevo LA, too. She would have been perversely comforted to have found her enemies in power somewhere. It would have given her an easy way to calculate her duty. However, Mada was quite certain that what this mystery meant was that twenty thousand millennia had conquered both the revolution *and* the Utopians and that she and her sibling batch had been designed in vain.

Still, she had nothing better to do with eternity than to try to find out what had become of her species.

a never-ending vacation

The Atlantic Ocean was now larger than the Pacific. The Mediterranean Sea had been squeezed out of existence by the collision of Africa, Europe and Asia. North America floated free of South America and was nudging Siberia. Australia was drifting toward the equator.

The population of Earth was about what it had been in the fifteenth century CE, according to the ship. Half a billion people lived on the home world and, as far as Mada could see, none of them had anything important to do. The means of production and distribution, of energy-generation and waste disposal were in the control of Dependent Intelligences like the ship. Despite repeated scans, the ship could detect no sign that any independent sentience was overseeing the system.

There were but a handful of cities, none larger than a quarter of a million inhabitants. All were scrubbed clean and kept scrupulously ordered by the DIs; they reminded Mada of databases populated with people instead of information. The majority of the population spent their bucolic lives in pretty hamlets and quaint towns overlooking lakes or oceans or mountains.

Humanity had booked a never-ending vacation.

"The brain clans could be controlling the DIs," said Mada. "That would make sense."

"Doubtful," said the ship. "Independent sentients create a signature disturbance in the sixth dimension."

"Could there be some secret dictator among the humans, a hidden oligarchy?"

"I see no evidence that anyone is in charge. Do you?"

She shook her head. "Did they choose to live in a museum," she said, "or were they condemned to it? It's obvious there's no

First Right here; these people have only the *illusion* of individuality. And no Second Right either. Those bodies are as plain as uniforms—they're still slaves to their biology."

"There's no disease," said the ship. "They seem to be functionally immortal."

"That's not saying very much, is it?" Mada sniffed. "Maybe this is some scheme to start human civilization over again. Or maybe they're like seeds, stored here until someone comes along to plant them." She waved all the screens off. "I want to go down for a closer look. What do I need to pass?"

"Clothes, for one thing." The ship displayed a selection of current styles on its screen. They were extravagantly varied, from ballooning pastel tents to skin-tight sheaths of luminescent metal, to feathered camouflage to jumpsuits made of what looked like dried mud. "Fashion design is one of their principal pastimes," said the ship. "In addition, you'll probably want genitalia and the usual secondary sexual characteristics."

It took her the better part of a day to flow ovaries, fallopian tubes, a uterus, cervix, and vulva and to rearrange her vagina. All these unnecessary organs made her feel bloated. She saw breasts as a waste of tissue; she made hers as small as the ship thought acceptable. She argued with it about the several substantial patches of hair it claimed she needed. Clearly, grooming them would require constant attention. She didn't mind taming her claws into fingernails but she hated giving up her whiskers. Without them, the air was practically invisible. At first her new vulva tickled when she walked, but she got used to it.

The ship entered Earth's atmosphere at night and landed in what had once been Saskatchewan, Canada. It dumped most of its mass into the empty dimensions and flowed itself into baggy black pants, a moss-colored boat neck top and a pair of brown, gripall loafers. It was able to conceal its complete sensorium in a canvas belt.

It was 9:14 in the morning on June 23, 19,834,004 CE when Mada strolled into the village of Harmonious Struggle.

the devil's apple

Harmonious Struggle consisted of five clothing shops, six restaurants, three jewelers, eight art galleries, a musical instrument maker, a crafts workshop, a weaver, a potter, a woodworking shop, two candle stores, four theaters with capacities ranging from twenty to three hundred and an enormous sporting goods store attached to a miniature domed stadium. There looked to be apartments over most of these establishments; many had views of nearby Rabbit Lake.

Three of the restaurants—Hassam's Palace of Plenty, The Devil's Apple, and Laurel's—were practically jostling each other for position on Sonnet Street, which ran down to the lake. Lounging just outside of each were waiters eyeing handheld screens. They sprang up as one when Mada happened around the corner.

"Good day, Madame. Have you eaten?"

"Well met, fair stranger. Come break bread with us."

"All natural foods, friend! Lightly cooked, humbly served."

Mada veered into the middle of the street to study the situation as the waiters called to her. ~*So I can choose whichever I want?*~ she subvocalized to the ship.

~*In an attention-based economy,*~ subbed the ship in reply, ~*all they expect from you is an audience.*~

Just beyond Hassam's, the skinny waiter from The Devil's Apple had a wry, crooked smile. Black hair fell to the padded shoulders of his shirt. He was wearing boots to the knee and loose rust-colored shorts, but it was the little red cape that decided her.

As she walked past her, the waitress from Hassam's was practically shouting. "Madame, *please*, their batter is dull!" She waved her handheld at Mada. "Read the *reviews*. Who puts shrimp in *muffins*?"

The waiter at The Devil's Apple was named Owen. He showed her to one of three tables in the tiny restaurant. At his suggestion, Mada ordered the poached peaches with white cheese mousse, an asparagus breakfast torte, baked orange walnut French toast and coddled eggs. Owen served the peaches, but it was the chef and owner, Edris, who emerged from the kitchen to clear the plate.

"The mousse, Madame, you liked it?" she asked, beaming.

"It was good," said Mada.

Her smile shrank a size and a half. "Enough lemon rind, would you say that?"

"Yes. It was very nice."

Mada's reply seemed to dismay Edris even more. When she came out to clear the next course, she blanched at the corner of breakfast torte that Mada had left uneaten.

"I knew this." She snatched the plate away. "The pastry wasn't fluffy enough." She rolled the offending scrap between thumb and forefinger.

Mada raised her hands in protest. "No, no, it was delicious." She could see Owen shrinking into the far corner of the room.

"Maybe too much Colby, not enough Gruyère?" Edris snarled. "But you have no comment?"

"I wouldn't change a thing. It was perfect."

"Madame is kind," she said, her lips barely moving, and retreated.

A moment later Owen set the steaming plate of French toast before Mada.

"Excuse me." She tugged at his sleeve.

"Something's wrong?" He edged away from her. "You must speak to Edris."

"Everything is fine. I was just wondering if you could tell me how to get to the local library."

Edris burst out of the kitchen. "What are you doing, bean-headed boy? You are distracting my patron with absurd chitterchat. Get out, get out of my restaurant now."

"No, really, he . . ."

But Owen was already out the door and up the street, taking Mada's appetite with him.

~*You're doing something wrong,*~ the ship subbed.

Mada lowered her head. ~*I know that!*~

Mada pushed the sliver of French toast around the pool of maple syrup for several minutes but could not eat it. "Excuse me," she called, standing up abruptly. "Edris?"

Edris shouldered through the kitchen door, carrying a tray with a silver egg cup. She froze when she saw how it was with the French toast and her only patron.

"This was one of the most delicious meals I have ever eaten." Mada backed toward the door. She wanted nothing to do with eggs, coddled or otherwise.

Edris set the tray in front of Mada's empty chair. "Madame, the art of the kitchen requires the tongue of the patron," she said icily.

She fumbled for the latch. "Everything was very, very wonderful."

no comment

Mada slunk down Lyric Alley, which ran behind the stadium, trying to understand how exactly she had offended. In this attention-based economy, paying attention was obviously not enough. There had to be some other cultural protocol she and the ship were missing. What she probably ought to do was go back and explore the clothes shops, maybe pick up a pot or some candles and see what additional information she could blunder into. But making a fool of herself had never much appealed to Mada as a learning strategy. She wanted the map, a native guide—some edge, preferably secret.

~Scanning,~ subbed the ship. ~Somebody is following you. He just ducked behind the privet hedge twelve-point-three meters to the right. It's the waiter, Owen.~

"Owen," called Mada, "is that you? I'm sorry I got you in trouble. You're an excellent waiter."

"I'm not really a waiter." Owen peeked over the top of the hedge. "I'm a poet."

She gave him her best smile. "You said you'd take me to the library." For some reason, the smile stayed on her face. "Can we do that now?"

"First listen to some of my poetry."

"No," she said firmly. "Owen, I don't think you've been paying attention. I said I would like to go to the library."

"All right then, but I'm not going to have sex with you."

Mada was taken aback. "Really? Why is that?"

"I'm not attracted to women with small breasts."

For the first time in her life, Mada felt the stab of outraged hormones. "Come out here and talk to me."

There was no immediate break in the hedge, so Owen had to squiggle through. "There's something about me that you don't like," he said as he struggled with the branches.

"Is there?" She considered. "I like your cape."

"That you *don't* like." He escaped the hedge's grasp and brushed leaves from his shorts.

"I guess I don't like your narrow-mindedness. It's not an attractive quality in a poet."

There was a gleam in Owen's eye as he went up on his tiptoes and began to declaim:

> "That spring you left I thought I might expire
> And lose the love you left for me to keep.
> To hold you once again is my desire
> Before I give myself to death's long sleep."

He illustrated his poetry with large, flailing gestures. At "death's long sleep" he brought his hands together as if to pray, laid the side of his head against them and closed his eyes. He held that pose in silence for an agonizingly long time.

"It's nice," Mada said at last. "I like the way it rhymes."

He sighed and went flat-footed. His arms drooped and he fixed her with an accusing stare. "You're not from here."

"No," she said. ~*Where am I from?*~ she subbed. ~*Someplace he'll have to look up.*~

~*Marble Bar. It's in Australia.*~

"I'm from Marble Bar."

"No, I mean you're not one of us. You don't comment."

At that moment, Mada understood. ~*I want to skip downwhen four minutes. I need to undo this.*~

~.this undo to need I .minutes four down-
when skip to want I~ .understood Mada,
moment that At ".comment don't You .us
of one not you're mean I, No" ".Bar
Marble from I'm" *~.Australia in It's .Bar*
Marble~ ~.up look to have he'll Someplace~
.subbed she *~?from I am Where~* .said she
",No" ".here from not You're" .stare accusing an with her fixed he and drooped
arms His .flatfooted went and sighed He
".rhymes it way the like I" .last at said
Mada ",nice It's" .time long agonizingly
an for silence in pose that held He .eyes
his closed and them against head his of
side the laid ,pray to if as together hands
his brought he "sleep long death's" At
.gestures flailing ,large with poetry his illustrated He ".sleep long death's to myself
give I Before desire my is again once you
hold To .keep to me for left you love the
lose And expire might I thought I left you
spring That" :declaim to began and tiptoes his on up went he as eye Owen's in
gleam a was There ".poet a in quality attractive an not It's .narrow-mindedness
your like don't I guess I" .shorts his from
leaves brushed and grasp hedge's the escaped He ".like *don't* you That" ".cape
your like I" .considered She "?there Is"
.branches the with struggled he as said he
",like don't you that me about something
There's" .through squiggle to had Owen
so ,hedge the in break immediate no was
There ".me to talk and here out Come"
.hormones outraged of stab the felt Mada
,life her in time first the For ".breasts
small with women to attracted not I'm"
"?that is Why ?Really" .aback taken was
Mada ".you with sex have to going not
I'm but ,then right All" ".library the to go
to like would I said I .attention paying
been you've think don't I ,Owen" .firmly
said she ",No" ".poetry my of some to
listen First"

As the ship surged through the empty dimensions, three space became as liquid as a dream. Leaves smeared and buildings ran together. Owen's face swirled.

"They want criticism," said Mada. "They like to think of themselves as artists but they're insecure about what they've accomplished. They want their audience to engage with what they're doing, help them make it better—the comments they both seem to expect."

"I see it now," said the ship. "But is one person in a backwater worth an undo? Let's just start over somewhere else."

"No, I have an idea." She began flowing more fat cells to her breasts. For the first time since she had skipped upwhen, Mada had a glimpse of what her duty might now be. "I'm going to need a big special effect on short notice. Be ready to reclaim mass so you can resubstantiate the hull at my command."

"First listen to some of my poetry."

"Go ahead." Mada folded her arms across her chest. "Say it then."

Owen stood on tiptoes to declaim:

"That spring you left I thought I might expire
And lose the love you left for me to keep.

To hold you once again is my desire
Before I give myself to death's long sleep."

He illustrated his poetry with large, flailing gestures. At "death's long sleep" he brought his hands together as if to pray, moved them to the side of his head, rested against them and closed his eyes. He had held the pose for just a beat before Mada interrupted him.

"Owen," she said. "You look ridiculous."

He jerked as if he had been hit in the head by a shovel.

She pointed at the ground before her. "You'll want to take these comments sitting down."

He hesitated, then settled at her feet.

"You hold your meter well, but that's purely a mechanical skill." She circled behind him. "A smart oven could do as much. Stop fidgeting!"

She hadn't noticed the anthills near the spot she had chosen for Owen. The first scouts were beginning to explore him. That suited her plan exactly.

"Your real problem," she continued, "is that you know nothing about death and probably very little about desire."

"I know about death." Owen drew his feet close to his body and grasped his knees. "Everyone does. Flowers die, squirrels die."

"Has anyone you've ever known died?"

He frowned. "I didn't know her personally, but there was the woman who fell off that cliff in Merrymeeting."

"Owen, did you have a mother?"

"Don't make fun of me. Everyone has a mother."

Mada didn't think it was time to tell him that she didn't; that she and her sibling batch of a thousand revolutionaries had been autoflowed. "Hold out your hand." Mada scooped up an ant. "That's your mother." She crunched it and dropped it onto Owen's palm.

Owen looked down at the dead ant and up again at Mada. His eyes filled.

"I think I love you," he said. "What's your name?"

"Mada." She leaned over to straighten his cape. "But loving me would be a very bad idea."

all that's left

Mada was surprised to find a few actual books in the library, printed on real plastic. A primitive DI had catalogued the rest of the collection, billions of gigabytes of print, graphics, audio, video, and VR files. None of it told Mada what she wanted to know. The library had sims of Egypt's New Kingdom, Islam's Abbasid dynasty, and the International Moonbase—but then came an astonishing void. Mada's searches on Trueborn, the Utopians, Tau Ceti, intelligence engineering and dimensional extensibility theory turned up no results. It was only in the very recent past that history resumed. The DI could reproduce the plans that the workbots had left when they built the library twenty-two years ago, and the menu The Devil's Apple had offered the previous summer, and the complete won-lost record of the Black Minks, the local scatterball club, which had gone 533–905 over the last century. It knew that the name of the woman who died in Merrymeeting was Agnes and that two years after her death, a replacement baby had been born to Chandra and Yuri. They named him Herrick.

Mada waved the screen blank and stretched. She could see Owen draped artfully over a nearby divan, as if posing for a portrait. He was engrossed by his handheld. She noticed that his lips moved as he read. She crossed the reading room and squeezed onto it next to him, nestling into the crook in his legs. "What's that?" she asked.

He turned the handheld toward her. "Nadeem Jerad's *Burning the Snow*. Would you like to hear one of his poems?"

"Maybe later." She leaned into him. "I was just reading about Moonbase."

"Yes, ancient history. It's sort of interesting, don't you think? The Greeks and the Renaissance and all that."

"But then I can't find any record of what came after."

"Because of the nightmares." He nodded. "Terrible things happened, so we forgot them."

"What terrible things?"

He tapped the side of his head and grinned.

"Of course," she said, "nothing terrible happens anymore."

"No. Everyone's happy now." Owen reached out and pushed a strand of her hair off her forehead. "You have beautiful hair."

Mada couldn't even remember what color it was. "But if something terrible did happen, then you'd want to forget it."

"Obviously."

"The woman who died, Agnes. No doubt her friends were very sad."

"No doubt." Now he was playing with her hair.

~*Good question,*~ subbed the ship. ~*They must have some mechanism to wipe their memories.*~

"Is something wrong?" Owen's face was the size of the moon; Mada was afraid of what he might tell her next.

"Agnes probably had a mother," she said.

"A mom and a dad."

"It must have been terrible for them."

He shrugged. "Yes, I'm sure they forgot her."

Mada wanted to slap his hand away from her head. "But how could they?"

He gave her a puzzled look. "Where are you from, anyway?"

"Trueborn," she said without hesitation. "It's a long, long way from here."

"Don't you have libraries there?" He gestured at the screens that surrounded them. "This is where we keep what we don't want to remember."

~*Skip!*~ Mada could barely sub; if what she suspected were true . . . ~*Skip downwhen two minutes.*~

~.minutes two downwhen Skip~ . . . true were suspected she what if ;sub barely could Mada ~!Skip~ ".remember to want don't we what keep we where is This" .them surrounded that screen the at gestured He "?there libraries have you Don't" ".here from way long ,long a It's" .hesitation without said she ",Trueborn" "?anyway, from you are Where" .look puzzled a her gave He "?they could how But" .head her from away hand his slap to wanted Mada ".her forgot they sure I'm, Yes" .shrugged He ".them for terrible been have must It" ".dad a and mom A".said she ",mother a had probably Agnes" .next her tell might he what of afraid was Mada; moon the of size of the was face Owen's "?wrong something Is" ~.memories their wipe to mechanism some have mustThey" .ship the subbed ~,question Good~ .hair her with playing was he Now ".doubt No" ".sad very were friends her doubt No .Agnes ,died who woman The" ".Obviously" ".it forget to want you'd then ,happen did terrible something if But" .was it color what remember even couldn't even Mada

She wrapped her arms around herself to keep the empty dimensions from reaching for the emptiness inside her. Was something wrong?

Of course there was, but she didn't expect to say it out loud. "I've lost everything and all that's left is *this*."

Owen shimmered next to her like the surface of Rabbit Lake.

"Mada, what?" said the ship.

"Forget it," she said. She thought she could hear something cracking when she laughed.

Mada couldn't even remember what color her hair was. "But if something terrible did happen, then you'd want to forget it."

"Obviously."

"Something terrible happened to me."

"I'm sorry." Owen squeezed her shoulder. "Do you want me to show you how to use the headbands?" He pointed at a rack of metal-mesh strips.

~Scanning,~ subbed the ship. ~Microcurrent taps capable of modulating post-synaptic outputs. I thought they were some kind of virtual reality I/O.~

"No." Mada twisted away from him and shot off the divan. She was outraged that these people would deliberately burn memories. How many stubbed toes and unhappy love affairs had Owen forgotten? If she could have, she would have skipped the entire village of Harmonious Struggle downwhen into the identity mine. When he rose up after her, she grabbed his hand. "I have to get out of here *right now*."

She dragged him out of the library into the innocent light of the sun.

"Wait a minute," he said. She continued to tow him up Ode

Street and out of town. "Wait!" He planted his feet, tugged at her and she spun back to him. "Why are you so upset?"

"I'm not upset." Mada's blood was hammering in her temples and she could feel the prickle of sweat under her arms. ~*Now I need you*,~ she subbed. "All right then. It's time you knew." She took a deep breath. "We were just talking about ancient history, Owen. Do you remember back then that the gods used to intervene in the affairs of humanity?"

Owen goggled at her as if she were growing beans out of her ears.

"I am a goddess, Owen, and I have come for you. I am calling you to your destiny. I intend to inspire you to great poetry."

His mouth opened and then closed again.

"My worshippers call me by many names." She raised a hand to the sky. ~*Help?*~

~*Try Athene? Here's a databurst.*~

"To the Greeks, I was Athene," Mada continued, "the goddess of cities, of technology and the arts, of wisdom and of war." She stretched a hand toward Owens's astonished face, forefinger aimed between his eyes. "Unlike you, I had no mother. I sprang full-grown from the forehead of my maker. I am Athene, the virgin goddess."

"How stupid do you think I am?" He shivered and glanced away from her fierce gaze. "I used to live in Maple City, Mada. I'm not some simple-minded country lump. You don't seriously expect me to believe this goddess nonsense?"

She slumped, confused. Of course she had expected him to believe her. "I meant no disrespect, Owen. It's just that the truth is . . ." This wasn't as easy as she had thought. "What I expect is that you believe in your own potential, Owen. What I expect is that you are brave enough to leave this place and come with me. To the stars, Owen, to the stars to start a new world." She crossed her arms in front of her chest, grasped the hem of her moss-colored top, pulled it over her head and tossed it behind her. Before it hit the ground the ship augmented it with enough reclaimed mass from the empty dimensions to resubstantiate the command and living mods.

Mada was quite pleased with the way Owen tried—and

failed—not to stare at her breasts. She kicked the gripall loafers off and the deck rose up beneath them. She stepped out of the baggy, black pants; when she tossed them at Owen, he flinched. Seconds later, they were eyeing each other in the metallic light of the ship's main companionway.

"Well?" said Mada.

duty

Mada had difficulty accepting Trueborn as it now was. She could see the ghosts of great cities, hear the murmur of dead friends. She decided to live in the forest that had once been the Green Sea, where there were no landmarks to remind her of what she had lost. She ordered the ship to begin constructing an infrastructure similar to that they had found on Earth, only capable of supporting a technologically advanced population. Borrowing orphan mass from the empty dimensions, it was soon consumed with this monumental task. She missed its company; only rarely did she use the link it had left her—a silver ring with a direct connection to its sensorium.

The ship's first effort was the farm that Owen called Athens. It consisted of their house, a flow works, a gravel pit and a barn. Dirt roads led to various mines and domed fields that the ship's bots tended. Mada had it build a separate library, a little way into the woods, where, she declared, information was to be acquired only, never destroyed. Owen spent many evenings there. He said he was trying to make himself worthy of her.

He had been deeply flattered when she told him that, as part of his training as a poet, he was to name the birds and beasts and flowers and trees of Trueborn.

"But they must already have names," he said, as they walked back to the house from the newly tilled soya field.

"The people who named them are gone," she said. "The names went with them."

"Your people." He waited for her to speak. The wind sighed through the forest. "What happened to them?"

"I don't know." At that moment, she regretted ever bringing him to Trueborn.

He sighed. "It must be hard."

"You left *your* people," she said. She spoke to wound him, since he was wounding her with these rude questions.

"For you, Mada." He let go of her. "I know you didn't leave them for *me*." He picked up a pebble and held it in front of his face. "You are now Mada-stone," he told it, "and whatever you hit . . ." He threw it into the woods and it *thwocked* off a tree. ". . . is Mada-tree. We will plant fields of Mada-seed and press Mada-juice from the sweet Mada-fruit and dance for the rest of our days down Mada Street." He laughed and put his arm around her waist and swung her around in circles, kicking up dust from the road. She was so surprised that she laughed too.

Mada and Owen slept in separate bedrooms, so she was not exactly sure how she knew that he wanted to have sex with her. He had never spoken of it; other than on that first day when he had specifically said that he did not want her. Maybe it was the way he continually brushed up against her for no apparent reason. This could hardly be chance, considering that they were the only two people on Trueborn. For herself, Mada welcomed his hesitancy. Although she had been emotionally intimate with her batch siblings, none of them had ever inserted themselves into her body cavities.

But, for better or worse, she had chosen this man for this course of action. Even if the galaxy had forgotten Trueborn two-tenths of a spin ago, the revolution still called Mada to her duty.

"What's it like to kiss?" she asked that night, as they were finishing supper.

Owen laid his fork across a plate of cauliflower curry. "You've never kissed anyone before?"

"That's why I ask."

Owen leaned across the table and brushed his lips across hers. The brief contact made her cheeks flush, as if she had just jogged in from the gravel pit. "Like that," he said. "Only better."

"Do you still think my breasts are too small?"

"I never said that." Owen's face turned red.

"It was a comment you made—or at least thought about making."

"A comment?" The word *comment* seemed to stick in his throat; it made him cough. "Just because you make comment on some aspect doesn't mean you reject the work as a whole."

Mada glanced down the neck of her shift. She hadn't really increased her breast mass all that much, maybe ten or twelve grams, but now vasocongestion had begun to swell them even more. She could also feel blood flowing to her reproductive organs. It was a pleasurable weight that made her feel light as pollen. "Yes, but do you think they're too small?"

Owen got up from the table and came around behind her chair. He put his hands on her shoulders and she leaned her head back against him. There was something between her cheek and his stomach. She heard him say, "Yours are the most perfect breasts on this entire planet," as if from a great distance and then realized that the *something* must be his penis.

After that, neither of them made much comment.

nine hours

Mada stared at the ceiling, her eyes wide but unseeing. Her concentration had turned inward. After she had rolled off him, Owen had flung his left arm across her belly and drawn her hip toward his and given her the night's last kiss. Now the muscles of his arm were slack, and she could hear his seashore breath as she released her ovum into the cloud of his sperm squiggling up her fallopian tubes. The most vigorous of the swimmers butted its head through the ovum's membrane and dissolved, releasing its genetic material. Mada immediately started raveling the strands of DNA before the fertilized egg could divide for the first time. Without the necessary diversity, they would never revive the revolution. Satisfied with her intervention, she flowed the blastocyst down her fallopian tubes where it locked onto the wall of her uterus. She prodded it and the ball of cells became a comma with a big head and a thin tail. An array of cells specialized and folded into a tube that ran the length of the embryo, weaving into nerve fibers. Dark pigment swept across two cups in the blocky head and then bulged into eyes. A mouth slowly opened; in it was a one-chambered, beating heart. The front end of the neural tube blossomed into the vesicles that would become the brain. Four buds swelled, two near the head, two at the tail. The uppermost pair sprouted into paddles, pierced by rays of cells that Mada immediately began to ossify into fingerbone. The lower buds stretched into delicate legs. At midnight, the embryo was as big as a her fingernail; it began to move and so became a fetus. The eyes opened for a few minutes, but then the eyelids fused. Mada and Owen were going to have a son; his penis was now a nub of flesh. Bubbles of tissue blew inward from the head and became his ears. Mada listened to him listen to her heartbeat. He lost his tail and his intestines slithered down the umbilical cord into his abdomen. As his fingerprints looped and whorled, he stuck his thumb into his mouth. Mada was having trouble breathing because the fetus was floating so high in her uterus. She eased herself into a sitting position and Owen grumbled in his sleep. Suddenly the curry in the cauliflower was giving her heartburn. Then the muscles of her uterus tightened and pain sheeted across her swollen belly.

~Drink this.~ The ship flowed a tumbler of nutrient nano onto the bedside table. *~The fetus gains mass rapidly from now on.~* The stuff tasted like rusty nails. *~You're doing fine.~*

When the fetus turned upside down, it felt like he was trying out a gymnastic routine. But then he snuggled headfirst into her pelvis, and calmed down, probably because there wasn't enough room left inside her for him to make large, flailing gestures like his father. Now she could feel electrical buzzes down her legs and inside her vagina as the baby bumped her nerves. He was big now, and growing by almost a kilogram an hour, laying down new muscle and brown fat. Mada was tired of it all. She dozed. At six thirty-seven her water broke, drenching the bed.

"Hmm." Owen rolled away from the warm, fragrant spill of amniotic fluid. "What did you say?"

The contractions started; she put her hand on his chest and pressed down. "Help," she whimpered.

"Wha . . . ?" Owen propped himself up on his elbows. "Hey, I'm wet. How did I get . . . ?"

"*O-Owen!*" She could feel the baby's head stretching her vagina in a way mere flesh could not possibly stretch.

"Mada! What's wrong?" Suddenly his face was very close to hers. "Mada, what's happening?"

But then the baby was slipping out of her, and it was *sooo* much better than the only sex she had ever had. She caught her breath and said, "I have begotten a son."

She reached between her legs and pulled the baby to her breasts. They were huge now, and very sore.

"We will call him Owen," she said.

begot

And Mada begot Enos and Felicia and Malaleel and Ralph and Jared and Elisa and Tharsis and Masahiko and Thema and Seema and Casper and Hevila and Djanka and Jennifer and Jojo and Regma and Elvis and Irina and Dean and Marget and Karoly and Sabatha and Ashley and Siobhan and Mei-Fung and Neil and Gupta and Hans and Sade and Moon and Randy and Genevieve and Bob and Nazia and Eiichi and Justine and Ozma and Khaled and Candy and Pavel and Isaac and Sandor and Veronica and Gao and Pat and Marcus and Zsa Zsa and Li and Rebecca.

Seven years after her return to Trueborn, Mada rested.

ever after

Mada was convinced that she was not a particularly good mother, but then she had been designed for courage and quick-thinking, not nurturing and patience. It wasn't the crying or the dirty diapers or the spitting-up, it was the utter uselessness of the babies that the revolutionary in her could not abide. And her maternal instincts were often skewed. She would offer her children the wrong toy or cook the wrong dish, fall silent when they wanted her to play, prod them to talk when they needed to withdraw. Mada and the ship had calculated that fifty of her genetically manipulated offspring would provide the necessary diversity to repopulate Trueborn. After Rebecca was born, Mada was more than happy to stop having children.

Although the children seemed to love her despite her awkwardness, Mada wasn't sure she loved them back. She constantly teased at her feelings, peeling away what she considered pretense and sentimentality. She worried that the capacity to love might not have been part of her emotional design. Or perhaps begetting fifty children in seven years had left her numb.

Owen seemed to enjoy being a parent. He was the one whom the children called for when they wanted to play. They came to Mada for answers and decisions. Mada liked to watch them snuggle next to him when he spun his fantastic stories. Their father picked them up when they stumbled, and let them climb on his shoulders so they could see just what he saw. They told him secrets they would never tell her.

The children adored the ship, which substantiated a bot companion for each of them, in part for their protection. All had inherited their father's all-but-invulnerable immune system; their chromosomes replicated well beyond the Hayflick limit with integrity and fidelity. But they lacked their mother's ability to flow tissue and were therefore at peril of drowning or breaking their necks. The bots also provided the intense individualized attention that their busy parents could not. Each child was convinced that his or her bot companion had a unique personality. Even the seven-year-olds were too young to realize that the bots were reflecting their ideal personality back at them. The bots were in general as intelligent as the ship, although it had programmed into their DIs a touch of naïveté and a tendency to literalness that allowed the children to play tricks on them. Pranking a brother or sister's bot was a particularly delicious sport.

Athens had begun to sprawl after seven years. The library had tripled in size and grown a wing of classrooms and workshops. A new gym overlooked three playing fields. Owen had asked the ship to build a little theater where the children could put on shows for each other. The original house became a ring of houses, connected by corridors and facing a central courtyard. Each night Mada and Owen moved to their bedroom in a different house. Owen thought

it important that the children see them sleeping in the same bed;
Mada went along.

After she had begotten Rebecca, Mada needed something to
do that didn't involve the children. She had the ship's farmbots
plow up a field and for an hour each day she tended it. She resisted
Owen's attempts to name this "Mom's Hobby." Mada grew vegetables; she had little use for flowers. Although she made a specialty
of root crops, she was not a particularly accomplished gardener.
She did, however, enjoy weeding.

It was at these quiet times, her hands flicking across the dark soil,
that she considered her commitment to the Three Universal
Rights. After two-tenths of a spin, she had clearly lost her zeal. Not
for the first, that independent sentients had the right to remain individual. Mada was proud that her children were as individual as any
intelligence, flesh or machine, could have made them. Of course,
they had no pressing need to exercise the second right of manipu-
lating their physical structures—she had taken care of that for them.
When they were of age, if the ship wanted to introduce them to
molecular engineering, that could certainly be done. No, the real
problem was that downwhen was forever closed to them by the
identity mine. How could she justify her new Trueborn society if it
didn't enjoy the third right: free access to the timelines?

undone

"Mada!" Owen waved at the edge of her garden. She blinked; he
was wearing the same clothes he'd been wearing when she had
first seen him on Sonnet Street in front of The Devil's Apple—
down to the little red cape. He showed her a picnic basket. "The
ship is watching the kids tonight," he called. "Come on, it's our
anniversary. I did the calculations myself. We met eight Earth years
ago today."

He led her to a spot deep in the woods, where he spread a blanket. They stretched out next to each other and sorted through the
basket. There was a curley salad with alperts and thumbnuts, brain-
boy and chive sandwiches on cheese bread. He toasted her with
Mada-fruit wine and told her that Siobhan had let go of the couch

and taken her first step and that Irina wanted everyone to learn to play an instrument so that she could conduct the family orchestra and that Malaleel had asked him just today if ship was a person.

"It's not a person," said Mada. "It's a DI."

"That's what I said." Owen peeled the crust off his cheese bread. "And he said if it's not a person, how come it's telling jokes?"

"It told a joke?"

"It asked him, 'How come you can't have everything?' and then it said, 'Where would you put it?'"

She nudged him in the ribs. "That sounds more like you than the ship."

"I have a present for you," he said after they were stuffed. "I wrote you a poem." He did not stand; there were no large, flailing gestures. Instead he slid the picnic basket out of the way, leaned close and whispered into her ear.

"Loving you is like catching rain on my tongue.
You bathe the leaves, soak indifferent ground;
Why then should I get so little of you?
Yet still, like a flower with a fool's face,
I open myself to the sky."

Mada was not quite sure what was happening to her; she had never really cried before. "I like that it doesn't rhyme." She had understood that tears flowed from a sadness. "I like that a lot." She sniffed and smiled and daubed at edges of her eyes with a napkin. "Never rhyme anything again."

"Done," he said.

Mada watched her hand reach for him, caress the side of his neck, and then pull him down on top of her. Then she stopped watching herself.

"No more children." His whisper seemed to fill her head.

"No," she said, "no more."

"I'm sharing you with too many already." He slid his hand between her legs. She arched her back and guided him to her pleasure.

When they had both finished, she ran her finger through the

sweat cooling at the small of his back and then licked it. "Owen," she said, her voice a silken purr. "That was the one."

"Is that your comment?"

"No." She craned to see his eyes. "This is my comment," she said. "You're writing love poems to the wrong person."

"There is no one else," he said.

She squawked and pushed him off her. "That may be true," she said, laughing, "but it's not something you're supposed to say."

"No, what I meant was . . ."

"I know." She put a finger to his lips and giggled like one of her babies. Mada realized then how dangerously happy she was. She rolled away from Owen; all the lightness crushed out of her by the weight of guilt and shame. It wasn't her duty to be happy. She had been ready to betray the cause of those who had made her for what? For this man? "There's something I have to do." She fumbled for her shift. "I can't help myself, I'm sorry."

Owen watched her warily. "Why are you sorry?"

"Because after I do it, I'll be different."

"Different how?"

"The ship will explain." She tugged the shift on. "Take care of the children."

"What do you mean, take care of the children? What are you doing?" He lunged at her and she scrabbled away from him on all fours. "Tell me."

"The ship says my body should survive." She staggered to her feet. "That's all I can offer you, Owen." Mada ran.

She didn't expect Owen to come after her—or to run so fast.

~*I need you.*~ she subbed to the ship. ~*Substantiate the command mod.*~

He was right behind her. Saying something. Was it to her? "No," he panted, "no, no, no."

~*Substantiate the com. . . .*~

Suddenly Owen was gone; Mada bit her lip as she crashed into the main screen, caromed off it and dropped like a dead woman. She lay there for a moment, the cold of the deck seeping into her cheek. "Goodbye," she whispered. She struggled to pull herself up and spat blood.

"Skip downwhen," she said, "six minutes."

".minutes six" ,said she ",downwhen Skip" .blood spat and up herself pull to struggled She .whispered she ",Goodbye" .cheek her into seeping deck the of cold the ,moment a for there lay She .woman dead a like dropped and it off caromed ,screen main the into crashed she as lip her bit Mada ;gone was Owen Suddenly ~. . . . *com the Substantiate~* ".no ,no ,no" ,panted he ",No" ?her to it Was .some-thing Saying .her behind right was He ~.*mod command the Substantiate~* .ship the to subbed she ~.*you need I~* .fast so run to or—her after come to Owen expect didn't She .ran Mada ".Owen ,you offer can I all That's" .feet her to staggered She ".survive should body my says ship The" ".me Tell" .fours all on him from away scrabbled she and her at lunged He "?doing you are What ?children the of care take ,mean you do What." ".children the of care Take" .on shift the tugged She ".explain will ship The" "?how Differ-ent" ".different be I'll ,it do I after Be-cause" "?sorry you are Why" .warily her watched Owen. ".sorry I'm ,myself help can't I" .shift her for fumbled She ".do to have I something There's" ?man this For ?what for her made had who those of cause the betray to ready been had She .happy be to duty her wasn't It .shame and guilt of weight the by her of out crushed lightness the all ,Owen from away rolled She .was she happy danger-ously how then realized Mada .babies her of one like giggled and lips his to finger a put She ".know I" ". . . . was meant I what ,No" ".say to supposed you're something not it's but" ,laughing, said she ",true be may That" .her off him pushed and squawked She .said he ",else one no is There" ".person wrong the to poems love writing You're" .said she ",comment my is This" .eyes his see to craned She ".No" "?comment your that Is" ".one the was That".purr silken a voice her ,said she ",Owen"

When threespace went blurry, it seemed that her duty did too. She waved her hand and watched it smear.

"You know what you're doing," said the ship.

"What I was designed to do. What all my batch siblings pledged to do." She waved her hand again; she could actually see through herself. "The only thing I can do."

"The mine will wipe your identity. There will be nothing of you left."

"And then it will be gone and the timelines will open. I believe that I've known this was what I had to do since we first skipped upwhen."

"The probability was always high," said the ship. "But not certain."

"Bring me to him, afterward. But don't tell him about the timelines. He might want to change them. The timelines are for the children, so that they can finish the revol . . . .

"Owen," she said, her voice a silken purr. Then she paused.

The woman shook her head, trying to clear it. Lying on top of her was the handsomest man she had ever met. She felt warm and sexy and wonderful. What was this? "I . . . I'm . . . ," she said. She reached up and touched the little red cloth hanging from his shoulders. "I like your cape."

done

"".minutes six" ,said she ",downwhen Skip" .blood spat and up herself pull to struggled She .whispered she ",Goodbye" .cheek her into seeping deck the of cold the ,moment a for there lay She .woman dead a like dropped and it off caromed ,screen main the into crashed she as lip her bit Mada ;gone was Owen Suddenly ~ . . . com the Substantiate~ "no ,no ,no" ,panted he ",No" ?her to it Was .something Saying .her behind right was He ~.mod command the Substantiate~ .ship the to subbed she ~.you need I~ .fast so run to or—her after come to Owen expect didn't She .ran Mada ".Owen ,you offer can I all That's" .feet her to staggered She ".survive should body my says ship The" ".me Tell" .fours all on him from away scrabbled she and her at lunged He "?doing you are What ?children the of care take ,mean you do What." ".children the of care Take" .on shift the tugged She ".explain will ship The" "?how Different" ".different be I'll ,it do I after Because" "?sorry you are Why" .warily her watched Owen. ".sorry I'm ,myself help can't I" .shift her for fumbled She ".do to have I something There's" ?man this For ?what for her made had who those of cause the betray to ready been had She .happy be to duty her wasn't It .shame and guilt of weight the by her of out crushed lightness the all ;Owen from away rolled She .was she happy dangerously how then realized Mada .babies her of one like giggled and lips his to finger a put She ".know I" ". . . . was meant I what ,No" ".say to supposed you're something not it's but" ,laughing, said she ",true be may That" .her off him pushed and squawked She .said he ",else one no is There" ".person wrong the to poems love writing You're" .said she ",comment my is This" .eyes his see to craned She ".No" "?comment your that Is" ".one the was That" .purr silken a voice her ,said she ",Owen"

Mada waved her hand and saw it smear in threespace. "What are you doing?" said the ship.

"What I was designed to do." She waved; she could actually see through herself. "The only thing I can do."

"The mine will wipe your identity. None of your memories will survive."

"I believe that I've known that's what would happen since we first skipped upwhen."

"It was probable," said the ship "But not certain."

Trueborn scholars pinpoint what the ship did next as its first step forward independent sentience. In its memoirs, the ship credits the children with teaching it to misbehave.

It played a prank.

"Loving you," said the ship, "is like catching rain on my tongue. You bathe . . ."

"Stop," Mada shouted. "Stop right now!"

"Got you!" The ship gloated. "Four minutes, fifty-one seconds."

"Owen," she said, her voice a silken purr. "That was the one."

"Is that your comment?"

"No." Mada was astonished—and pleased—that she still existed. She knew that in most timelines her identity must have been obliterated by the mine. Thinking about those brave, lost selves made her more sad than proud. "This is my comment," she said. "I'm ready now."

Owen coughed uncertainly. "Umm, already?"

She squawked and pushed him off her. "Not for *that*." She sifted his hair through her hands. "To be with you forever."

The Rhysling Awards for science fiction poetry, voted on by members of the Science Fiction Poetry Association, have been given continuously since their inception in 1978. Since the 1980s, they have usually been included in the Nebula anthology. There are two Rhyslings, one for a poem of up to fifty lines, one for more than fifty lines. This year's winners follow a distinguished list that includes Ursula K. Le Guin, Gene Wolfe, Lucius Shepard, and Michael Bishop.

Bruce Boston is the author of thirty books and chapbooks. His poems and stories have appeared in hundreds of publications and won numerous awards, including the prestigious Pushcart Prize and an Asimov's Readers' Award. In 1999 the Science Fiction Poetry Association honored him with its first Grand Master Award. "My Wife Returns As She Would Have It" delicately embodies a grieving man's wishes—and, perhaps, something else as well.

Joe Haldeman has won five Hugos, four Nebulas, and three Rhyslings. Having grown up in such far-flung places as Puerto Rico, Alaska, and Washington, D.C., Joe and wife Gay now bicycle across continents for fun. He is the author of twenty-four books, including such modern classics as *The Forever War*, *Forever Peace*, *Mindbridge*, and *Worlds*. His most recent work is the much-anticipated *Guardian*. "January Fires" is a powerful and unflinching look at what disaster can do to the human mind.

for Maureen

Bruce Boston

"I'd come back as a butterfly,"
she often told me, "a Monarch
or something equally as beautiful."

Eleven days after her death it happens.
I am walking a block from our house
when a quick flutter of velvet wings,
dark against the pale dome of the sky,
passes left to right inches from my face,
causing me to pull up short in mid-stride.

Turning to the right I see a butterfly
has landed on the sidewalk at my feet.
Black and brown shadings striated by
vermilion bands, speckled with white.
(Not a Monarch but a Red Admiral,
I later discover in one of her books.)

"Is that you, sweetheart?" I whisper.
I am a fifty-six-year-old man suddenly
kneeling on the cement spilling out
his love and regrets to a lone insect
he hopes is a reincarnation of his wife.

Clearly as beautiful as any Monarch,
an epiphany of color in my flat world,
the butterfly appears to be listening.
Brilliantly hued wings shift slowly
up and down as if they sense the
coarse human sounds filling the air.

Even once language deserts me,
it/she remains a moment by my side
(together like partners after a dance!)
before soaring into a sky all-at-once blue,
vanishing into her future and my past,
alive and free as our finest memories.

JANUARY FIRES

Joe Haldeman

27 January 1967

precisely one month before I'd leave for Vietnam

the TV went silent

we all looked   into the white noise

    news bulletin
    the Apollo One astronauts
    Grissom Chaffee White
    have died in a freak fire

    (killed by pure oxygen and one spark
    on a wire's cheap cotton insulation)

    no pictures   please   no pictures

years later   tempered by combat I saw those grim
unheroic pictures   ugly and real as napalm death

one almost got the door open

28 January 1986

Daytona Beach
  tropic morning   winter cold
   rigid splash of icy breakers

freezing seabirds
　stalk annoyed
　　on cold sand

three launch holds　 no more patience
　coffee cold and bitter　 gritty
　　waiting and grit and cold
　　　that's all we talked about
　　　　talking to keep warm

　　　　　　　　　　　it finally went up

　　　　　　　　　　　six jocks and one schoolteacher

　　　　　　　　　　　riding a white column of steam

　　　　　　　　　　　to a solid spasm of fire

　　　　　　　　　　　cloud tombstone on the edge of space

the tourists cheering madly　 madly
　thinking it was part of the show
　　　　booster separation or　　　　the rest
　　　　whatever they call it　　　　of us
　　　　　　　　　　　　　　　　　　　in shock

　　　　　　watching pieces fall
　　　　　　into the frigid water

　　　　　　no parachutes　　 no parachutes

two hours later　　　　　　　　　　numb
the resident expert
　　　　　　　　　　　　　　　I sat down in front of a microphone
　　　　　　　　　　　　　　　and the pale talkshow woman
　　　　　　　　　　　　　　　asked whether I would still go up

　　　　sure　 I said　 twenty-five to one odds
　　　　did you ever draw to an inside straight
　　　　　and did you expect to make it

while something inside

 still stalking jungle trail

  said liar liar liar

   you know

    you would kill anything

    to stay alive you

     would even kill a dream

There is no overlooking Mike Resnick, ever. Exuberant, large, and big-hearted, he is as delighted to discover and encourage new talent as he is quick to praise good work from established writers. Mike enlivens any party, one way or another (his style of flirting runs to invitations to mud wrestle). Some of my most memorable SF dinners have been spent with Mike and his wife, Carol.

His literary range is astonishing, from raucous adventure to the bittersweet "Kirinyaga" stories, with their memorable characters trapped in an unworkable and quixotic re-creation of a dead past. The author of over forty novels, twelve story collections, and more than 140 stories, Mike apparently never sleeps. He has edited over twenty-five anthologies, won four Hugos and a Nebula, and had his work translated into twenty-two languages.

"The Elephants on Neptune" is an unclassifiable short story, sui generis. It invites us to look at ourselves from an entirely new perspective, with very disquieting results.

THE ELEPHANTS ON NEPTUNE

Mike Resnick

The elephants on Neptune led an idyllic life.

None ever went hungry or were sick. They had no predators. They never fought a war. There was no prejudice. Their birth rate exactly equaled their death rate. Their skins and bowels were free of parasites.

The herd traveled at a speed that accommodated the youngest and weakest members. No sick or infirm elephant was ever left behind.

They were a remarkable race, the elephants on Neptune. They lived out their lives in peace and tranquility, they never argued among themselves, the old were always gentle with the young. When one was born, the entire herd gathered to celebrate. When one died, the entire herd mourned its passing. There were no animosities, no petty jealousies, no unresolved quarrels.

Only one thing stopped it from being Utopia, and that was the fact that an elephant never forgets.

Not ever.

No matter how hard he tries.

When men finally landed on Neptune in A.D. 2473, the elephants were very apprehensive. Still, they approached the spaceship in a spirit of fellowship and goodwill.

The men were a little apprehensive themselves. Every survey of Neptune told them it was a gas giant, and yet they had landed on solid ground. And if their surveys were wrong, who knew what else might be wrong as well?

A tall man stepped out onto the frozen surface. Then another.

Then a third. By the time they had all emerged, there were almost as many men as elephants.

"Well, I'll be damned!" said the leader of the men. "You're elephants!"

"And you're men," said the elephants nervously.

"That's right," said the men. "We claim this planet in the name of the United Federation of Earth."

"You're united now?" asked the elephants, feeling much relieved.

"Well, the survivors are," said the men.

"Those are ominous-looking weapons you're carrying," said the elephants, shifting their feet uncomfortably.

"They go with the uniforms," said the men. "Not to worry. Why would we want to harm you? There's always been a deep bond between men and elephants."

That wasn't exactly the way the elephants remembered it.

326 b.c.

Alexander the Great met Porus, King of the Punjab of India, in the Battle of the Jhelum River. Porus had the first military elephants Alexander had ever seen. He studied the situation, then sent his men out at night to fire thousands of arrows into extremely sensitive trunks and underbellies. The elephants went mad with pain and began killing the nearest men they could find, which happened to be their keepers and handlers. After his great victory, Alexander slaughtered the surviving elephants so that he would never have to face them in battle.

217 b.c.

The first clash between the two species of elephants. Ptolemy IV took his African elephants against Antiochus the Great's Indian elephants.

The elephants on Neptune weren't sure who won the war, but they knew who lost. Not a single elephant on either side survived.

Later that same 217 b.c.

While Ptolemy was battling in Syria, Hannibal took thirty-seven elephants over the Alps to fight the Romans. Fourteen of them froze to death, but the rest lived just long enough to absorb the enemy's spear thrusts while Hannibal was winning the Battle of Cannae.

■

"We have important things to talk about," said the men. "For example, Neptune's atmosphere is singularly lacking in oxygen. How do you breathe?"

"Through our noses," said the elephants.

"That was a serious question," said the men, fingering their weapons ominously.

"We are incapable of being anything *but* serious," explained the elephants. "Humor requires that someone be the butt of the joke, and we find that too cruel to contemplate."

"All right," said the men, who were vaguely dissatisfied with the answer, perhaps because they didn't understand it. "Let's try another question. What is the mechanism by which we are communicating? You don't wear radio transmitters, and because of our helmets we can't hear any sounds that aren't on our radio bands."

"We communicate through a psychic bond," explained the elephants.

"That's not very scientific," said the men disapprovingly. "Are you sure you don't mean a telepathic bond?"

"No, though it comes to the same thing in the end," answered the elephants. "We know that we sound like we're speaking English to you, except for the man on the left who thinks we're speaking Hebrew."

"And what do we sound like to you?" demanded the men.

"You sound exactly as if you're making gentle rumbling sounds in your stomachs and your bowels."

"That's fascinating," said the men, who privately thought it was a lot more disgusting than fascinating.

"Do you know what's *really* fascinating?" responded the elephants.

"The fact that you've got a Jew with you." They saw that the men didn't comprehend, so they continued: "We always felt we were in a race with the Jews to see which of us would be exterminated first. We used to call ourselves the Jews of the animal kingdom." They turned and faced the Jewish spaceman. "Did the Jews think of themselves as the elephants of the human kingdom?"

"Not until you just mentioned it," said the Jewish spaceman, who suddenly found himself agreeing with them.

42 b.c.

The Romans gathered their Jewish prisoners in the arena at Alexandria, then turned fear-crazed elephants loose on them. The spectators began jumping up and down and screaming for blood—and, being contrarians, the elephants attacked the spectators instead of the Jews, proving once and for all that you can't trust a pachyderm.

(When the dust had cleared, the Jews felt the events of the day had reaffirmed their claim to be God's chosen people. They weren't the Romans' chosen people, though. After the soldiers killed the elephants, they put all the Jews to the sword, too.)

■

"It's not his fault he's a Jew any more than it's your fault that you're elephants," said the rest of the men. "We don't hold it against either of you."

"We find that difficult to believe," said the elephants.

"You do?" said the men. "Then consider this: the Indians—that's the good Indians, the ones from India, not the bad Indians from America—worshipped Ganesh, an elephant-headed god."

"We didn't know that," admitted the elephants, who were more impressed than they let on. "Do the Indians still worship Ganesh?"

"Well, we're sure they would if we hadn't killed them all while we were defending the Raj," said the men. "Elephants were no longer in the military by then," they added. "That's something to be grateful for."

■

Their very last battle came when Tamerlane the Great went to war against Sultan Mahmoud. Tamerlane won by tying branches to buffaloes' horns, setting fire to them, and then stampeding the buffalo herd into Mahmoud's elephants, which effectively ended the elephant as a war machine, buffalo being much less expensive to acquire and feed.

All the remaining domesticated elephants were then trained for elephant fighting, which was exactly like cock-fighting, only on a larger scale. Much larger. It became a wildly popular sport for thirty or forty years until they ran out of participants.

■

"Not only did we worship you," continued the men, "but we actually named a country after you—the Ivory Coast. *That* should prove our good intentions."

"You didn't name it after *us*," said the elephants. "You named it after the parts of our bodies that you kept killing us for."

"You're being too critical," said the men. "We could have named it after some local politician with no vowels in his name."

"Speaking of the Ivory Coast," said the elephants, "did you know that the first alien visitors to Earth landed there in 1883?"

"What did they look like?"

"They had ivory exoskeletons," answered the elephants. "They took one look at the carnage and left."

"Are you sure you're not making this all up?" asked the men.

"Why would we lie to you at this late date?"

"Maybe it's your nature," suggested the men.

"Oh, no," said the elephants. "Our nature is that we always tell the truth. Our tragedy is that we always remember it."

The men decided that it was time to break for dinner, answer calls of nature, and check in with Mission Control to report what they'd found. They all walked back to the ship, except for one man, who lingered behind.

All of the elephants left too, except for one lone bull. "I intuit that you have a question to ask," he said.

"Yes," replied the man. "You have such an acute sense of smell, how did anyone ever sneak up on you during the hunt?" ·

"The greatest elephant hunters were the Wanderobo of Kenya and Uganda. They would rub our dung all over their bodies to hide their own scent, and would then silently approach us."

"Ah," said the man, nodding his head. "It makes sense."

"Perhaps," conceded the elephant. Then he added, with all the dignity he could muster, "But if the tables were turned, I would sooner die than cover myself with *your* shit."

He turned away and set off to rejoin his comrades.

•

Neptune is unique among all the worlds in the galaxy. It alone recognizes the truism that change is inevitable, and acts upon it in ways that seem very little removed from magic.

For reasons the elephants couldn't fathom or explain, Neptune encourages metamorphosis. Not merely adaptation, although no one could deny that they adapted to the atmosphere and the climate and the fluctuating surface of the planet and the lack of acacia trees—but *metamorphosis*. The elephants understood at a gut level that Neptune had somehow imparted to them the ability to evolve at will, though they had been careful never to abuse this gift.

And since they were elephants, and hence incapable of carrying a grudge, they thought it was a pity that the men couldn't evolve to the point where they could leave their bulky space suits and awkward helmets behind, and walk free and unencumbered across this most perfect of planets.

The elephants were waiting when the men emerged from their ship and strode across Neptune's surface to meet them.

"This is very curious," said the leader.

"What is?" asked the elephants.

The leader stared at them, frowning. "You seem smaller."

"We were just going to say that you seemed larger," replied the elephants.

"This is almost as silly as the conversation I just had with Mission Control," said the leader. "They say there aren't any elephants on Neptune."

"What do they think we are?" asked the elephants.

"Hallucinations or space monsters," answered the leader. "If you're hallucinations, we're supposed to ignore you."

He seemed to be waiting for the elephants to ask what the men were supposed to do if they were space monsters, but elephants can be as stubborn as men when they want to be, and that was a question they had no intention of asking.

The men stared at the elephants in silence for almost five minutes. The elephants stared back.

Finally the leader spoke again.

"Would you excuse me for a moment?" he said. "I suddenly have an urge to eat some greens."

He turned and marched back to the ship without another word.

The rest of the men shuffled their feet uncomfortably for another few seconds.

"Is something wrong?" asked the elephants.

"Are we getting bigger or are you getting smaller?" replied the men.

"Yes," answered the elephants.

"I feel much better now," said the leader, rejoining his men and facing the elephants.

"You look better," agreed the elephants. "More handsome, somehow."

"Do you really think so?" asked the leader, obviously flattered.

"You are the finest specimen of your race we've ever seen," said the elephants truthfully. "We especially like your ears."

"You do?" he asked, flapping them slightly. "No one's ever mentioned them before."

"Doubtless an oversight," said the elephants.

"Speaking of ears," said the leader, "are you African elephants or Indian? I thought this morning you were African—they're the ones with the bigger ears, right?—but now I'm not sure."

"We're Neptunian elephants," they answered.

"Oh."

They exchanged pleasantries for another hour, and then the men looked up at the sky.

"Where did the sun go?" they asked.

"It's night," explained the elephants. "Our day is only fourteen hours long. We get seven hours of sunlight and seven of darkness."

"The sun wasn't all that bright anyway," said one of the men with a shrug that set his ears flapping wildly.

"We have very poor eyesight, so we hardly notice," said the elephants. "We depend on our senses of smell and hearing."

The men seemed very uneasy. Finally they turned to their leader.

"May we be excused for a few moments, sir?" they asked.

"Why?"

"Suddenly we're starving," said the men.

"And I gotta use the john," said one of them.

"So do I," said a second one.

"Me too," echoed another.

"Do you men feel all right?" asked the leader, his enormous nose wrinkled in concern.

"I feel great!" said the nearest man. "I could eat a horse!"

The other men all made faces.

"Well, a small forest, anyway," he amended.

"Permission granted," said the leader. The men began walking rapidly back to the ship. "And bring me a couple of heads of let-tuce, and maybe an apple or two," he called after them.

"You can join them if you wish," said the elephants, who were coming to the conclusion that eating a horse wasn't half as disgust-ing a notion as they had thought it would be.

"No, my job is to make contact with aliens," explained the leader. "Although when you get right down to it, you're not as alien as we'd expected."

"You're every bit as human as we expected," replied the ele-phants.

"I'll take that as a great compliment," said the leader. "But then, I would expect nothing less from traditional friends such as yourselves."

"Traditional friends?" repeated the elephants, who had thought nothing a man said could still surprise them.

"Certainly. Even after you stopped being our partners in war, we've always had a special relationship with you."

"You have?"

"Sure. Look how P. T. Barnum made an international superstar out of the original Jumbo. That animal lived like a king—or at least he did until he was accidentally run over by a locomotive."

"We don't want to appear cynical," said the elephants, "but how do you *accidentally* run over a seven-ton animal?"

"You do it," said the leader, his face glowing with pride, "by inventing the locomotive in the first place. Whatever else we may be, you must admit we're a race that can boast of magnificent accomplishments: the internal combustion engine, splitting the atom, reaching the planets, curing cancer." He paused. "I don't mean to denigrate you, but truly, what have you got to equal that?"

"We live our lives free of sin," responded the elephants simply. "We respect each other's beliefs, we don't harm our environment, and we have never made war on other elephants."

"And you'd put that up against the heart transplant, the silicon chip, and the three-dimensional television screen?" asked the leader with just a touch of condescension.

"Our aspirations are different from yours," said the elephants. "But we are as proud of our heroes as you are of yours."

"You have heroes?" said the leader, unable to hide his surprise.

"Certainly." The elephants rattled off their roll of honor: "The Kilimanjaro Elephant. Selemundi. Mohammed of Marsabit. And the Magnificent Seven of Krueger Park: Mafunyane, Shingwedzi, Kambaki, Joao, Dzombo, Ndlulamithi, and Phelwane."

"Are they here on Neptune?" asked the leader as his men began returning from the ship.

"No," said the elephants. "You killed them all."

"We must have had a reason," insisted the men.

"They were there," said the elephants. "And they carried magnificent ivory."

"See?" said the men. "We *knew* we had a reason."

The elephants didn't like that answer much, but they were too polite to say so, and the two species exchanged views and white lies all through the brief Neptunian night. When the sun rose again, the men voiced their surprise.

"Look at you!" they said. "What's happening?"

"We got tired of walking on all fours," said the elephants. "We decided it's more comfortable to stand upright."

"And where are your trunks?" demanded the men.

"They got in the way."

"Well, if that isn't the damnedest thing!" said the men. Then they looked at each other. "On second thought, *this* is the damnedest thing! We're bursting out of our helmets!"

"And our ears are flapping," said the leader.

"And our noses are getting longer," said another man.

"This is most disconcerting," said the leader. He paused. "On the other hand, I don't feel nearly as much animosity toward you as I did yesterday. I wonder why?"

"Beats us," said the elephants, who were becoming annoyed with the whining quality of his voice.

"It's true, though," continued the leader. "Today I feel like every elephant in the universe is my friend."

"Too bad you didn't feel that way when it would have made a difference," said the elephants irritably. "Did you know you killed sixteen million of us in the twentieth century alone?"

"But we made amends," noted the men. "We set up game parks to preserve you."

"True," acknowledged the elephants. "But in the process you took away most of our habitat. Then you decided to cull us so we wouldn't exhaust the park's food supply." They paused dramatically. "That was when Earth received its second alien visitation. The aliens examined the theory of preserving by culling, decided that Earth was an insane asylum, and made arrangements to drop all their incurables off in the future."

Tears rolled down the men's bulky cheeks. "We feel just terrible about that," they wept. A few of them dabbed at their eyes with short, stubby fingers that seemed to be growing together.

"Maybe we should go back to the ship and consider all this," said the men's leader, looking around futilely for something large enough in which to blow his nose. "Besides, I have to use the facilities."

"Sounds good to me," said one of the men. "I got dibs on the cabbage."

"Guys?" said another. "I know it sounds silly, but it's much more comfortable to walk on all fours."

The elephants waited until the men were all on the ship, and then went about their business, which struck them as odd, because before the men came they didn't *have* any business.

"You know," said one of the elephants. "I've got a sudden taste for a hamburger."

"I want a beer," said a second. Then: "I wonder if there's a football game on the subspace radio."

"It's really curious," remarked a third. "I have this urge to cheat on my wife—and I'm not even married."

Vaguely disturbed without knowing why, they soon fell into a restless, dreamless sleep.

■

Sherlock Holmes once said that after you eliminate the impossible, what remains, however improbable, must be the truth.

Joseph Conrad said that truth is a flower in whose neighborhood others must wither.

Walt Whitman suggested that whatever satisfied the soul was truth.

Neptune would have driven all three of them berserk.

"Truth is a dream, unless my dream is true," said George Santayana.

He was just crazy enough to have made it on Neptune.

■

"We've been wondering," said the men when the two groups met in the morning. "Whatever happened to Earth's last elephant?"

"His name was Jamal," answered the elephants. "Someone shot him."

"Is he on display somewhere?"

"His right ear, which resembles the outline of the continent of Africa, has a map painted on it and is in the Presidential Mansion in Kenya. They turned his left ear over—and you'd be surprised how many left ears were thrown away over the centuries before someone somewhere thought of turning them over—and another map was painted, which now hangs in a museum in Bombay. His feet were turned into a matched set of barstools, and currently grace the Aces High Show Lounge in Dallas, Texas. His scrotum serves as a tobacco pouch for an elderly Scottish politician. One tusk is on display at the British Museum. The other bears a scrimshaw and resides in a store window in Beijing. His tail has been turned into a fly swatter, and is the proud possession of one of the last *vaqueros* in Argentina."

"We had no idea," said the men, honestly appalled.

"Jamal's very last words before he died were, 'I forgive you,'" continued the elephants. "He was promptly transported to a sphere higher than any man can ever aspire to."

The men looked up and scanned the sky. "Can we see it from here?" they asked.

"We doubt it."

The men looked back at the elephants—except that they had evolved yet again. In fact, they had eliminated every physical feature for which they had ever been hunted. Tusks, ears, feet, tails, even scrotums, all had undergone enormous change. The elephants looked exactly like human beings, right down to their space suits and helmets.

The men, on the other hand, had burst out of their space suits (which had fallen away in shreds and tatters), sprouted tusks, and found themselves conversing by making rumbling noises in their bellies.

"This is very annoying," said the men who were no longer men. "Now that we seem to have become elephants," they continued, "perhaps you can tell us what elephants *do?*"

"Well," said the elephants who were no longer elephants, "in our spare time, we create new ethical systems based on selflessness, forgiveness, and family values. And we try to synthesize the work of Kant, Descartes, Spinoza, Thomas Aquinas, and Bishop Berkeley into something far more sophisticated and logical, while never forgetting to incorporate emotional and aesthetic values at each stage."

"Well, we suppose that's pretty interesting," said the new elephants without much enthusiasm. "Can we do anything else?"

"Oh, yes," the new spacemen assured them, pulling out their .550 Nitro Expresses and .475 Holland & Holland Magnums and taking aim. "You can die."

"This can't be happening! You yourselves were elephants yesterday!"

"True. But we're men now."

"But why kill us?" demanded the elephants.

"Force of habit," said the men as they pulled their triggers.

Then, with nothing left to kill, the men who used to be elephants boarded their ship and went out into space, boldly searching for new life forms.

■

Neptune has seen many species come and go. Microbes have been spontaneously generated nine times over the eons. It has been visited by aliens thirty-seven different times. It has seen forty-three wars, five of them atomic, and the creation of 1,026 religions, none of which possessed any universal truths. More of the vast tapestry of galactic history has been played out on Neptune's foreboding surface than any other world in Sol's system.

Planets cannot offer opinions, of course, but if they could, Neptune would almost certainly say that the most interesting creatures it ever hosted were the elephants, whose gentle ways and unique perspectives remain fresh and clear in its memory. It mourns the fact that they became extinct by their own hand. Kind of.

A problem would arise when you asked whether Neptune was referring to the old–new elephants who began life as killers, or the new–old ones who ended life as killers.

Neptune just hates questions like that.

As I pointed out in my introduction, speculative fiction is actually many fields, each with its separate pleasures, difficulties, and histories both commercial and literary. No one will ever agree where the boundaries lie among these subsets of SF, least of all their practitioners. But let us pretend, for convenience's sake, that we can name the fields, and let us listen to the joys and jeremiads of those who resonate there in this early twenty-first century.

HARD SCIENCE FICTION

Geoffrey A. Landis

Geoffrey Landis is the author of much first-rate hard SF, including the well-received novel *Mars Crossing.*

I have a secret to tell you: Science is a game.

It's a team sport, for the most part, although there are occasional superstars who dazzle all with their speed and skill. And it's a game where, for the most part, the opponent is not really the other player. Like golf, I suppose: all the players are aiming for the same goal, and it's only a question of which one gets there a bit faster, a bit more elegantly. (Although it would be an amusing game of golf indeed in which all of the players were in the woods, and none quite sure in which direction was the hole.)

Science is an exciting game with bold strokes of skillful play, blending meticulously crafted strategy and wild improvisation; full of sudden reverses and agonizing fumbles and unexpected goals.

The universe is the real opponent, and the rules of the game are always changing, but the objective is always the same: trying to understand a universe of infinite subtlety. The trophy isn't a medallion given away in Stockholm; that's just an afterthought, no more the actual game than the summary in the morning paper the day after a baseball game. The real prize is to understand something that has never before been understood.

People liken science to a puzzle more often than to a game, but, puzzle or game, it's the ultimate sport, one which athletes devote decades to training for, a sport which will consume them for the rest of their lives.

It's a very slow game—a single play can take decades; one match can take a lifetime. Some of us train hard and play hard but never score a goal. It's a slow sport for spectators, but for an aficionado, it has more subtlety than chess, more thrills than a bullfight, more chained horsepower than the Indy 500.

Science fiction—or the stuff we call "hard" science fiction—then, is a way for amateurs to join the sport. The universe, in hard science fiction, is a puzzle, and the challenge the author sets is, Can you understand it? Science fiction invents worlds to match wits against and in which the match can take less than a lifetime.

Like science, hard science fiction is always changing. The atomic spaceships of the 1940s have given way to puzzles of alien ecologies and wormhole physics, with cosmology and quantum physics taking the place of orbital mechanics. As science gets more sophisticated, hard SF is getting harder to write (or perhaps I should say that *good* hard SF is getting harder to write; there certainly is still enough fiction with the trappings of hard SF, with marvelous machines and blazing buzzwords of science flying majestically through the purple sky). But as we unlearn much of the things we once knew about the planets and about the universe, we learn new things about our own solar system and others, and the new solar system we are entering is as strange and wonderful as the old—perhaps stranger—and no less a place for science fiction. For the best hard SF engages the edges of real science and poses puzzles that draw on all that we now know about the universe. Good hard science fiction makes us think about the universe we live in, with all its possibilities and weirdness and wonder.

Kenneth Brewer once asked Freeman Dyson what it felt like when he had put together the puzzle of quantum electrodynamics and for a moment knew something that nobody else in the world knew. "Well," Dyson said, "you have to know that it's the greatest feeling in the world."

SOFT- AND MEDIUM-VISCOSITY SCIENCE FICTION

Scott Edelman

Scott Edelman is a longtime SF editor.

Science keeps marching on, and for the past century (or perhaps even longer, depending upon which critic does the carbon dating) science fiction has been by its side, marching merrily along with it. In fact, one of science fiction's proudest achievements has always been that we're usually a few steps ahead, with science struggling to catch up, huffing and puffing as it attempts to weave reality out of our dreams. Often we even find ourselves light-years ahead, in danger of losing sight of science all together.

The distance that separates the dreamers and the facilitators hardly matters. What matters is our role in this relationship. And the part we have chosen to play is that of prophet. With our stories, we walk before science with a metaphorical lantern, guiding, inspiring, illuminating the possible destinations. And then, spurred by these seductive vapors, science does go on, choosing some of our possible futures to make real, discarding others as—at least for now—either impossibly ridiculous or sadly out of reach.

Some of the paths turn out to be dead ends. But others lead to the Moon.

How the world loves science fiction at times such as those, when we turn out to have been right! The world sure does love its winners, and we've hit the bull's-eye many times. Hugo Gernsback would have been proud of us. But to be embraced only when science delivers on science fiction's predictions seems a little hollow to me, as if the general public needs to be bribed with successes in order to give us their love. In literature, as in life, I'd prefer my love to be a little less one-sided and a little more unconditional.

I don't want science fiction to be loved only when we look forward with it, before we can possibly know which stories got it right and which did not, but also when we're looking back at it from a further future. But how can we create a work that is not just for its own time but also for all time, when so many generations have gotten it wrong? At one time, phlogiston was widely believed to be the true matter of the universe, and atomic theory was seen as just a myth. How are we to know at any given moment whether, by arming our futures with technological and scientific details, we will be seen by later generations as prescient—or just plain silly?

We can't. As much as we dream of time machines, we are too much of our own time. Which means that like it or not, some of our hardest science fiction will ooze to mere putty in the hands of the future.

Some will call it heresy, but I've come to see that the only futures that the future will be able to stomach will be the soft ones. Rigorous, but soft nonetheless.

So I say, All hail the black box. What powers the ships hurtling across the galaxies, the engines that keep towering cities floating high above the alien seas below, or the mechanical brains that motivate a race of robots? Does it truly matter? The hardest of SF writers want to worry about how they and other miracles work. But those who worry instead about how what works affects us are likelier to last into the future as more than museum curiosities. That is why though I enjoy hard SF, and have certainly bought much of it as an editor, I worry that it can only be written for the writer's generation alone, and so I do not practice it when I wear my own writer's hat.

That is why I choose the black box. What's inside? Who knows? Each generation will choose differently in filling it. Sometimes there have been wires inside, or vacuum tubes, or printed circuitry. Who knows what the future will bring and with what technology our descendants will choose to inhabit the black boxes that we build in our stories? That is why I only need to be made to believe. I do not need so much information as to be capable of building it. Verisimilitude should be enough, for, after all, we do not seek out reality itself in fiction but rather the semblance of reality.

We cannot truly blueprint the future, only dream it. And that in itself should be enough of a reward. Or else we will end up speaking a language that will be coherent only to the people already in the room.

There is, of course, a downside for those who choose to write other than the hardest sort of SF. This pitfall comes from certain subsets of our audience and of our peers. There are those who will say that by focusing on the affect rather than the effect, we are embracing ignorance, that we are "less than," or indeed, not writing science fiction at all.

But that is a small price to pay for the accompanying joys.

This I know:

The future will bring miracles, and the world will change because of it. And the world will change whether those miracles come powered by steam or electricity or atomics or some method as yet unknown. The miracles themselves are only the catalysts for the sense of wonder that future folks will feel. And it is that which we must examine.

Or else we shall suffer as most of our spiritual forebears have done, and our ghosts will watch as all the fruits of our field turn into artifacts that to our children are nothing more than quaint.

SF HUMOR: A LOOK AT THE NUMBERS

(condensed from Writers Booty *magazine)*

Terry Bisson

Terry Bisson is a multiple award winner for his quirky, intelligent SF.

For only pennies a day, you can be writing and selling SF humor from your own home. Sound too good to be true? Read on! A necessarily partial phone survey (11.43 percent don't have working phones, and 8.54 percent don't answer intelligibly) of SFWA's humor writers shows the top five earning considerably more than a dollar a day (how does $1.39 sound to you?) while the average ($0.39) still holds a comfortable lead over the related but low-paying genres of Industrial Erotica, Adventure Travel, and Trash.

SF is unique among America's low-flying lits in that it is almost one-fourth humor: 23.45 percent funny, to be precise. This is considerably less than Romantic Sports which is almost 30 (29.23) percent funny, but well above both Romance (18.24) and Sports (15.32). Humor itself, the flagship as it were, is only 51.76 percent funny, and that average is artificially inflated by Mark Twain, who would be a SFWA member if he weren't so dead.

Much of SF's considerable smile factor is due to the high-spirited young writers it attracts. SF and Fantasy together induct an average of almost sixteen new scribblers a year (15.42), of whom more than six (6.19) are funny. Let's look at a typical year—2001. Nationally, 118 writers went pro that year, an above-average eighteen of whom were picked up by SFWA, which handles the draft for the related fields of SF, Fantasy and Low Slipstream. Of these rookies, seven were funny, four almost funny, and two were just weird. By way of comparison, the mainstream gained forty-one new pros, of whom only six were a little funny and two were actually depressing.

Who says you can't tell a book by its cover? The high risibility-index of SF is due in large part to appearances. Many (254 total) SF writers dress funny, often intentionally. There are no gender distinctions here with the women being fully (99.44 percent) as funny-looking as the men. Author photos are of course the "wings" that bring these laughs to the readers, which is why trade books are not as funny as hardcovers, and mass market paperbacks get less funny every day.

It's not all personnel, however. The impressive display of humor in modern SF is due in large measure to tradition. From the high comedy of *Frankenstein* to the rollicking chase scenes of *Dune* (who can forget those goofy worms?), humor has played an important role in SF. And it's becoming more rather than less important: of the 1,786,873 dialogue interchanges added to the literature since *Apollo 11*, fully 987,543 have contained puns, jokes, or wry rejoinders, and this is discounting the narrative drollery (more troublesome to quantify) that is a staple of the field.

But tradition, though honored, can play only a supporting role in an innovative genre. Many of the laughs in SF (33.78 percent of the total) have to do with the material itself. SF is quite correctly considered a literature of ideas, and ideas are funny, at least some of them; and even the ones that aren't funny are funnier than manners, morals, or money, the mainstream obsessions that still (go figure!) account for 64.87 percent of America's printed matter.

It must be noted that within the linked fields of Fantasy and SF, the playing field is far from level. Robots and rocket ships are almost always funny (68.98 percent of the time), but monsters? Not! Elves are not funny at all (perhaps because they try so hard). Aliens are funnier than unicorns by a factor of ten, and castles are funny only to those who have not lived in them for five or more consecutive days.

Of course, a career in SF doesn't automatically bring laughs, except from the immediate family. If a robot whines in the forest and no one laughs, is it funny? The SF humorist needs an agent, and SF agents are a special breed (65.67 percent special, in fact) known for their ability to laugh at as well as with their clients. The best of them (32.65 percent) actively seek sarcastic rejections, and the worst (27.87 percent, allowing for overlap) like to receive small dead animals in the mail.

These agents can't afford to waste their time on the trade mags like *Locus* and *SF Chronicle*, which rarely print humor (1.456

laughs per page, not counting ads), nor on the all-humor mags like *The New Yorker* and *Analog*, which are written in-house by lunatics. For speedy, top-penny sales, SF deal-makers go straight for the prestige 'zines like *Asimov's*, *F&SF*, and *SciFiction,* whose editors are so eager to please that they have been known (987 documented incidents) to laugh at their own jokes.

Agents can't do it all, though, which brings us to the most powerful weapon in any SF writer's arsenal: the personal touch. Successful SF and Fantasy pros understand that the best time to make an editor laugh is after midnight. Between ten and two a.m. is best, when all but the most hopeless (three at last count) are home in bed. Remember to keep it light: the last thing an editor wants is a collect call from a writer who runs out of funny stories after only twenty minutes on the phone!

So now you know the ropes. Isn't it about time you put on your funny hat, powered up your word processor, and joined the ranks of the SF pros who are turning laughs into dollars at the rate of pennies a day?

CONTEMPORARY FANTASY

Andy Duncan

Andy Duncan's story "The Chief Designer" won the 2002 Sturgeon Award.

For me, the great lure of fantasy as a reader and as a writer, is the chance to explore the truly *weird*—weirder even than the most way-out science fiction stories, which must necessarily ride, in relative comfort, the rails of scientific, technological, and social extrapolation. By contrast, the fantasy story is free to set off on foot without a map, whistling a jaunty tune as dark clouds roll in from the west, shadows reach out from alleyways, street signs become few and far between, and the first fat drops splash down the back of the neck: unnerving, yes, but exhilarating, too.

The two great fantasy magazines of the early twentieth century

right in their very titles: *Weird Tales* and *Unknown*. The titles
[t]ee terrific recent collections nail it, too: *Stranger Things Hap-*
pen, Tales of Pain, and *Wonder,* and *Magic Terror.* And all of the above
exemplify a relatively new approach to fantasy, finding the uncanny
not just in the pastoral long ago and far away but also next door,
down the street, around the corner, the day before yesterday.

Today, the field of contemporary fantasy is full of wild talents,
visionaries, writers of the marvelously and necessarily weird—and
in lo, what numbers! *Never before have first-rate contemporary fantasists*
so many and so varied written at the peak of their powers simultaneously.
To name a few favorites among them is to leave out too many, but
even the most preliminary list indicates that these are extraordinary
times in the field of contemporary fantasy, as in the world at large.

Consider the past few years. Kelly Link's marvelous and inde-
scribable collection *Stranger Things Happen* declares a new genre,
one so far occupied only by *Stranger Things Happen* and perhaps by
nothing else, ever, at least until Link's next book comes along.
From *The Sandman* through *American Gods,* Neil Gaiman has
demonstrated an uncanny ability not only to channel and revive
old myths but to create new ones. The novels of Jonathan Carroll—*The Wooden Sea* being a recent example—never stop opening
doors in the reader's head, not even after the book itself is closed.

The artists, aesthetes, and angst-ridden adolescents who com-
pellingly people Elizabeth Hand's *Black Light* and *Last Summer at*
Mars Hill are as fabulous as gryphons and as timely as the tabloids.
John Crowley, who tempts even the hardheaded to retrieve the
word *genius* from the dustbin, wrote *Little, Big* and then, instead of
resting on the seventh day, just kept going, into the majestic series
that includes, most recently, *Daemonomania.* Tim Powers's *Declare*
reads like an Indiana Jones vehicle written by John Le Carré or, in
other words, like nothing else in this world, but it also manages to
be an epic *Zhivago*-style love story chockablock with jaw-dropping
notions, my favorite being the revelation of a sinister second Ark
that shadowed Noah's. How's that for High Concept?

Peter Straub is the best horror writer since Herman Melville.
"Mr. Clubb and Mr. Cuff," the highlight of his collection *Magic*
Terror, demonstrates anew that fantasy need not include a single

supernatural element. Don't ask me; ask *him*. Caitlín R. Kiernan, author of *Tales of Pain and Wonder*, is a mesmerizing stylist with an unerring sense of place; Anne Rice's New Orleans has nothing on Kiernan's Birmingham, Alabama. Kiernan is also a Goth queen and a mosasaur expert. How cool is that? Another prose magician is Jeffrey Ford, who managed to get his collection *The Fantasy Writer's Assistant and Other Stories* and his novel *The Portrait of Mrs. Charbuque* published at the same time, the show-off.

See what I mean? I'm running out of space, and I haven't even mentioned Graham Joyce, Nalo Hopkinson, Ray Vukcevich, Glen David Gold, Philip Pullman, China Miéville, Ted Chiang, Alan Moore, Louise Erdrich, Steven Millhauser, Lisa Goldstein . . .

(many more names go here)

. . . or J. K. Rowling, whose multivolume Harry Potter saga, when complete, will make all the grumblers, potshotters, and naysayers look even sillier than they look now.

Whence this explosion of cutting-edge contemporary fantasy, this embarrassment of riches? Well. Tolkien famously argued that a chief function of "fairy-stories" was Escape, which he both lauded as a heroic act and capitalized, as he did "its companions, Disgust, Anger, Condemnation, and Revolt." Most of us don't share Tolkien's Disgust at the modern world; he went on, in the next paragraph of that famous essay, to Condemn electric street-lamps. But as I write this in summer 2002, I can think of any number of things we writers and readers might justifiably be Escaping from these days—into the pastoral long ago and far away, no doubt, but also into more contemporary realms: our world, straight up, with a twist. The long-term benefits of this literary and psychological trend, if it continues, are interesting to contemplate, but it's late, and I'm sleepy. After a good night's rest and a great many dreams, informed by all those writers named above, I will rise and mow the lawn, and then come inside and do my part: I will write a fantasy story.

TRADITIONAL FANTASY

Mindy L. Klasky

Relative newcomer Mindy L. Klasky has been making a splash in fantasy with her *Glasswright* series.

"Traditional fantasy": Readers outside of the speculative fiction crowd often regard the phrase with suspicion, their reactions ranging from polite confusion (from people who have no idea what is included in the genre) to knowing leers (from people who assume that "fantasies" are hidden in plain brown wrappers, available only behind the sales counter). Nevertheless, the past few years have introduced millions of people to traditional fantasy through the cinematic blockbusters of *Harry Potter* and *The Lord of the Rings*. As if in reaction to those media visions (and, in some cases, the traditional novels on which they were based), written traditional fantasy has pushed new boundaries, exploring intimate relationships between characters and focusing on sexual identity and power as major tools of storytelling.

The juggernaut of traditional fantasy rolls onward, continuing to appeal to children (both chronological youngsters and nostalgic adults). The first four books in the *Harry Potter* series proved so popular that the *New York Times* Bestseller list created a new category of "Children's Literature" to open up slots for some other—any other—novels. *The Lord of the Rings* and its prequel, *The Hobbit*, have occupied four of the top ten slots on *Locus* magazine's mass market paperback bestseller list for the majority of the past few years. People who have never dreamed of reading in the speculative fiction ghetto have proudly boasted of their literary excursions into cinematic "novelizations"—novels that have, in some cases, been available for more than half a century.

The public seems to embrace these media fantasies for the archetypes they present—the struggles of good against evil, the stories of growth from childhood to adulthood, the hope of magic in our daily affairs. And yet many adults have a desire to push beyond those childhood dreams, to edge past the old struggles. There is a movement in print fantasy to confront new challenges, to address more complex problems, to create new solutions. Many of these novels address the uniquely adult world of complex sexuality to explore their new parameters.

Anne Bishop's *Black Jewels Trilogy* exemplifies the new, adult aspect of traditional fantasy. The dominant race of her world, the Blood, are virile vampires, humanlike creatures whose sexuality is central to their means of communication. Women often control men, holding them as sexual slaves and forcing them to serve as unpaid gigolos. Men can be controlled by magical rings—channels that convey great pain—placed directly on their genitals. Witches—the strongest and most dangerous of women—can be destroyed if they are deflowered by brutal or careless men. Throughout the novels, sexuality is the currency of power, a driving force that sweeps up characters, the plot, and the author's themes.

Similarly, in Lynn Flewelling's *The Bone Doll's Twin* sexuality is twined about the core of power. In that well-received novel, a prophesied princess is hidden from her murderous royal uncle, disguised as a boy. The disguise, however, goes far beyond the traditional fairy-tale vision of a girl wearing pants and clipping her hair. Flewelling's princess is physically transformed into a male child; in a blood rite, her body is manipulated through magic. The resulting tale traces the confused princess's friendships and feudal relationships, yielding a complex and fascinating examination of gender politics, all wrapped up in an ostensibly traditional fantasy story of succession, usurpation, and feudal loyalty.

Even fiction that is generally marketed to children in the United States has been shaped by the examination of sexual roles and mores. Phillip Pullman's acclaimed trilogy, which began with *The Golden Compass* and continued with *The Subtle Knife*, concluded with *The Amber Spyglass*. In that novel, an alien race is dying because it has lost the secret of its reproduction. Two human children are enlisted in a battle between good and evil that spans several worlds. Their innocent discovery of their own sexual natures is crucial to the resolution of the novel's intertwined plots.

In each of the examples cited above, sexuality is a major element of the story, woven into the plot, the characters, and even the physical setting. It is not a fillip added to a tale to otherwise attract adult readers. It is not a lurid sidelight, designed to bring in a few prurient purchasers. Rather, it is a crucial element, vital and essential to the storytelling.

As in the past, traditional fantasy provides readers a chance to explore the meaning of their worlds through very different societies. Some aspects of the genre remain stable: the vast majority of novels are published in series. The vast majority of fantasy works contain magic, with strict rules about its application and usefulness. The vast majority of traditional fantasy explores essential conflicts between forces of good and forces of evil.

And yet the field is expanding, growing, defining itself to exist in a field separate from the media, separate from the exuberant—if occasionally simplistic—youthful audience attracted by cinema. Traditional fantasy is growing up, shaping itself for grown-up readers with grown-up concerns.

DARK FANTASY

Ellen Datlow

Venerable SF editor Ellen Datlow currently edits the online magazine SCI FICTION.

I've been interested in dark literature all my life. As a child I read everything around the house from *Bulfinch's Mythology* to Guy de Maupassant's and Nathaniel Hawthorne's short fiction. I watched the original *Twilight Zone* television series as soon as my parents would let me stay up late. Later, I read *The Playboy Book of Horror and the Supernatural* with stories by Ray Russell, Ray Bradbury, Robert Bloch, Gahan Wilson, and a host of other names familiar to horror readers, and Richard Matheson's *Shock* collections. Those are the books that hooked me on horror.

I still read a lot of dark fiction—horror/dark fantasy—as my reading for the annual *Year's Best Fantasy and Horror*, of course, but also because I love this subgenre of fantastic literature. Just as in science fiction, there are arguments as to what constitutes "horror"—is it *only* supernatural fiction, or does it encompass psychological horror? And what about terror fiction, crime fiction? I and other aficionados of the dark literary tradition embrace a dictum comparable to Damon Knight's: "If I as an editor point to it, it's SF." My personal rule of thumb is, if it's dark enough—if I as a horror reader and editor read a piece of fiction that gives me a certain frisson, promotes a specific unease or feeling of dread while reading it—I'll call it horror. Horror is the only literature that is defined by its effect on the reader rather than on its subject matter. Which is why great science fiction classics such as *Frankenstein* by Mary Shelley, "Who Goes There?" by John W. Campbell, and great psychological horror works by Robert Bloch and Richard Matheson (both of whom also have published supernatural fiction) fit comfortably into the horror field.

Horror has gone through growing pains similar to SF's, although unlike SF it originally began as part of the mainstream, and in the 1980s, as a result of Stephen King's popularity, it was made into a marketing category. And because many publishers decided they needed a horror line with a set number of slots to fill, a lot of bad horror was written and published, saturating a market that really wanted more Stephen King but not necessarily more horror. The horror lines crashed and burned relatively quickly, and soon few commercial publishers would touch horror—overtly—although a flurry and then an avalanche of literary/crime/psychological horror novels were published throughout the nineties.

But unlike SF, horror has never really had more than one or two professional magazines. *Weird Tales*, although publishing dark fantasy for many years, does not publish what I consider horror. The difference? A matter of degree. *Twilight Zone Magazine* and its sister *Night Cry* existed for relatively short periods of time. Some of the SF magazines have published and continue to publish a bit of horror. But out of this vacuum the small press grew.

The proliferation of desktop publishing and the Internet have made it possible for anyone to self-publish or publish their friends on a shoestring budget. This innovation has produced some quality magazines and webzines and a lot of dreck. The worst problem facing the horror field today is being able to distinguish between quality and junk. I don't mean entertaining junk. I mean stuff like hairballs caught in a cat's throat. A lot of small-press horror magazines are just abominable, though I know the editors *must* believe in what they're doing. But not everyone can or should be an editor. Editing is a calling—not something you just dabble in—if you want to produce anything of consistent quality. I think that the young and clueless are too caught up in the gore of it.

Here we come to the negative side of today's horror field. Although horror should elicit emotion from the reader, what's forgotten by the purveyors of a tiny subgenre that's been screaming for attention—gross out/extreme horror—is that they're taking the easy way out. Eliciting disgust and repelling readers might be a charge in the short run but in the long run it's self-defeating, a stylistic choice more than a thematic one—and a dead end. They've left behind the idea that the gore needs to be integrated into a story in which you care about what's happening. They've forgotten that gore for gore's sake becomes numbing. This sort of horror has a limited audience within the horror community and an even tinier audience outside the horror community. I believe that most of the writers writing it now will tire of it and move on—or stop writing. And if they don't move on? That just means they have nothing to say.

But whenever I feel discouraged by the shouting, I know I can cleanse my literary palate by reading the work of newer writers who excite me—voices of the dark short story such as Glen Hirshberg, Kelly Link, Tia V. Travis, Marion Arnott, Tim Lebbon, and Gemma Files—and by reading the dark stories and novellas by some of my favorite writers, such as Elizabeth Hand, Steve Rasnic Tem, Melanie Tem, Kathe Koja, Terry Dowling, Tanith Lee, Paul McAuley, Lucius Shepard, P. D. Cacek, Kim Newman, Terry Lamsley, Peter Straub, Gene Wolfe, and a host of others who are creating chilling dark fiction with verve, a graceful use of language, and imagination. And over the years, while reading for the *Year's Best Fantasy and Horror* series, I've read brilliant horror novels by Stewart O'Nan (*A Prayer for the Dying*), Jack O'Connell (*Word Made Flesh*), China Miéville (*King Rat* and *Perdido Street Station*), Janette Turner Hospital (*Oyster* and *The Last Magician*), and everything by Jonathan Carroll.

Whenever you have so many writers (and others who I didn't

mention for reasons of space) producing and publishing their best work, you've got a healthy field.

ALTERNATE HISTORY

Harry Turtledove

Harry Turtledove has set his award-winning novels in many alternate times and places.

A friend of mine once claimed that alternate history was the most fun you could have with your clothes on. I don't know that I'd go that far—and I do suspect I could get my face slapped for experimenting—but the subgenre certainly does have its attractions.

First, of course, are the pleasures any good story offers: evocative writing, interesting characters, and a well-made plot. Right behind those is the peculiar fillip you get only from science fiction: seeing if the author's extrapolation from the change he or she has made to the so-called real world is plausible and persuasive. Though alternate history changes the past rather than the present or the future, it usually plays by the same sort of rules as the rest of science fiction once the change is made.

But alternate history also has a special kick all its own. It looks at the world in a funhouse mirror no other form of fiction can match. In it, we can look at not only fictional characters but real characters in fictional settings, bouncing what we already know about them off the paddles of a new pinball machine. If the Spanish Armada had won, what would have happened to Shakespeare's career? If the Union had lost, what would have happened to Abraham Lincoln's? If Muhammad hadn't founded Islam, what might he have done? And what would the world look like then?

Most science fiction projects onto a blank screen. You know only what the author tells you about the world and its inhabitants. Like mainstream historical fiction, alternate history assumes you know more; some of the people and situations involved will be familiar to you ahead of time. But, where historical fiction deals with pieces of the world as it was, alternate history demands more of its readers: it asks them to look into that funhouse mirror and see things as they might have been.

And it can do more than that. It can turn whole societies upside down. If a plague completely destroyed Western Europe at the end of the fourteenth century, what would the world have looked like afterwards? Could there have been an industrial revolution? If blacks had enslaved whites in North America rather than the other way around, how might they have treated them? (Reversing roles and looking at consequences is one of the things science fiction does particularly well.) If fascism or communism had triumphed during the turbulent century just past, how might things look?

From a writer's point of view, there's one other joy to doing alternate history: the research. If you aren't into digging up weird things for the fun of digging them up, this probably isn't the subgenre for you. If you are, though, you can transpose Newton and Galileo into Central Asia, make obscure references that ninety-nine out of a hundred of your readers will never notice but that will horrify or crack up the hundredth, or make all your readers feel as if they're looking at a trompe l'oeil painting. Perhaps the finest compliment I ever got was from a reviewer who said a novel of mine made him think he was reading an accurate portrayal of a world that in fact never existed.

Jeremiads? What goes wrong in alternate history is the flip side of what goes right. Bad writing and inept characterization can and too often do afflict any fiction. But the subgenre's besetting sins are failure of research and failure of extrapolation. A few years back, there was a novel (marketed as mainstream fiction rather than SF) that had to do with Jefferson Davis's reelection bid after a Southern victory in the Civil War. Lovely—except that the Confederate Constitution limited the president of the CSA to a single six-year term. There's another book about a world where the Romans conquered Germany and the Empire survived into the twentieth century. Unfortunately, it's also a world where Roman society never changed even though the Empire had an industrial revolution . . . and a world where, despite the immense changes a successful conquest and assimilation of Germany would have caused,

Constantine still gets born three centuries after the breakpoint and still plays a role recognizably similar to the one he had in real history.

Suspension of disbelief is probably harder to pull off in alternate history than in most other forms of fiction, not least because you're playing in part with what your readers already know. If they think *She'd never act that way, not even under those changed circumstances, because she did thus-and-so in the real world* or *Even if they had invented Silly Putty then, that doesn't mean we'd all be going around with hula hoops twenty years later*, you've lost them. Once disbelief comes crashing down, a steroid-laced weightlifter can't pick it up again.

Done well, alternate history is some of the most thought-provoking, argument-inducing fiction around. It also often inspires those who read it to go find out what really happened, which isn't a bad thing, either. Done not so well, it reminds people how painfully true Sturgeon's Law is. And I expect we'll all go on arguing about what is good and what's not so good and why or why not for a long, long time to come.

FILM AND TELEVISION

Michael Cassutt

Michael Cassutt successfully writes both SF and television scripts.

In my increasingly distant youth, a science fiction or fantasy film was a rarity, either a low-budget wonder that happened to sneak out of Hollywood early one morning or, like *2001*, a major studio event that got made only because a powerful director wouldn't take no for an answer.

Now, a year into Kubrick and Clarke's millennium, five or six of the ten top-grossing motion pictures of all time are science fiction or fantasy, depending on what megablockbuster has opened lately. SF and fantasy are part of the motion picture landscape—a lucrative part.

Television is also our playground, if you believe a recent *USA Today* poll, in which baby boomers named *The Twilight Zone* and *Star Trek* as two of their top three favorite series of all time. More recently, several generations of *Star Trek* sequels have had long, loving runs—*Next Generation, Deep Space Nine, Voyager,* and now *Enterprise.* Intriguing series such as *Babylon 5* and *Max Headroom* have come and gone. *The X-Files* lasted for nine seasons. *Buffy the Vampire Slayer* is still kicking satanic butt. *Farscape* sails on through its peculiar universe, low-rated but critically approved.

What is there to complain about? Well, for one thing, most SF or fantasy films and television are still written and produced by mainstream talents, not by SF writers who have published in the magazines or written novels. (*Babylon 5's* J. Michael Straczynski is the notable exception.)

Which means that the cutting-edge concepts on display in *Asimov's, Analog,* or *Interzone* don't make it to the screen. Well, make that rarely: there was this movie called *The Matrix* . . .

It may be that cutting-edge SF is, by its nature, limited to a more elite (which is to say, smaller) audience.

Look at the finalists for the Nebula script category, as selected by the membership of the Science Fiction and Fantasy Writers of America: *X-Men* (based on the famed Marvel comic book), the wonderful Chinese fantasy *Crouching Tiger, Hidden Dragon,* the Coen Brothers' *O Brother, Where Are Thou?* and (from *Buffy the Vampire Slayer*) Joss Whedon's television script "The Body."

Four fantasies. If you wanted to be tough about it, you could say *three* fantasies: *O Brother* is a musical comedy that continues the Coen Brothers' exploration of the American yokel.

The Spielberg–posthumous Kubrick collaboration, *A.I.,* based on material by Brian Aldiss and Ian Watson, and emerging from the core of traditional science fiction, didn't make the cut. Nor was it particularly successful, certainly not by Spielbergian standards. It's not hard to see why: the treatment of the subject matter was slow and obvious. Worse, Kubrick's cold, unflinching, and unforgiving view of human nature fits with Spielberg's warmth and sentimentality like a shot of gin with a slice of tiramisu. Yuck.

Perhaps the most rigorously traditional and successful SF film or television production of 2001 was Sci Fi Channel's miniseries *Dune*, adapted and directed by John Harrison from the classic Frank Herbert novel. It was not as artistic as David Lynch's critically battered (yet, by some, secretly appreciated) 1984 feature film, but it made more sense, helped, no doubt, by a six-hour running time.

Buffy the Vampire Slayer, the only prime-time drama series to approach the very mainstream *West Wing* in having a clear writer's voice, suffered somehow in moving from the WB to UPN for fall 2001. It would require more moral character than I possess to give WB network execs credit for *Buffy*'s success; perhaps Whedon and his talented staff are tired or, with the spin-off *Angel* series, stretched too thin.

Enterprise, which is simultaneously a follow-on to *Voyager* and a prequel to the original series, premiered strongly in fall 2001, though it has yet to become "appointment" television. Well, *Next Generation* and *Deep Space Nine* took two seasons to find themselves. *Enterprise* has the outlandish luxury of a five-year, 120-episode commitment.

Syndicated science fiction continued to fill Saturday afternoons, with varying degrees of success. *Gene Roddenberry's Andromeda* prospered in its second season; *Gene Roddenberry's Earth: Final Conflict*, ran out of gas in its fifth. The superhero series *Mutant X* arrived, aimed squarely at the audience that enjoyed the *X-Men* movie but was impatient for the sequel.

Not all the SF on television held its own as well as these series. *The X-Files* tottered into the television equivalent of old age. *Roswell* squandered a terrific concept (alienated teenaged aliens here on Earth). The Sci Fi Channel and UPN had notable failures, best left undescribed.

The failures and even the successful series suffer from a conceptual sameness: they all deal with heroic starship captains, alien hunters, or superheroes. Where are the stories set on our world in a future we might see? Where are adaptations of SF?

I think they're on the way. The explosive growth in computer-generated special effects has made it possible to create almost any sort of world on the screen, even on a series television budget and schedule.

Certainly, feature films show astonishing promise. In the fall of 2001, *Harry Potter and the Sorcerer's Stone* and *The Fellowship of the Ring* opened to huge box office success. *Harry Potter*, based on the megaselling novel by J. K. Rowling, was perhaps as good a movie as one could expect, but *The Fellowship of the Ring* was successful in almost every way. Simply *committing* to the three movies—at a cost of more than half a billion dollars—was an act of astonishing courage by New Line. For an effects-laden fantasy film with no big stars? And a relatively unknown director (Peter Jackson)?

Yet it all worked. Even the pickiest Tolkien fans seemed pleased with *Fellowship*. This picky viewer certainly was.

If anything can be made, in film or television, how long can it be before we see real science fiction?

Catherine Asaro—quantum physicist, mother, and former ballet dancer—zips around Maryland from NASA to ballet classes at practically light speed. Born in California, she received her Ph.D. in chemical physics from Harvard. She has done research at, among other places, the University of Toronto and the Max Planck Institut fur Astrophysik in Germany. She was a physics professor until 1990, when she established her own consulting company, Molecudyne Research.

Catherine's novels combine hard science, space adventure, and romance. She makes her ideas do double duty; some of the science in her popular SF series made a more sober appearance in her 1996 paper for *The American Journal of Physics*, "Complex Speeds and Special Relativity."

First serialized in *Analog* in 1999, *The Quantum Rose* is part of Catherine's well-received *Skolian Empire* series. This excerpt is the novel's exciting opening.

THE QUANTUM ROSE

Catherine Asaro

1

IRONBRIDGE
First Scattering Channel

Kamoj Quanta Argali, the governor of Argali Province, shot through the water and broke the surface of the river. Basking in the day's beauty, she tilted her face up to the violet sky. The tiny disk of Jul, the sun, was so bright she didn't dare look near it. Curtains of green and gold light shimmered across the heavens in an aurora visible even in the afternoon.

Her bodyguard Lyode stood on the bank, surveying the area. Lyode's true name was a jumble of words from the ancient language Iotaca, which scholars pronounced as *light emitting diode*. No one knew what it meant, though, so they all called her Lyode.

Unease prickled Kamoj. She treaded water, her hair swirling around her body, wrapping her slender waist and then letting go. Her reflection showed a young woman with black curls framing a heart-shaped face. She had dark eyes, as did most people in the province of Argali, though hers were larger than usual, with long lashes that right now sparkled with droplets of water.

Nothing seemed wrong. Reeds as red as pod-plums nodded on the bank, and six-legged lizards scuttled through them, glinting blue and green among the stalks. A few paces behind Lyode, the prismatic forest began. Up the river, in the distant north, the peaks of the Rosequartz Mountains floated like clouds in the haze. She drifted around to the other bank, but saw nothing amiss there either. Tubemoss covered the hills in a turquoise carpet broken by stone outcroppings that gnarled up like the knuckles of a buried giant.

What bothered her wasn't unease exactly, more a troubled anticipation. She supposed she should feel guilty about swimming here, but it was hard to summon that response on such a lovely day. The afternoon hummed with life, golden and cool.

Kamoj sighed. As much as she enjoyed her swim, invigorated by the chill water and air, she did have her position as governor to consider. Swimming naked, even in this secluded area, hardly qualified as dignified. She glided to the bank and clambered out, reeds slapping against her body.

Her bodyguard continued to scan the area. Lyode suddenly stiffened, staring across the water. She reached over her shoulder for the ballbow strapped to her back.

Puzzled, Kamoj glanced back. A cluster of greenglass stags had appeared from behind a hill on the other side of the river, each animal with a rider astride its long back. Sun rays splintered against the green scales that covered the stags. Each stood firm on its six legs, neither stamping nor pawing the air. With their iridescent antlers spread to either side of their heads, they shimmered in the blue-tinged sunshine.

Their riders were all watching her.

Sweet Airys, Kamoj thought, mortified. She ran up the slope to where she had left her clothes in a pile behind Lyode. Her bodyguard was taking a palm-sized marble ball out of a bag on her belt. She slapped it into the targeting tube of her crossbow, which slid inside an accordion cylinder. Drawing back the bow, Lyode sighted on the watchers across the river.

Of course, here in the Argali, Lyode's presence was more an indication of Kamoj's rank than an expectation of danger. Indeed, none of the watchers drew his bow. They looked more intrigued than anything else. One of the younger fellows grinned at Kamoj, his teeth flashing white in the streaming sunshine.

"I can't believe this," Kamoj muttered. She stopped behind Lyode and scooped up her clothes. Drawing her tunic over her head, she added, "Thashaverlyster."

"What?" Lyode said.

Kamoj jerked down the tunic, covering herself with soft gray cloth as fast as possible. Lyode stayed in front of her, keeping her bow poised to shoot. Kamoj counted five riders across the river, all in copper breeches and blue shirts, with belts edged by feathers from the blue-tailed quetzal.

One man sat a head taller than the rest. Broad-shouldered and long-legged, he wore a midnight-blue cloak with a hood that hid his face. His stag lifted its front two legs and pawed the air, its bi-hooves glinting like glass, though they were a hardier material, hornlike and durable. The man ignored its restless motions, keeping his cowled head turned toward Kamoj.

"That's Havyrl Lionstar," Kamoj repeated as she pulled on her gray leggings. "The tall man on the big greenglass."

"How do you know?" Lyode asked. "His face is covered."

"Who else is that big? Besides, those riders are wearing Lionstar colors." Kamoj watched the group set off, cantering into the blue-green hills. "Hah! You scared them away."

"With five against one? I doubt it." Lyode gave her a dry look. "More likely they left because the show is over."

Kamoj winced. She hoped her uncle didn't hear of this. As the only incorporated man in Argali, Maxard Argali had governed the province for Kamoj in her youth. In the years since she had become an adult, Kamoj had shouldered the responsibility of leading her people and province. But Maxard, her only living kin, remained a valued advisor.

Lionstar's people were the only ones who might reveal her indiscretion, though, and they rarely came to the village. Lionstar had "rented" the Quartz Palace in the mountains for more than a hundred days now, and in that time no one she knew had seen his face. Why he wanted a ruined palace she had no idea, given that he refused all visitors. When his emissaries had inquired about it, she and Maxard had been dismayed by the suggestion that they let a stranger take residence in the honored, albeit disintegrating, home of their ancestors. Kamoj still remembered how her face had heated as she listened to the outlanders explain their leige's "request."

However, no escape had existed from the "rent" Lionstar's people put forth. The law was clear: she and Maxard had to best his challenge or bow to his authority. Impoverished Argali could never match such an offer: shovels and awls forged from fine metals, stacks of firewood, golden bridle bells, dewhoney and molasses, dried rose-leeks, cobber-wheat, tri-grains, and reedflour that poured through your fingers like powdered rubies.

So they yielded—and an incensed Maxard had demanded that Lionstar pay a rent of that same worth every fifty days. It was a lien so outrageous, all Argali had feared Lionstar would send his soldiers to "renegotiate."

Instead, the cowled stranger had paid.

With Lyode at her side, Kamoj entered the forest. Walking among the trees, with tubemoss under her bare feet, made her even more aware of her precarious position. Why had he come riding here? Did he also have an interest in her lands? She had invested his rent in machinery and tools for farms in Argali. As much as she disliked depending on a stranger, it was better than seeing her people starve. But she couldn't bear to lose more to him, especially not this forest she loved.

So. She would have to inquire into his activities and see what she could discover.

The beauty of the forest helped soothe her concern. Drapes of moss hung on the trees, and shadow-ferns nodded around their trunks. Argali vines hung everywhere, heavy with the blush-pink roses that gave her home its name. Argali. It meant "vine rose" in Iotaca.

At least, most scholars translated it as rose. One fellow insisted it meant resonance. He also claimed they misspelled Kamoj's middle name, Quanta, an Iotaca word with no known translation. The name *Kamoj* came from the Iotaca word for *bound*, so if this odd scholar was correct, her name meant *Bound Quantum Resonance*. She smiled at the absurdity. *Rose* made more sense, of course.

The vibrant life in the autumnal woods cheered Kamoj. Camouflaged among the roses, puff lizards swelled out their red sacs. A ruffling breeze parted the foliage to let a sunbeam slant through the forest, making the scale-bark on the trees sparkle. Then the ray vanished and the forest returned to its dusky violet shadows. A thornbat whizzed by, wings beating furiously. It homed in on a lizard and stabbed its needled beak into the red sac. As the puff deflated with a whoosh of air, the lizard scrambled away, leaving the disgruntled thornbat to dart on without its prey.

Powdered scales drifted across Kamoj's arm. She wondered why people had no scales. The inconsistency had always puzzled her, since her early childhood. Most everything else on Balumil, the world, had them. Scaled tree roots swollen with moisture churned the soil. The trees grew slowly, converting water into stored energy to use during the long summer droughts and endless winter snows. Unlike people, who fought to survive throughout the grueling year, seasonal plants grew only in the gentler spring and autumn. Their big, hard-scaled seeds lay dormant until the climate was to their liking.

Sorrow brushed Kamoj's thoughts. If only people were as well adapted to survive. Each Long Year they struggled to replenish their population after the endless winter decimated their numbers. Last winter they had lost even more than usual to the blizzards and brutal ices.

Including her parents.

Even after so long, that loss haunted her. She had been a small child when she and Maxard, her mother's brother, became sole heirs to the impoverished remains of a province that had once been proud.

Will Lionstar take what little we have left? She glanced at Lyode, wondering if her bodyguard shared her concerns. A tall woman with lean muscles, Lyode had the dark eyes and hair common in Argali. Here in the shadows, the vertical slits of her pupils widened until they almost filled her irises. She carried Kamoj's boots dangling from her belt. She and Kamoj had been walking together in comfortable silence.

"Do you know the maize-girls who do chores in the kitchen?" Kamoj asked.

Lyode turned from her scan of the forest and smiled at Kamoj. "You mean the three children? Tall as your elbow?"

"That's right." Kamoj chuckled, thinking of the girls' bright energy and fantastic stories. "They told me, in solemn voices, that Havyrl Lionstar came here in a cursed ship that the wind chased across the sky, and that he can never go home because he's so loathsome the elements refuse to let him sail again." Her smile faded. "Where do these stories come from? Apparently most of Argali believes it. They say he's centuries old, with a metal face so hideous it will give you nightmares."

The older woman spoke quietly. "Legends often have seeds in truth. Not that he's supernatural, but that his behavior makes people fear him."

Kamoj had heard too many tales of Lionstar's erratic behavior to dismiss them. Since he had come to Argali, she had several times seen his wild rides herself, from a distance. He tore across the land like a madman.

Watching her closely, Lyode lightened her voice. "Well, you know, with the maize-girls, who can say? They tried to convince me that Argali is haunted. They think that's why all the light panels have gone dark."

Kamoj gave a soft laugh, relieved to change the subject. "They told me that too. They weren't too specific on who was haunting what, though." Legend claimed the Current had once lit all the houses here in the Northern Lands. But that had been centuries past, even longer in the North Sky Islands, where the Current had died thousands of years ago. The only reason one light panel worked in Argali House, Kamoj's home, was because her parents had found a few intact fiber-optic threads in the ruins of the Quartz Palace.

The panel intrigued Kamoj as much as it baffled her. It linked to cables that climbed up inside the walls of the house until they reached the few remaining sun-squares on the roof. No one understood the panel, but Lyode's husband, Opter, could make it work. He had no idea why, nor could he fix damaged components, but given undamaged parts he had an uncanny ability to fit them into the panels.

"Hai!" Kamoj winced as a twig stabbed her foot. Lifting her leg, she saw a gouge between her toes welling with blood.

"A good reason to wear your shoes," Lyode said.

"Pah." Kamoj enjoyed walking barefoot, but it did have drawbacks.

A drumming that had been tugging at her awareness finally intruded enough to make her listen. "Those are greenglass stags."

Lyode tilted her head. "On the road to Argali."

Kamoj grinned. "Come on. Let's go look." She started to run, then hopped on her good foot and settled for a limping walk. When they reached the road, they hid behind the trees, listening to the thunder of hooves.

"I'll bet it's Lionstar," Kamoj said.

"Too much noise for only five riders," Lyode said.

Kamoj gave her a conspiratorial look. "Then they're fleeing bandits. We should nab them!"

"And just why," Lyode inquired, "would these nefarious types be fleeing up a road that goes straight to the house of the central authority in this province, hmmm?"

Kamoj laughed. "Stop being so sensible."

Lyode still didn't look concerned. But she slipped out a bow-ball anyway and readied her bow.

Down the road, the first stags came around a bend. Their riders made a splendid sight. The men wore gold diskmail, ceremonial, too soft for battle, designed to impress. Made from beaten disks, the vests were layered to create an airtight garment. They never attained that goal, of course. Why anyone would want airtight mail was a mystery to Kamoj, but tradition said to do it that way, so that was how they made the garments.

On rare occasions, stagmen also wore leggings and a hood of mail. Some ancient drawings even showed mail covering the entire body, including gauntlets, knee boots, and a transparent cover for the face. Kamoj thought the face cover must be artistic fancy. She saw no reason for it.

Her uncle's stagmen gleamed today. Under their vests, they wore bell-sleeved shirts as gold as suncorn. Their gold breeches tucked into dark red knee-boots fringed by feathers from the green-tailed quetzal. Twists of red and gold ribbon braided their reins, and bridle bells chimed on their greenglass stags. Sunlight slanted down on the road, drawing sparkles from the dusty air.

Lyode smiled. "Your uncle's retinue makes a handsome sight."

Kamoj didn't answer. Normally she enjoyed watching Maxard's honor guard, all the more so because of her fondness for the riders, most of whom she had known all her life. They served Maxard well. His good-natured spirit made everyone like him, which was why a wealthy merchant woman from the North Sky Islands was courting him despite his small corporation. However, today he wasn't with his honor guard. He had sent them to Ironbridge a few days ago, and now they returned with an esteemed guest— someone Kamoj had no desire to see.

The leading stagmen were riding past her hiding place, the bi-hooves of their mounts stirring up scale dust from the road. She recognized the front rider. Gallium Sunsmith. Seeing him made her day brighten. A big, husky man with a friendly face, Gallium worked with his brother Opter in a sunshop, engineering gadgets that ran on light, like the mirror-driven pepper mill Opter had invented. Gallium also made a good showing for himself each year in the swordplay exhibition at festival. So when Maxard needed an honor guard, Gallium became a stagman.

Down the road, more of the party came into view. These new riders wore black mail, with dark purple shirts and breeches, and black boots fringed by silver fur. Jax Ironbridge, the governor of Ironbridge Province, rode in their center. Long-legged and muscu-lar, taller than the other stagmen, he had a handsome face with strong lines, chiseled like granite. Silver streaked his black hair. He sat astride Mistrider, a huge greenglass stag with a rack of cloud-tipped antlers and scales the color of the opal-mists that drifted in the northern mountains.

Kamoj's pleasure in the day faded. Still hidden, she turned away from the road. She leaned against the tree with her arms crossed, staring into the forest while she waited for the riders to pass.

A flight-horn sounded behind her, its call winging through the air. She jumped, then spun around. Apparently she wasn't as well-concealed as she thought; Jax had stopped on the road and was watching her, the curved handle of a horn in his hand.

Kamoj flushed, knowing she had given offense by hiding. Her merger with Jax had been planned for most of her life. He had the largest corporation in the northern provinces, which consisted of Argali, the North Sky Islands, and Ironbridge. Argu-ment existed about the translation of the Iotaca word *corporation*: for lack of a better interpretation, most scholars assumed it meant a man's dowry, the property and wealth he brought into mar-riage. A corporation as big as Jax's became a political tool, invoking the same law of "Better the offer or yield" as had Lionstar's rent.

Ironbridge, however, had given Argali a choice. Jax made an offer Kamoj and Maxard could have bettered. It would have meant borrowing from even the most impoverished Argali farmers, but besting the amount by one stalk of bi-wheat was all it took. Then they could have declined the marriage offer and repaid the loans. She had been tempted to try. But Argali was her responsibility, and her province needed this merger with flourishing Ironbridge. So she had agreed.

Jax watched her with an impassive gaze. He offered his hand. "I will escort you back to Argali House."

"I thank you for you kind offer, Governor Ironbridge," she said. "But you needn't trouble yourself."

He gave her a cold smile. "I am pleased to see you as well, my love."

Hai! She hadn't meant to further the insult. She stepped forward and took his hand. He lifted her onto the stag with one arm, a feat of strength few other riders could manage even with a child, let alone an adult. He turned her so she ended up sitting sideways on the greenglass, her hips fitted in front of the first boneridge that curved over its back. Jax sat behind her, astride the stag, between its first and second boneridges, his muscular legs pressed against her hips and leg.

The smell of his diskmail wafted over her, rich with oil and sweat. As he bent his head to hers, she drew back in reflex. She immediately regretted her response. Although Jax showed no outward anger, a muscle in his cheek twitched. She tried not to flinch as he took her chin in his hand and pulled her head forward. Then he kissed her, pressing her jaw until it forced her mouth open for his tongue. Despite her efforts, she tensed and almost clamped her mouth shut. He clenched his fist around her upper arm to hold her in place.

A rush of air thrummed past Kamoj, followed by the crack of a bowball hitting a tree and the shimmering sound of falling scales. Jax raised his head. Lyode stood by the road, a second ball knocked in her bow, her weapon aimed at Jax.

The Argali and Ironbridge stagmen had all drawn their bows and trained their weapons on Lyode. They looked acutely uncomfortable. No one wanted to shoot Kamoj's bodyguard. The Argali stagmen had grown up with her, and Gallium was her brother-in-law. Jax had visited Kamoj at least twice each short-year for most of her life, since their betrothal, so the Ironbridge stagmen also knew Lyode well. However, they couldn't ignore that she had just sent a bowball hurtling within a few hand-spans of the two governors.

In a chill voice only Kamoj could hear, Jax said, "Your hospitality today continues to amaze me." Turning to Gallium Sunsmith, he spoke in a louder voice. "You. Escort Lyode back to Argali House."

Gallium answered carefully. "It is my honor to serve you, sir. But perhaps Governor Argali would also like to do her best by Ironbridge, by accompanying her bodyguard back."

Kamoj almost swore. She knew Lyode and Gallium meant well, and she valued their loyalty, but she wished they hadn't interfered. It would only earn them Jax's anger. She and Jax had to work this out. Although their merger favored Ironbridge, it gave control to neither party. They would share authority, she focused on Argali and he on Ironbridge. It benefited neither province if their governors couldn't get along.

Perhaps she could still mollify Jax. "Please accept my apologies, Governor Ironbridge. I will discuss Lyode's behavior with her on the walk back. We'll straighten this out."

He reached down and grasped her injured foot, bending her leg at the knee so he could inspect her instep. "Can you walk on this?"

"Yes." The position he was holding her leg in was more uncomfortable than the gouge itself.

"Very well." As he let go, his fingers scraped the gash between her toes. Kamoj stiffened as pain shot through her foot. She didn't think he had done it on purpose, but she couldn't be sure.

She slid off the stag, taking care to land on her other foot. As she limped over to Lyode, bi-hooves scuffed behind her. She turned to see the riders thundering away, up the road to Argali.

2

THE OFFER
Incoming Wave

Jul, the sun, had sunk behind the trees by the time Kamoj and Lyode walked around the last bend of the road, into view of Argali House. Seeing her home, Kamoj's spirits lifted.

Legend claimed the house had once been luminous pearl, all one surface with no seams. According to the temple scholar, who could read bits of the ancient codices, Argali House had been grown in a huge vat of liquid, on a framework of machines called *nanobots*, which were supposedly so tiny you couldn't see them even with a magnifying glass. After these machines completed the house, one was to believe they simply swam away and fell apart.

Kamoj smiled. Absurdities filled the old scrolls. During one of her visits to Ironbridge, about ten years ago, Jax had shown her one in his library. The scroll claimed that Balumil, the world, went around Jul in an "elliptical orbit" and rotated on a tilted axis. This tilt, and their living in the north, was purported to explain why nights were short in summer and long in winter, fifty-five hours of darkness on the longest night of the year, leaving only five hours of sunlight.

She had always thought it strange how her people counted time. One year consisted of four seasons, of course: spring, summer, autumn, winter. They called it the Long Year. A person could be born, reach maturity, wed, and have a baby within one Long Year. For some reason her ancestors considered this a long time: hence the name. Even more inexplicable, they divided the Long Year into twenty equal periods called short-years, five per season. People usually just called those "years." But really, it made no sense. Why call it a short-*year*? The scroll claimed this odd designation came about because the time span came close to a "standard" year.

Standard for what?

Still, she found it more credible than too-little-to-see machines. Whatever the history of Argali House, it was wood and stone now, both the main building and the newer wings that rambled over the cleared land. Huge stacks of firewood stood along one side, stores for winter. Seeing them gave her satisfaction, knowing that preparations for the harsh season were well under way.

Bird-shaped lamps hung from the eaves, rocking in the breezes, their glass tinted in Argali colors—rose, gold, and green. Their radiance created a dam against the purple shadows pooled under the trees. The welcome sight spread its warmth over Kamoj. Here in the road, a fluted post stood like a sentinel. A lantern molded and tinted like a rose hung from a scalloped hook at its top, its glow beckoning them home.

They entered the front courtyard by a gate engraved with vines. Five stone steps ran the length of the house, leading up to a terrace, and five doors were set at even intervals along the front. The center door was larger than the others, stuccoed white and bordered by hieroglyphs in rose, green, and gold, with luminous blue accents.

As they neared the house, Kamoj heard voices. By the time they reached the steps, it resolved into two men arguing.

"That sounds like Ironbridge," Lyode said.

"Maxard too." Kamoj paused, her foot on the first step. Now silence came from within the house.

Above them, the door slammed open. Maxard stood framed in its archway, a burly man in old farm clothes. His garb startled Kamoj more than his sudden appearance. By now he should have been decked out in ceremonial dress and mail, ready to greet Ironbridge. Yet he looked as if he hadn't even washed up since coming in from the fields.

He spoke to her in a low voice. "You'd better get in here."

Kamoj hurried up the steps. "What happened?"

He didn't answer, just moved aside to let her enter a small foyer paved with white tiles bordered by Argali rose designs.

Boots clattered in the hall beyond. Then Jax swept into the entrance foyer with five stagmen. He paused in midstride when he saw Kamoj. He stared at her, caught in a look of fury, and surprise too, as if he hadn't expected to reveal the intensity of his reaction to her. Then he went to Maxard, towering over the younger man.

"We aren't through with this," Jax said.

"The decision is made," Maxard told him.

"Then you are a fool." Jax glanced at Kamoj, his face stiff now with a guarded emotion, one he hid too well for her to identify. In all the years she had known him, he had never shown such a strong response, except in anger. But this was more than rage. Shock? Emotional *pain?* Surely not from Jax, the pillar of Ironbridge. Before she had a chance to speak, he strode out of the house with his stagmen, ignoring Lyode, who stood just outside the door.

Kamoj turned to her uncle. "What's going on?"

He shook his head, his motion strained. Lyode came up the stairs, but when she tried to enter, Maxard braced his hand against the door frame, blocking her way. He spoke with uncharacteristic anger. "What blew into your brain, Lyode? Why did you have to *shoot* at him? Of all days I didn't need Jax Ironbridge angry, this was it."

"He was mistreating Kamoj," Lyode replied.

"So Gallium Sunsmith says." Maxard frowned at Kamoj. "What were you doing running around the woods like a wild animal?"

She would have bristled at the rebuke, except it was too far outside his usual congenial nature to make sense. She always walked in the woods after she finished working in the stables. He often came with her, the two of them discussing projects for Argali or enjoying each other's company.

She spoke quietly. "What is it, Uncle? What's wrong?"

He pushed his hand through his dark hair. "We can meet later in the library. You've several petitioners waiting for you now."

She studied his face, trying to fathom what troubled him. No hints showed. So she nodded, to him and to Lyode. Then she limped into her house.

■

For her office, Kamoj had chosen a large room on the ground floor. Its tanglebirch paneling glimmered with blue and green highlights in scale patterns. The comfortable old armchairs were upholstered in gold, with a worn pattern of roses. Stained-glass lanterns hung on the walls. She didn't sit behind her tanglebirch desk; she had always felt it distanced her from people.

A carafe of water waited on one table, with four finely cut tumblers. Kamoj was pouring herself a drink when the housemaid showed in her first visitors, Lumenjack Donner, a broad-shouldered man with brown eyes, and Photax Prior, a much slimmer man who could juggle light-spheres like no one else in Argali. Both were wearing freshly cleaned homespun clothes and carrying their best hats, with their dark hair uncut but well-brushed for this meeting. They bowed to her.

Kamoj beamed at them, a smile warming her face. She had known both farmers all her life. "My greetings, Goodmen."

Lumenjack's deep voice rumbled. "And to you, Governor."

"Tidings, Gov'ner." Photax's hands moved restlessly on his hat as if he wanted to juggle.

She indicated the armchairs. "Have a seat, please. Would either of you like water?"

Both declined as they settled in the chairs. Kamoj sat in one at right angles to theirs, so she could watch their faces and judge their moods. "What can I do for you today?"

Lumenjack spoke up. "Photax be cheating me, ma'am. I come to ask your help."

"It's a twiddling lie, it is," Photax declared.

Kamoj suspected that if they had agreed to seek an arbitrator, the situation was probably salvageable. "What seems to be the problem?"

Lumenjack crossed his arms, accenting his husky build. "Photax is plowing my land and taking my crops."

"It's my land!" Photax gave Kamoj his most sincere look. "He traded it to me last year when I juggled for his daughter at the festival."

Lumenjack made an incredulous noise. "I wouldn't give you my *land* for throwing pretty gigags in the air." He turned to Kamoj. "I said he could have the crops, just last year, from a strip of my land that borders his."

"You said the land!"

"I meant the crops!"

Photax shot Kamoj a beseeching look. "He be going back on his bargain, Gov'nor."

Kamoj rubbed her chin. "Photax, do you really think such a parcel of land is a fair trade for a juggling show?"

"That's not the point. He made a deal and now he's reneging."

Photax glowered at Lumenjack. "You're as crazy as that madman Lionstar." To Kamoj, he added, "Begging your pardon, ma'am. Lionstar rode through my fields yesterday and tore up my bi-grains."

Kamoj didn't like the implications. Lionstar seemed to be stirring from his borrowed palace more often lately. "Did he recompense you for the damage?"

"Nary a bridal bell. He doesn't even stop." Photax gave a theatrical shudder. "He was riding like a man possessed. He's a cursed one, he is."

She doubted it involved any curses. Lionstar's destructive behavior was problem enough by itself. "I will send a messenger to the palace. If he wrecked your crops, he owes you for them."

Photax looked mollified. "I'd be right obliged if you would do that, Gov'ner."

"That's why you're so set on Lumenjack's land, isn't it? Because you're going to be short this year."

"I can't feed a family by juggling balls," Photax said.

"So if you get your recompense," Lumenjack said, "will you quit trying to steal my land?"

"*Steal?*" Photax bristled at him. "I don't steal. You *gave* it to me!"

"Why would I do something so stupid?" Lumenjack demanded. "What, I'm going to feed my family rocks?"

Photax shifted in his chair, his mobile face showing less confidence now. "I heard you say it. So did my wife and other people."

Lumenjack made an exasperated noise. "If I said the land, instead of last year's crops on the land, it was a mistake."

"You gave your word," Photax repeated.

Kamoj sighed. Technically, if Lumenjack had given his word, he did owe Photax the land. But the mistake was so obvious, she couldn't imagine Photax holding him to it if he hadn't already been in trouble due to Lionstar's rampage. "How about this? Photax, I will see to your compensation for the crop damage. For the disputed land, why don't you and Lumenjack split the yield this year and then call the debt done, with Lumenjack keeping his land. That way, neither of you suffers unduly from the mix-up."

"I don't like giving him half my crops for nothing," Lumenjack grumbled. After a pause, he added, "But I will agree."

Photax moved his hands as if he were feeling the weight of light-spheres. "All right." He stopped his ghost juggling and frowned at Kamoj. "Do you think Lionstar will make good?"

"I can't say." She doubted it, but she didn't want to sound negative. "If he doesn't, Argali House can help you from our yield this year."

"It be right decent of you, Gov'ner."

"I wish I could do more." Her province needed so much. Not for the first time, she wondered if she should hasten her merger with Jax, to ensure Ironbridge support. After what had happened today, though, she dreaded facing his temper.

She talked more with Photax and Lumenjack, catching up on news of their families. They took their leave on better terms than when they had entered, though now they were arguing about whose son could throw a bowball farther.

She next met with the representatives of several committees she had set up: the storage group, which worked to ensure Argali had stocks of grain for the coming winter, when the village would live off crops grown during autumn; the midwives, who discussed childbirth techniques, with the hope that sharing knowledge would decrease Argali's heartbreaking infant mortality rate; and the festival group that planned the harvest celebrations.

The housemaid finally announced her last visitor, Lystral, or *Liquid Crystal*, an older woman who was well-liked in the village. Instead of arriving with her usual good nature, today Lystral stalked into the room. She wasted no time on amenities. "Well, so, Governor, have you done anything about that maniac?"

Standing by her armchair, Kamoj blinked. "Maniac?"

"Lionstar!" Lystral's scowl deepened the lines around her eyes. "That misbegotten demon-spawn of a maddened spirit raised from the dead to bedevil the good folk of this land."

Kamoj held back her smile. Granted, Lionstar was a problem, but she suspected it had more to do with human misdeeds than misbegotten spirits. "What happened?"

"He and a pack of his stagmen stopped at my daughter's house in the country, where my grandchildren were playing. He jumped down at the well, helped himself to water, and broke the chain on the bucket. He's a demonic one, I tell you. No normal man could break that chain—and Lionstar didn't even notice! He scared the little ones so much, they almost jumped from here to the Thermali Coast. Then he just got on his greenglass and rode off. Never even pulled down his cowl. Not that any of us *want* to see his pud-ugly face." She put her fists on her hips. "At least his stagman had the decency to apologize before they went tearing after him."

"I'm sorry he frightened your family, Lystral. I'm sending an emissary to the palace. I will include a protest about his behavior and a statement of the recompense he owes you for fixing the well."

"I be thanking you, ma'am." Lystral shook her head. "I wish he would leave Argali alone."

Kamoj also wished so. However, he had a right to the palace as long as he paid the rent. She just hoped Argali could weather his tenancy.

■

The centuries had warped the library door-arch beyond simple repair. Kamoj leaned her weight into the door to shove it closed. Inside the library, shelves filled with codices and books covered the walls. The lamp by Maxard's favorite armchair shed light over a table. A codex lay there, a parchment scroll made from the soft inner bark of a sunglass tree and painted with gesso, a smooth plaster. Glyphs covered it, delicate symbols inked in Argali colors. Kamoj could decipher almost none of the symbols. Now that she had taken primary responsibility for Argali, Maxard had more time for his scholarship.

He was learning to read.

Behind her the door scraped open, and she turned to see her uncle. With no preamble, he said, "Come see this."

Puzzled, she went with him to an arched door in the far wall. The storeroom beyond had once held carpentry tools, but those were long gone, sold by her grandparents to buy grain. Maxard fished a skeleton key out of his pocket and opened the moongloss door. Unexpectedly, oil lamps lit the room beyond. Kamoj stared past him—and gasped.

Urns, boxes, chests, huge pots, finely wrought buckets: they crammed the storeroom full to overflowing. Gems filled baskets, heaped like fruits, spilling onto the floor, diamonds that split the light into rainbows, opals as brilliant as greenglass scales, rose-rubies the size of fists, sapphires, topazes, amethysts, star-eyes, jade, turquoise. She walked forward, and her foot kicked an emerald the size of a polestork egg. It rolled across the floor and hit a bar of metal.

Metal. Bars lay in tumbled piles: gold, silver, copper, bronze. Sheets of rolled platinum sat on cornucopias filled with fruits, flowers, and grains. Glazed pots brimmed with vegetables and spice racks hung from the wall. Bracelets, anklets, and necklaces lay everywhere, wrought from gold and studded with jewels. A chain of diamonds lay on top a silver bowl heaped with eider plums. Just as valuable, dried foodstuffs filled cloth bags and woven baskets. Nor had she ever seen so many bolts of rich cloth: glimsilks, brocades, rose-petal satins, gauzy scarves shot through with metallic threads, scale-velvets, plush and sparkling.

And light strings! At first Kamoj thought she mistook the clump on a pile of crystal goblets. But it was real. She picked up the bundle of threads. They sparkled in the lamplight, perfect, no damage at all. This one bundle could repair broken Current threads throughout the village, and it was only one of several in the room.

Turning to Maxard, she spread out her arms, the threads clutched in one fist. "This is—it's—is this *ours?*"

He spoke in a cold voice. "Yes. It's ours."

"But Maxard, why do you look so dour!" A smile broke out on her face. "This could support Argali for years! How did it happen?"

"You tell me." He came over to her. "Just what did he give you out there today?"

He? She lowered her arms. "Who?"

"Havyrl Lionstar."

She would never have guessed Lionstar would see to his debts with such phenomenal generosity. This was so far beyond any expected recompense for Photax and Lystral's family, she couldn't begin to comprehend his intent. "Why did he send it here?"

"You tell me. You're the one who saw him."

Hai! So Maxard had heard about the river. "I didn't know he was watching."

"Watching what?"

"Me swimming."

"Then what?"

Baffled, she said, "Then nothing."

"Nothing?" Incredulity crackled in his voice. "What did you promise him, Kamoj? What sweet words did you whisper to compromise his honor?"

She couldn't imagine any woman having the temerity to try compromising the huge, brooding Lionstar. "What are you talking about?"

"You promised to marry him if he gave you what you wanted, didn't you?"

"What?"

His voice snapped. "Isn't that why he sent this dowry?"

Dowry? Sweet Airys, now what? "That's crazy."

"He must have liked whatever the two of you did."

"We did nothing. You know I would never jeopardize our alliance with Ironbridge."

Her uncle exhaled. In a quieter voice he said, "Then why did he send this dowry? Why does he insist on a merger with you tomorrow?"

Kamoj felt as if she had stepped into a bizarre skit played out for revelers during a harvest festival. This couldn't be real. "He wants *what?*"

Maxard motioned at the storeroom. "His stagmen brought it today while I was tying up stalks in the tri-grain field. They spoke as if the arrangement were already made."

It suddenly became all too clear to Kamoj. Lionstar didn't want the ruins of an old palace, the trees in their forest, or Photax's crops.

He wanted Argali. All of it.

Strange though his methods were, they made a grim sort of sense. He had demonstrated superiority in forces; many stagmen served him, over one hundred, far more than Maxard had, more even than Ironbridge. With his damnable "rent" he had established his wealth. He had even laid symbolic claim to her province by living in the Quartz Palace, the ancestral Argali home. Any way they looked at it, he had set himself up as an authority. Today he added the final, albeit unexpected, ingredient—a merger bid so far beyond the pale that the combined resources of all the Northern Lands could never best his offer.

"Gods," Kamoj said. "No wonder Jax is angry." She set down the light threads, the remnants of her good mood vanishing like a doused candle. "There must be a way I can refuse this."

"I've already asked the temple scholar," Maxard said. "And I've looked through the old codices myself. We've found nothing. You know the law. Better the offer or yield."

She stared at him in disbelief. "I'm not going to marry that crazy man."

Maxard brushed back the disarrayed locks of his hair, his forehead furrowed with lines that hadn't shown anywhere near as much yesterday. "Then he will be within his rights to take Argali by force. That was how it was done, Kamoj, in the time of the sky ships." He squinted at her. "I'm not sure my stagmen even know how to fight a war. Argali has never had one, at least not that I know about."

"There must be some way out."

It was a moment before her uncle answered. Then he spoke with care, as if treading through shards of glass. "The merger could do well for Argali."

Kamoj was sure she must have misheard. "You *want* me to go through with it?"

He spread his hands out from his body. "And what of survival, Governor?"

So. Maxard's words came with sobering force, as he finally spoke aloud what they dealt with implicitly in every discussion about the province. Drought, famine, killing winters, high infant mortality, failing machines no one understood, lost medical knowledge, and overused fields: it all added up to one inescapable fact, the long slow dying of Argali.

The province wouldn't end this Long Year, or next, maybe not even in a century. But their slide into oblivion was relentless. With the Ironbridge merger, they still might struggle, but their chances improved. She and Jax had regularly visited each other to discuss the merger. At worst, Jax would annex her province, making it part of Ironbridge. She would do her best to keep Argali separate, but if she did lose it to him, at least her people would have the protection and support of the strongest province on this continent. Although Jax didn't inspire love among his people, he was a good leader who earned loyalty and respect.

And Lionstar? Yes, he had wealth. That said nothing about his ability to lead. For all she knew he would drive her province into famine and ruin.

"Hai, Maxard." She rubbed her hand over her eyes. "I need to think about all this."

He nodded, the tension of the day showing on his face. "Go on upstairs. I'll send a maize-girl to tend you."

She went stiff, understanding his unspoken implication. "Lyode always tends to me."

"I need her elsewhere tonight."

"*You* need her? Or Jax?" When he didn't answer, her pulse surged. "I won't have my people flogged." Kamoj headed toward the door. "If you won't tell him, I will." She dreaded confronting Jax, but this time it had to be done.

Maxard grabbed her arm, stopping her. He held up his other hand, a tiny space between his thumb and index finger. "Ironbridge is this close to declaring a rite of battle against us. I've barely thirty stagmen, Kamoj. He has over eighty, all better trained." He dropped her arm. "It would be a massacre. And you know Lyode. She would insist on fighting with them. Will you save Lyode and Gallium from a few lashes so they can die in battle?"

Kamoj shuddered. "Don't say that."

His voice quieted. "With the mood Ironbridge is in now, seeing you will only enrage him. He can't touch you yet, so Gallium and Lyode are the ones he will take out his rage on."

Knowing Maxard was right made it no easier to hear. Kamoj wondered, too, if her uncle realized what else he had just revealed. *He can't touch you yet.* She spoke with difficulty. "And after the merger, when the rages take Ironbridge? Who will pay the price of his anger then?"

Maxard watched her with a strained expression, one that reminded her of the wrenching day he had come to tell her that the village patrol had found the bodies of her parents frozen beneath masses of ice in a late winter storm. She had never forgotten that wounded time of loss.

He spoke now in an aching voice. "Does it occur to you that you might be better off with Lionstar?"

She rubbed her arms as if she were cold. "What have I seen about him to make me think such a thing?"

"Hai, Kami." He started to reach for her, to offer comfort, but she shook her head. She loved him for his concern, but she feared to accept it. Taking shelter from the pain now would only make her responsibilities that much harder to face when that shelter was gone.

Maxard had caught her off-guard with his insight into her relationship with Jax. Her uncle had always claimed he delayed her merger to give her experience at governing, lest Ironbridge be tempted to take advantage of a child bride. Now she wondered if Maxard had a better idea than he let on about the life she faced with Jax. As an adult she had more emotional resources to deal with Jax's temper.

But Maxard hadn't guessed the whole of it. Last year, in Ironbridge, she had enraged Jax when she visited the city outside his fortress without his permission. Nor had that been the first time she bore the brunt of his temper. Most people saw him as the strong, inspired leader who had built Ironbridge into a great power. Kamoj also knew his other side, the Jax who would make Lyode and Gallium pay for defying him. The only difference was that in this case he would have a stagman mete out the punishment rather than taking care of it himself, as he did in private with Kamoj, when he used his hands or riding quirt against her.

In her childhood, he had never touched her in anger, instead using censure or cold silence to reproach behaviors that offended him. But since she had become an adult, his temper had turned physical. She had never told Maxard, knowing it would drive her uncle to break the betrothal no matter what price it cost Argali. She could never set her personal situation before the survival of her people.

Gentle one moment, violent the next, Jax kept her on the edge between love and hatred. She dreaded his rage, savored his wisdom, feared his cruelty, longed for his mercurial tenderness, resented his need to control, and admired his remarkable intellect. But beyond her conflicted emotions, she knew one fact: Argali needed him. Her loyalty and love for her people came first, above all else, including her personal happiness. So she had learned to cope with Jax. The situation wasn't perfect, but it would *work*. Lionstar threatened that careful balance like a plow tearing up their world.

"Can you talk to Jax?" she asked. "Mollify him? Maybe you can keep him from hurting them."

"I'll do what I can." He watched her, his dark eyes filled with concern. "This will work out, Kami."

"Yes. It will." She wished she believed those comforting words.

After she left her uncle, she walked through the house, down halls paneled in tanglebirch, then up to a second floor balcony. At the top of the stairs, she gazed out over the foyer below, treasuring the sight of this home where she had lived all her life—the home she might soon leave. The entrance to the living room arched to the right. A chandelier hung from the room's ceiling like an inverted rose aglow with candles. It reflected in a polished table, drawing blue scale-gleams from the wood. Near the table, a light panel glowed in the wall, the last working one in all the Northern Lands.

Regret and longing for all that her people had lost washed over Kamoj. When that panel failed, a thousand new light threads would do no good. Even Opter Sunsmith couldn't fix a broken panel. The knowledge had been lost long ago, even from the Sunsmith line.

Kamoj walked along the balcony to her room. Candlelight filled the chamber, welcoming her. It glowed on the parquetry floors, worn furniture, and her old doll collection on the table, which she kept in memory of her mother, who had given her the beloved toys. Her bed stood in a corner, each of its four posts a totem of rose blossoms and fruits, ending at the top with a closed bud.

A voice spoke behind her. "Ev'ning, ma'am."

She turned to see Ixima Ironbridge, a young woman with a smudge of flour on one cheek. Jax had sent the Ironbridge maize-girl to Argali last year, so Kamoj could get to know her. That way, whenever Kamoj traveled to Ironbridge, she would bring a familiar face with her, someone who already knew the province and could help Kamoj feel more at home. The thoughtful gesture had both touched and confused Kamoj. How could Jax be so considerate one moment and so harsh the next?

Ixima spoke in her Ironbridge dialect. "Shall I be a'helpin' you change, ma'am?"

"Thank you." Kamoj sat tiredly on her bed.

Ixima slid off the boot and peeled away the sock. Kamoj winced as the cloth ripped away from her toes. The gouge must have bled and then dried her sock to her skin. Lifting her foot, she saw dirt in the cut. "We better clean it."

The maize-girl tilted her head, considering Kamoj's foot. "I donnee see how a'rubbin' it would help. You rest, hai, ma'am? Tomorrow it be feeling better enough to scrub."

Her lack of knowledge troubled Kamoj. Dirty wounds festered. Nor was Ixima the only person she had known to make mistakes on health matters. She thought of asking the healer in the village about setting up a program to educate people. He was already overworked, and she hated to add to his load, but in the long run this might help ease his burden.

"We must treat it now." Kamoj kept her voice kind so Ixima didn't take it as a rebuke.

The maize-girl fetched a bowl of warm water and soap. While she cleaned Kamoj's foot, Kamoj leaned against the bed post, struggling to stay awake. After Ixima helped her prepare for sleep, Kamoj settled in bed. The maize-girl darkened the room and left quietly, leaving one candle flickering on the windowsill.

Kamoj lay on her back, her hands behind her head, staring at the ceiling. She would always remember the first time she had met Jax, not long after her parents had died. Tall and powerful, his mail gleaming, his handsome face kind, he had knelt to speak to her, bringing his eyes level with her own. He had seemed like an enchanted hero then, a shining savior come to rescue Argali. Over the years she had learned the truth, that under the hero's exterior burned a complicated, violent man whose clenched need to control contaminated his many good qualities.

If she refused the Lionstar merger, it would placate Jax but break the law. If Argali and Ironbridge combined forces, they could raise an army almost equal to that of Lionstar. But if Lionstar attacked, Kamoj would have to send people she loved into a rite of combat. A good chance existed they wouldn't come home. Lionstar might slaughter them; neither Ironbridge nor Argali had ever ridden into battle.

Kamoj knew what she had to do. As she made her decision, she felt as if a door closed. She had no way to predict what would happen in a Lionstar merger, but he had made it clear he could support her province. If she turned him down, the people and realm she loved could suffer, perhaps even die, at his whim.

Never again would Jax raise his hand or whip to her person. Never again would he use the survival of Argali as a weapon against her. It was a bitter victory, given what she had seen of Lionstar, but it was all she had.

3

LIONSTAR
Second Scattering Channel

Kamoj squinted at the mirror while the threadwoman fussed over her clothes. All this attention disconcerted her. She never dressed this way, in such formal garments. Leggings and a farm tunic were much more her preference, or a farm dress for more festive occasions. However, today was her wedding, and at one's wedding one wore a wedding dress no matter how dour the bride felt about that incipient marital status.

Despite everything, Kamoj treasured this dress. Knowing her mother and grandmother had worn it at their weddings made her feel close to them. Dyed the blush color of an Argali rose, it fit snug around her torso and fell to the floor in drapes of rose-scale satin. Lace bordered the neckline and sleeves, and her hair fell in glossy black curls to her waist. The Argali Jewels glittered at her throat, wrists, and ankles, gold chains designed like vines and inset with ruby roses.

With tugs and taps, the aged threadwoman tightened the dress at the waist and tried to make it stretch over Kamoj's breasts. She cackled at her reluctant model, her eyes almost lost in their nest of lines. "You've no boy's shape, Gov'ner. You be making Lionstar a happy man, I reckon."

Kamoj glowered at her, but the seamstress was saved from her retort by a knock on the door. Kamoj limped across the room in her unfamiliar shoes, heeled slippers sheathed in rose scale-leather. She opened the door to see Lyode.

Her bodyguard beamed. "Hai, Kamoj! You look lovely."

"It's for my wedding." She wondered what Lionstar would do if she showed up in a flour sack. Go away maybe. Then again, he was so odd he might like it.

Her guardian's enthusiasm waned. "Yes. Maxard told me."

Lyode's presence offered a welcome respite from all these wedding preparations. Kamoj dismissed the seamstress, then drew Lyode over to sit with her on the sofa. The older woman started to lean back, then jerked when her shoulders touched the cushions and sat forward again. Watching her, Kamoj felt another surge of anger at Jax, that he inflicted pain on the people she loved because they sought to protect her from his anger.

"You've huge bags under your eyes," Kamoj said.

"I had—a little trouble sleeping last night."

Kamoj wasn't fooled. It dismayed her to see Lyode's discomfort. But Maxard must have mollified Jax to some extent; otherwise Lyode wouldn't be able to move. "I'm so sorry."

The archer laid her hand on Kamoj's arm. "It's isn't your fault."

Isn't it? At times like this Kamoj felt trapped. "How is Gallium?"

Lyode spoke gently. "He's all right, Kami. We both are."

Kamoj crumpled her skirt in her fists. "I hate that all this has happened."

"Hate is a strong word. Give Lionstar a chance."

"I tell myself it will work out for the best. But after all we've heard about him—" She stopped, unable to voice her fears, as if saying them aloud would make real the tales of sorcery and dread that surrounded him.

"You've a kind heart," Lyode said. "He would be blind not to see that."

"Lyode—"

"Yes?"

"About tonight . . ." Although Kamoj knew what happened on a wedding night, it was only as vague concepts. She felt awkward asking advice on such matters even from Lyode. It touched a part of her life that would have given her both anticipation and apprehension even if she had gone into it with a man she knew, loved, and trusted. None of the three applied to Lionstar.

Lyode's face relaxed into the affectionate grin she always took on at the mention of her own husband, Opter. "Don't look so dour. Weddings are good things."

Kamoj smiled. "You look like a besotted fruitwing." When Lyode laughed, Kamoj said, "How will I know what to do?"

"Trust your instincts."

"My instincts tell me to run the other way."

Lyode touched her arm. "Don't judge Lionstar yet. Wait and see."

■

At sunset the Argali coach rolled into the courtyard, pulled by four greenglass stags and driven by a stagman. Shaped and tinted like a rose, it sat in a chassis of emerald-green leaves. Unlike Argali House, which had only legends attesting to its construction, the coach was inarguably one surface with no seams, glimmering like pearl. Its making was so long in the past, no one remembered how it had been done.

Watching from her bedroom window, Kamoj suddenly wanted to go down to the courtyard and tell them all that she had changed her mind, that they must cancel the wedding. Taking a deep breath, she calmed her thoughts. *You made the best decision you could. Trust your instincts.*

The door opened behind her. Turning, she saw Lyode framed in the archway. Her bodyguard wore a fine white shirt and soft suede trousers, with her ballbow in her hand instead of on her back. Her familiar presence reassured Kamoj.

Lyode's expression was both fond and sad. "It's time to go."

Kamoj crossed the room without a limp. Her foot had gone

numb. She had soaked and cleaned the wound again this morning, but it remained swollen. It didn't hurt now, though.

Maxard was waiting at the bottom of the stairs. A swell of pride filled Kamoj. Today no lack of splendor would shame Argali. She wished Maxard's lady in the North Sky Islands were here to see him. His mail gleamed, a gold contrast to his black hair and eyes. He wore a suncorn shirt, wine-red suede breeches, and a belt made from quetzal feathers in Argali colors. Green feathers lined the tops of his gold knee-boots, and a ceremonial sword hung at his side, its scabbard tooled with Argali designs.

As Kamoj descended the stairs, Maxard watched, his face filled with the affection that made her love him so. When she reached him, he said, "You look like a dream." His voice caught. "It seems just yesterday you were a child. How did you grow up so fast?"

"Hai, Maxard." She hugged him. "I don't know." It was true. A few years ago she had been a child. Then she became an adult. Almost nothing separated the two; her adolescence had lasted only a few tendays. It gave her an inexplicable sense of loss. Why should she want a longer time of transition? Most people had no adolescence at all.

She knew the stories, of course, of the rare child who took longer to reach adulthood. Rumor claimed Jax Ironbridge's youth had stretched out far longer than normal. Years after his peers had become adults, he had still been an adolescent, tall and gangly, with only the first signs of his beard. He continued to grow long past the age when most youths reached maturity. Jax came into full adulthood well after most men his age—and by that time he was taller, stronger, and smarter than everyone else.

If only it had made him kinder, too.

With Maxard and Lyode on either side, Kamoj left the house. A group of her childhood friends had gathered in the courtyard, young women with rose vines braided into their black hair. They waved and smiled, and Kamoj waved back, trying to appear in good spirits.

Arrayed around the coach, ten stagmen sat astride their mounts, including Gallium Sunsmith. A smudgebug flittered into the face of one animal and it pranced to the side, crowding Gallium's greenglass.

As the first rider pulled back his mount, his elbow bumped Gallium's back. Kamoj saw the grimace of pain Gallium tried to hide, just as Lyode had done on the sofa.

Kamoj's smile faded, lost to thoughts of Jax. He had shadowed so much of her life. She had treasured Gallium for as long as she could remember. The stagman had given her rides when she was a little girl and gave her his unwavering loyalty now.

As she passed him, she looked up. "My gratitude, Goodman Sunsmith. For everything. I won't forget."

His face gentled. "And you, Kami. You be a sight of beauty."

She managed to smile, not wanting to burden him with her fear. Lyode opened the door of the coach and Maxard entered first, followed by Kamoj. Lyode came last and closed them into the heart of the rose. The driver blew on his flight-horn, and its call rang through the evening air. Then they started off, bumping down the road.

Sitting between Lyode and Maxard, Kamoj took each of their hands. Maxard patted her arm and Lyode hugged her, but no one spoke. They needed no words; after so many years, they could speak with the simplest touch. She cherished this time with them. It felt ephemeral. She wished she could put this moment in a locket, a gold heart that would protect it, so she could take it out when the loneliness came and remember these two people who were her only family.

The coach rolled slowly, so the people walking could keep up. Even so, it seemed that far too little time passed before it stopped, bringing an end to their moment together.

The door swung back, leaving Gallium framed in its opening. Beyond him in the gathering dusk, the golden face of the Spectral Temple basked in the rays of the setting sun. Kamoj's retinue of stagmen and friends, and now many other villagers too, waited in the muddy plaza before the temple. It touched her to know that so many had come to see her wed Lionstar, especially given how much they feared him.

Lyode left the coach first. Kamoj gathered her skirts and followed—but froze in the doorway. Across the mud and cobblestones, a larger coach was rolling into view. Made from bronze and black metal, it had the shape of a roaring skylion's head with wind whipping back its feathered mane. Every burnished detail gleamed. The eyes were emeralds as large as fists. A blush spread across Kamoj's face at the imposing sight.

Her groom had arrived.

As soon as the coach stopped, its door opened. Two stagmen came out, decked in copper and dark blue, with cobalt diskmail that glittered in the sun's slanting rays. Sapphires lined the tops of their boots. Kamoj wondered where Lionstar found so many incredible gems. Argali's jewel master had checked and double-checked the ones in his dowry. They were real. Flawless and real.

Then a cowled man stepped down into the plaza.

Lionstar towered over everyone else, easily the largest man in the courtyard. Seeing his unusual height, she wondered if—like Jax—he too had spent years as an adolescent. What if he had other, harsher, similarities to her former betrothed? As always, he wore a blue cloak with a cowl pulled over his head. She wasn't sure she wanted to know what he hid under that shadowed hood. Only black showed inside; either he had a cloth over his face—or he had no face.

Maxard took her arm. "We should go."

His touch startled her into motion. She descended from the coach, onto a flagstone that glinted with mica even in the purple shadows. Her heels clicked as she stepped from stone to stone to avoid the mud.

Even tonight, the sight of the Spectral Temple gave her a thrill. The terraced pyramid stood surrounded by the Argali forest. When rays from the setting sun hit the stairs that ran up its side at just the right angle, it made light ripple down them to the statue of a starlizard's head at the bottom, creating a serpent of radiance and stone. In the front of the temple, a huge starlizard's head opened its mouth in a roar, forming an entrance. When a sun ray hit its crystal eyes, arcs of light glistened around its head like the Perihelia spirits, also called Sun Lizards, that guarded the temple.

Kamoj had always loved the sun lizards that appeared in the sky. They made halos on either side of the sun, like pale rainbows, each with a tail of white light. This was their favored time, as tiny Jul descended to the horizon, scantily dressed in wispy clouds. During winter, when ice crystals filled the air, Perihelia and Halo spirits graced the heavens in arcs and rings. They might even form around the head of a favored person's shadow as it stretched across dewy tubemoss at dawn. But she saw no nimbus now, no sign to portend good fortune for this merger.

Lionstar's group reached the temple first. He stopped under the overhang of the sun lizard's fanged mouth and waited, his cowled head turned toward Kamoj. She came up with her retinue and stopped. After they had all stood that way for a moment, she flushed. Didn't he know he should go in first? She shifted her weight, wondering how to balance courtesy with expediency. They couldn't stand here all night.

One of Lionstar's stagmen spoke to him in a low voice. He nodded, then entered the temple with his retinue. Relieved, Kamoj followed with her people. No one spoke. She wondered if Lionstar could even talk. No one she knew had ever heard him say a word.

Inside, light from the sunset trickled through slits high in the walls. Stone benches filled the interior, except for a dais at the far end, which supported a polished stone table. Carvings decorated the table, Argali vine designs, those motifs called *Bessel integrals* in ancient Iotaca.

Kamoj savored the scents in the temple. Rose vines and ferns heaped the table, filling the air with their fragrance, fresh and clean. Around the walls, garlands hung from the statues of several Current spirits: the Airy Rainbows, the Glories, and the Nimbi. In wall slits above the statues, light slanted through faceted windows with water misted between the double panes, creating rainbows. Music graced the air, coming from breezes that blew through fluted chambers on the ceiling, hidden within engravings of the Spherical Harmonic wraiths.

Most days, Kamoj enjoyed the Spectral Temple's beauty. Now it all seemed unreal, its ethereal quality untouched by the far less serene ceremony going on within it. As everyone else sat down on the benches, Kamoj walked to the dais with Maxard at her side and Lionstar preceding them. The priestess, Airysphere Prism, waited by the flower-bedecked table. Tall and lithe, she had large eyes and shiny black hair that poured to her waist.

After he stepped up onto the dais, Lionstar turned to watch

Kamoj approach. At least she assumed he was watching. His cowl hid his face. When she reached him, she saw only darkness within that hood, perhaps a glint of metal. She told herself she was mistaken. Surely a man couldn't have a metal face.

Maxard bowed to him. "Argali welcomes you, Governor Lionstar."

The taller man just nodded. After an awkward silence Maxard flushed, though whether from anger or shame, Kamoj didn't know. Did Lionstar realize the insult in his silence, or did he act out of ignorance? The answer to that question would have told her a great deal about her groom, but she had no way to judge from the unreadable shadows within his cowl.

When the silence became long, Maxard turned and took Kamoj's hands. He spoke tenderly. "May the Current always flow for you, Kami."

She curled her fingers around his. "And for you, dear Uncle."

He lingered a moment more, watching her face. But finally he released her hands. Then he left the dais, going to sit on the front bench with Lyode.

"It is done?" Lionstar asked.

Kamoj almost jumped. His voice rumbled, deep and resonant, with a heavy accent. On the word "is," it vibrated like a stringed instrument.

Airys blinked, the vertical slits of her pupils opened wide in the shadowed temple. "Do you refer to the ceremony?"

"Yes," Lionstar said.

"It hasn't begun." Airys took a scroll from the table and unrolled it. Glyphs covered the parchment in starlight blue ink. She offered it to Lionstar, and he accepted with black-gloved hands.

"Governor Argali," Airys said. "Give me your hand."

As Kamoj extended her arm, Airys said, "In the name of Spectra Luminous I give this man to you." She closed her hand around Kamoj's wrist. "Havyrl Lionstar, give me your hand." When he complied, Airys took a vine from the altar and tied his and Kamoj's wrists together, bedecking them in roses and scale-leaves.

It startled Kamoj to feel the leather of his glove against her skin. Why did he hide himself, even his hands? Surely he must realize it might disquiet his bride. Try as she might, she could find

few good reasons for his behavior, unless he really were the prover-
bial demon, in which case she preferred not to think about the details.

Airys spoke to Lionstar. "You may read the contract now."

Kamoj waited for him to decline. No one ever read the contract at a wedding. Only scholars could read, after all, and only the
most gifted knew ancient Iotaca. Most people considered the scroll
a fertility prayer. Kamoj had her doubts; Airys had managed to
translate a few parts for her, and it sounded more like a legal docu-
ment than a poem. In any case, the groom always returned the
scroll. Then the couple spoke a blessing they composed themselves. Kamoj hadn't prepared anything; what she felt about this
merger was better left unsaid. Unless Lionstar had his own poem,
which she doubted, they would continue the ceremony without
the blessing.

Except they didn't. Lionstar read the scroll.

As his voice rumbled with the Iotaca words, indrawn breaths
came from their audience. Kamoj doubted anyone had ever heard
the blessing spoken, let alone with such power. Lionstar had a deep
voice, with an unfamiliar accent and the burr of a vibrato. His
words also sounded slurred. The sounds rolled over her, so unexpected she had trouble absorbing them.

When he finished, the only sounds in the temple were the faint
calls of evening birds outside.

Finally he said, "This ceremony, is it done?"

Airys took a breath, as if coming back to herself. "The vows
are finished, if that is what you mean."

He gave her the scroll. Then he untied the vine joining his
and Kamoj's wrists and draped it around Kamoj's neck, spilling
the roses over her breasts. She blushed, jarred by the break with
tradition; they weren't supposed to undo the vine until they con-
summated the marriage. Before she could speak, he took her
elbow, turned her around, and headed for the entrance, pulling her
with him.

Murmurs came from the watchers, a rustle of clothes, the clink
of diskmail. Belatedly Kamoj realized that he had misunderstood;
he thought the ceremony was over when it had hardly begun. But
the rest was only ritual. They had said the vows. Argali and Lion-

star had their corporate merger. Whatever happened now, she had committed herself and her province to this man. She just hoped that future didn't tumble down around them.

They came out into a purple evening. She barely had time to catch her breath before they reached Lionstar's coach. This was happening too fast; she had thought she would have at least a little more time to accept the marriage before she was alone with her new husband.

Then he stopped, looking over her head. She turned to see Maxard coming up behind them, with Lyode and Gallium, their familiar faces a welcome sight.

Lionstar spoke to her uncle. "Good night, sir."

Kamoj wondered what he meant. Was "good night" a greeting or a farewell?

Maxard bowed. Lionstar just nodded, then motioned to his men. As he raised his arm, his cloak parted and revealed his diskmail, a sapphire flash of blue. What metal did he use, to create such a dramatic color?

As one of his stagmen opened the coach door, Lionstar put his hand on Kamoj's arm, ready to pass her inside. Before she even realized what she was doing, she balked, stepping back. She couldn't leave this way, not without making her farewells.

Kamoj went to Lyode and embraced her, taking care with Lyode's back, her head buried against the taller woman's shoulder. Lyode spoke softly. "You're like a daughter to me. You remember that. I will always love you." Her words had the sound of tears.

Kamoj's voice caught. "And I you."

Before she could go to Maxard, Lionstar drew her toward the coach. She almost pulled away again, but then she stopped herself. Antagonizing the man who had just taken over Argali would be a poor start to their merger and could endanger the province. She glanced at Maxard, her eyes misted with tears, and he nodded, moisture glimmering in his as well.

Then Lionstar passed her to his stagmen, who handed her up into the roaring lion. Black moongloss paneled its somber interior and dark leather upholstered the seat. A window showed in the wall across from the door. She turned as Lionstar entered and saw another window in the door behind him. Yet from outside, no panes had shown at all. *It has a reasonable explanation*, she told herself. She only wished she believed that.

A stagman closed the door, and Lionstar sat next to her, his long legs filling the car. His cloak fell open, revealing ceremonial dress much like Maxard's, except in dark sapphire. As the coach rolled forward, Kamoj turned to her window for a final glimpse of her home. But the "glass" had become a blank expanse of wood. Dismayed, she looked toward Lionstar's window, only to find it had vanished as well. With such a dark interior and no lamps, the coach should have been pitch black. But light still filled it. She was having more and more trouble believing that a normal explanation existed for all this.

"Here." Lionstar tapped the ceiling. His voice had a blurred quality.

Puzzled, she looked up. A glowing white strip bordered the roof of the coach. It resembled a light panel, but one made as thin as a finger and flexible enough to bend. She didn't know whether to be relieved that a reason existed for the light or disquieted by its unusual source.

"That's what you were looking for, wasn't it?" he said. "The light?"

How had he known? "Yes."

"Thought so." He reached into his cloak and brought out a bottle. Curved and slender, it was made from dark blue glass with a gold top. He unscrewed the top, then lifted the bottle into his cowl and tilted back his head. After a moment he lowered his arm and wiped his hand across whatever he had for a face. Then he returned the bottle to his cloak.

A whiff of rum tickled Kamoj's nose. Like a trick picture that changed if she looked at it in a new way, her perception shifted. She thought of his slurred words at the wedding and his actions at Lystral's well. Could *drink* be what made him act that way? That thought wasn't exactly reassuring either, but it was far more palatable than supernatural causes.

Lionstar sighed. As he turned toward her, she caught another glint of silver within his cowl. Then he slid his arms around her waist.

Hai! Kamoj's instincts clamored at her to push him away. *He is your husband*, she told herself. *Sit still*. He had a right to hug his wife. But she couldn't bring herself to return the embrace.

He rubbed the lace on her sleeve, then rolled it between his fingers. His black glove made a dark contrast against the rosy silk. She wondered if he would wear gloves when he made love to her. What if he never pulled off his cowl, even in the bedroom? She felt a blush spreading in her face. Maybe she had better not think about that right now.

Lionstar slid his hand up her torso, under the vine of roses around her neck, and folded his gloved palm around her breast. Kamoj froze, her logic vanishing like the windows in the coach. She didn't *care* if he was her husband; he was still a stranger. As he caressed her breast, she held back the urge to sock him. She wished he would speak or show her some sign that a human person existed in there.

He fondled her for a few moments, but gradually his hand slowed to a stop. Then it fell into her lap. He was leaning on her, his weight making it hard to sit up straight. She peered up at him, wondering what to do.

While she pondered, he gave a snore.

Her new husband, it seemed, had gone to sleep.

Kamoj rubbed her chin. What did one do in such a situation? Perhaps nothing, except thank the Spectral Harmonic spirits for this respite.

With Lionstar leaning against her, though, it was hard to sit straight. So she gave him a nudge. When he made no objection, she pushed him upright. He lay his head back against the seat, his mail-covered chest rising and falling in a deep, even rhythm, his cowl fallen over his face.

Just as Kamoj began to feel grateful for this unexpected reprieve, he tried to lie down. The seat of the coach had too little room for his legs, so he stretched out with his feet on the ground and his head in her lap. Then he went back to snoring.

Kamoj had no idea what to think. Of all the scenarios she had imagined for their ride to the palace, this wasn't one of them. She stared at his head in her lap and the hood lying across his face. Was he truly as hideous as rumor claimed? With one twitch of the cloth, she would know.

Your husband hides his face for a reason. He valued that reason enough to cover it even at his own wedding. If she looked now, she might antagonize him.

But he was asleep.

A torment of curiosity swept over her. She touched the edge of his cowl. No, she couldn't take the chance. She withdrew her hand. He continued to sleep, a soft snore at the end of each breath. How would he know if she looked? Perhaps he would never find out. Then again, he might wake up if she uncovered him.

Finally Kamoj could take it no more. She tugged on his cowl. When he showed no sign of waking, she pulled the cloth more. Still no response. Emboldened, she brushed the hood back from his head—and nearly screamed.

1965

Best Novel: *Dune* by Frank Herbert
Best Novella: "The Saliva Tree" by Brian W. Aldiss and "He
  Who Shapes" by Roger Zelazny (tie)
Best Novelette: "The Doors of His Face, the Lamps of His
  Mouth" by Roger Zelazny
Best Short Story: " 'Repent, Harlequin!' Said the Ticktock-
  man" by Harlan Ellison

1966

Best Novel: *Flowers for Algernon* by Daniel Keyes and *Babel-17*
  by Samuel R. Delany (tie)
Best Novella: "The Last Castle" by Jack Vance
Best Novelette: "Call Him Lord" by Gordon R. Dickson
Best Short Story: "The Secret Place" by Richard McKenna

1967

Best Novel: *The Einstein Intersection* by Samuel R. Delany
Best Novella: "Behold the Man" by Michael Moorcock
Best Novelette: "Gonna Roll the Bones" by Fritz Leiber
Best Short Story: "Aye, and Gomorrah" by Samuel R.
  Delany

1968

Best Novel: *Rite of Passage* by Alexei Panshin
Best Novella: "Dragonrider" by Anne McCaffrey

Best Novelette: "Mother to the World" by Richard Wilson
Best Short Story: "The Planners" by Kate Wilhelm

1969

Best Novel: *The Left Hand of Darkness* by Ursula K. Le Guin
Best Novella: "A Boy and His Dog" by Harlan Ellison
Best Novelette: "Time Considered as a Helix of Semi-Precious Stones" by Samuel R. Delany
Best Short Story: "Passengers" by Robert Silverberg

1970

√ Best Novel: *Ringworld* by Larry Niven
Best Novella: "Ill Met in Lankhmar" by Fritz Leiber
Best Novelette: "Slow Sculpture" by Theodore Sturgeon
Best Short Story: no award

1971

Best Novel: *A Time of Changes* by Robert Silverberg
Best Novella: "The Missing Man" by Katherine MacLean
Best Novelette: "The Queen of Air and Darkness" by Poul Anderson
Best Short Story: "Good News from the Vatican" by Robert Silverberg

1972

√ Best Novel: *The Gods Themselves* by Isaac Asimov
Best Novella: "A Meeting with Medusa" by Arthur C. Clarke
Best Novelette: "Goat Song" by Poul Anderson
Best Short Story: "When It Changed" by Joanna Russ

1973

√ Best Novel: *Rendezvous with Rama* by Arthur C. Clarke
Best Novella: "The Death of Doctor Island" by Gene Wolfe
Best Novelette: "Of Mist, and Grass, and Sand" by Vonda N. McIntyre
Best Short Story: "Love Is the Plan, the Plan Is Death" by James Tiptree Jr.
Best Dramatic Presentation: *Soylent Green*

Stanley R. Greenberg for screenplay (based on the novel *Make Room! Make Room!*), Harry Harrison for *Make Room! Make Room!*

1974

Best Novel: *The Dispossessed* by Ursula K. Le Guin
Best Novella: "Born with the Dead" by Robert Silverberg
Best Novelette: "If the Stars Are Gods" by Gordon Eklund and Gregory Benford
Best Short Story: "The Day Before the Revolution" by Ursula K. Le Guin
Best Dramatic Presentation: *Sleeper* by Woody Allen
Grand Master: Robert A. Heinlein

1975

Best Novel: *The Forever War* by Joe Haldeman
Best Novella: "Home Is the Hangman" by Roger Zelazny
Best Novelette: "San Diego Lightfoot Sue" by Tom Reamy
Best Short Story: "Catch That Zeppelin!" by Fritz Leiber
Best Dramatic Writing: Mel Brooks and Gene Wilder for *Young Frankenstein*
Grand Master: Jack Williamson

1976

Best Novel: *Man Plus* by Frederik Pohl
Best Novella: "Houston, Houston, Do You Read?" by James Tiptree Jr.
Best Novelette: "The Bicentennial Man" by Isaac Asimov
Best Short Story: "A Crowd of Shadows" by Charles L. Grant
Grand Master: Clifford D. Simak

1977

Best Novel: *Gateway* by Frederik Pohl
Best Novella: "Stardance" by Spider and Jeanne Robinson
Best Novelette: "The Screwfly Solution" by Raccoona Sheldon
Best Short Story: "Jeffty Is Five" by Harlan Ellison
Special Award: *Star Wars*

1978

Best Novel: *Dreamsnake* by Vonda N. McIntyre
Best Novella: "The Persistence of Vision" by John Varley
Best Novelette: "A Glow of Candles, a Unicorn's Eye" by
    Charles L. Grant
Best Short Story: "Stone" by Edward Bryant
Grand Master: L. Sprague de Camp

1979

Best Novel: *The Fountains of Paradise* by Arthur C. Clarke
Best Novella: "Enemy Mine" by Barry Longyear
Best Novelette: "Sandkings" by George R. R. Martin
Best Short Story: "giANTS" by Edward Bryant

1980

Best Novel: *Timescape* by Gregory Benford
Best Novella: "The Unicorn Tapestry" by Suzy McKee
    Charnas
Best Novelette: "The Ugly Chickens" by Howard Waldrop
Best Short Story: "Grotto of the Dancing Deer" by Clifford
    D. Simak
Grand Master: Fritz Leiber

1981

Best Novel: *The Claw of the Conciliator* by Gene Wolfe
Best Novella: "The Saturn Game" by Poul Anderson
Best Novelette: "The Quickening" by Michael Bishop
Best Short Story: "The Bone Flute" by Lisa Tuttle★

1982

Best Novel: *No Enemy But Time* by Michael Bishop
Best Novella: "Another Orphan" by John Kessel
Best Novelette: "Fire Watch" by Connie Willis
Best Short Story: "A Letter from the Clearys" by Connie
    Willis

★This Nebula Award was declined by the author.

1983

Best Novel: *Startide Rising* by David Brin
Best Novella: "Hardfought" by Greg Bear
Best Novelette: "Blood Music" by Greg Bear
Best Short Story: "The Peacemaker" by Gardner Dozois
Grand Master: Andre Norton

1984

Best Novel: *Neuromancer* by William Gibson
Best Novella: "Press Enter ■" by John Varley
Best Novelette: "Bloodchild" by Octavia E. Butler
Best Short Story: "Morning Child" by Gardner Dozois

1985

Best Novel: *Ender's Game* by Orson Scott Card
Best Novella: "Sailing to Byzantium" by Robert Silverberg
Best Novelette: "Portraits of His Children" by George R. R. Martin
Best Short Story: "Out of All Them Bright Stars" by Nancy Kress
Grand Master: Arthur C. Clarke

1986

Best Novel: *Speaker for the Dead* by Orson Scott Card
Best Novella: "R & R" by Lucius Shepard
Best Novelette: "The Girl Who Fell into the Sky" by Kate Wilhelm
Best Short Story: "Tangents" by Greg Bear
Grand Master: Isaac Asimov

1987

Best Novel: *The Falling Woman* by Pat Murphy
Best Novella: "The Blind Geometer" by Kim Stanley Robinson
Best Novelette: "Rachel in Love" by Pat Murphy
Best Short Story: "Forever Yours, Anna" by Kate Wilhelm
Grand Master: Alfred Bester

1988

Best Novel: *Falling Free* by Lois McMaster Bujold
Best Novella: "The Last of the Winnebagos" by Connie Willis
Best Novelette: "Schrödinger's Kitten" by George Alec
    Effinger
Best Short Story: "Bible Stories for Adults, No. 17: The
    Deluge" by James Morrow
Grand Master: Ray Bradbury

1989

Best Novel: *The Healer's War* by Elizabeth Ann Scarborough
Best Novella: "The Mountains of Mourning" by Lois
    McMaster Bujold
Best Novelette: "At the Rialto" by Connie Willis
Best Short Story: "Ripples in the Dirac Sea" by Geoffrey
    Landis

1990

Best Novel: *Tehanu: The Last Book of Earthsea* by Ursula K.
    Le Guin
Best Novella: "The Hemingway Hoax" by Joe Haldeman
Best Novelette: "Tower of Babylon" by Ted Chiang
Best Short Story: "Bears Discover Fire" by Terry Bisson
Grand Master: Lester del Rey

1991

Best Novel: *Stations of the Tide* by Michael Swanwick
Best Novella: "Beggars in Spain" by Nancy Kress
Best Novelette: "Guide Dog" by Mike Conner
Best Short Story: "Ma Qui" by Alan Brennert

1992

Best Novel: *Doomsday Book* by Connie Willis
Best Novella: "City of Truth" by James Morrow
Best Novelette: "Danny Goes to Mars" by Pamela Sargent
Best Short Story: "Even the Queen" by Connie Willis
Grand Master: Frederik Pohl

1993

Best Novel: *Red Mars* by Kim Stanley Robinson
Best Novella: "The Night We Buried Road Dog" by Jack
    Cady
Best Novelette: "Georgia on My Mind" by Charles Sheffield
Best Short Story: "Graves" by Joe Haldeman

1994

Best Novel: *Moving Mars* by Greg Bear
Best Novella: "Seven Views of Olduvai Gorge" by Mike
    Resnick
Best Novelette: "The Martian Child" by David Gerrold
Best Short Story: "A Defense of the Social Contracts" by
    Martha Soukup
Grand Master: Damon Knight

1995

Best Novel: *The Terminal Experiment* by Robert J. Sawyer
Best Novella: "Last Summer at Mars Hill" by Elizabeth Hand
Best Novelette: "Solitude" by Ursula K. Le Guin
Best Short Story: "Death and the Librarian" by Esther M.
    Friesner
Grand Master: A. E. van Vogt

1996

Best Novel: *Slow River* by Nicola Griffith
Best Novella: "Da Vinci Rising" by Jack Dann
Best Novelette: "Lifeboat on a Burning Sea" by Bruce Hol-
    land Rogers
Best Short Story: "A Birthday" by Esther M. Friesner
Grand Master: Jack Vance

1997

Best Novel: *The Moon and the Sun* by Vonda N. McIntyre
Best Novella: "Abandon in Place" by Jerry Oltion
Best Novelette: "The Flowers of Aulit Prison" by Nancy Kress
Best Short Story: "Sister Emily's Lightship" by Jane Yolen

Grand Master: Poul Anderson

1998
Best Novel: *Forever Peace* by Joe W. Haldeman
Best Novella: "Reading the Bones" by Sheila Finch
Best Novelette: "Lost Girls" by Jane Yolen
Best Short Story: "Thirteen Ways to Water" by Bruce Holland
    Rogers
Grand Master: Hal Clement

1999
Best Novel: *Parable of the Talents* by Octavia E. Butler
Best Novella: "Story of Your Life" by Ted Chiang
Best Novelette: "Mars Is No Place for Children" by Mary A.
    Turzillo
Best Short Story: "The Cost of Doing Business" by Leslie
    What
Best Script: *The Sixth Sense* by M. Night Shyamalan
Grand Master: Brian W. Aldiss

2000
Best Novel: *Darwin's Radio* by Grey Bear
Best Novella: "Goddesses" by Linda Nagata
Best Novelette: "Daddy's World" by Walter Jon Williams
Best Short Story: "macs" by Terry Bisson
Best Script: *Galaxy Quest* by Robert Gordon and David
    Howard